RAVE REVIEWS FOR THE AUTHORS OF
SILENT NIGHT!

CLAUDIA DAIN

"Claudia Dain writes with intelligence, sensuality, and heart and the results are extraordinary!"
—Connie Brockway, bestselling author

"[Claudia Dain writes] a red-hot romance."
—*Publishers Weekly*

"Claudia Dain weaves in tight suspense until the final, chilling climax."
—*Romantic Times* on *A Kiss to Die For*

DEE DAVIS

"Fans of contemporary romantic suspense should add Ms. Davis to their list of authors to watch for."
—*Romance Reviews Today*

"Dee Davis pours on the atmosphere and cranks up the danger in this terrific thriller."
—*Romantic Times* on *After Twilight*

"Author Dee Davis is making quite a name for herself in the romantic suspense field."
—*Romantic Times*

"A great romantic read from a wonderful romantic writer."
—Roundtable Reviews on *Wild Highland Rose*

EVELYN ROGERS

"Complex, fascinating romantic suspense.... Cleverly done. This is a suspenseful novel with some fairly spicy elements."
—*Romantic Times* on *More Than You Know*

"A wonderful romantic suspense thriller."
—Harriet Klausner on *More Than You Know*

CLAUDIA DAIN
DEE DAVIS
EVELYN ROGERS

SILENT NIGHT

LEISURE BOOKS   NEW YORK CITY

LEISURE BOOKS ®

October 2004

Published by

Dorchester Publishing Co., Inc.
200 Madison Avenue
New York, NY 10016

ISBN: 0-8439-5422-1

The name "Leisure Books" and the stylized "L" with design are trademarks of Dorchester Publishing Co., Inc.

Printed in the United States of America.

Visit us on the web at www.dorchesterpub.com.

SILENT NIGHT

TABLE OF CONTENTS

TRACKED

by Claudia Dain

CHAPTER ONE

She pulled off the highway and felt the rush in her blood. She was at the lake again. A turn, and then a turn again to take her back over Route 84 on the overpass and then she could see it: the lake glowing white and blue, frozen and crisp in the December night, ringed with dark trees and weathered cottages tucked safely beneath them. The lake. A place drowned in memory, thick with emotion. At least for her.

Always for her.

Even in winter the power of it was still strong.

Her car took the turns slowly, carefully, crushing the snowy slush on the road that was even now freezing, hardening again. These were country roads, back roads that wouldn't see a snowplow unless it *really* snowed. The last and first snow of the season had been two weeks ago;

what remained was a foot of snow that had been beaten into mild submission, forced to the sides of the road in mushy piles of brown and gray and murky white. Old snow. It had been warm today, warm enough to melt the snow huddled against the sides of the road so that every flat surface gleamed with snowmelt. But now it was dark and the temperature was dropping and the gleam of snowmelt was morphing into the glimmer of black ice.

She loved it up here, but the last thing she wanted was to slide off the road, stranded. She took the last turn with extreme care; the steep hill down to her family's cottage was the final hurdle in her race to get to the lake. The gravel crunched in frozen outrage beneath her tires, but then she was past it and she could see the dark shape of the cottage ahead of her, sitting expectantly in the dark, a small box resting on the snow. Behind it, the dull gleam of a lake buried in ice pushed against the darkness.

Her blood thumped slowly, electrically, in her veins. The lake. It wasn't home. No, it was more. It was like coming into a dream. A dream you dreamed again and again and wished only to dream yet one more time. And she always could.

And she always did.

She got out of her BMW, her feet sinking shin-deep into the snow, and then slogged her way over to the back door, the security light on the power pole helping her match the key to the lock. With a stiff creak, the door opened and she fell into the cottage, pounding the snow off her boots as she passed the threshold.

It was freezing inside, days of single-digit temperatures stored up within the cottage walls like an unwelcome gift. She stomped over to the thermostat and cranked it up to eighty. Her mom would kill her when she got the bill, but she'd be back at college by then, out of reach.

At least until spring break. Mom would have forgotten about it by then. Maybe.

She flipped on the lights and then, out of habit, turned on the floodlight that shone out over the lake. Green light swept over the snow and pierced the blue-white of ice. Of all the cottages on the lake, theirs was the only one that had a colored floodlight. It had started out as a joke, the only light they could find in the junk drawer, and then it had become tradition. Driving the boat home at night had become instantly easier with the green light to guide her over the blackened waters; it was like a wide green pathway that made finding home so easy.

No, not home. Finding the dream.

And just as in all good dreams, the phone rang.

Her heart jumped in her chest. Jumped and thumped and pounded. The green light. He had seen the light.

She picked up the wall-mounted phone and said, "Hello?"

"Hi," he said. That voice. That husky, sexy voice. She had turned on the light out of habit. *Yeah. Right.*

5

"Hi," she said softly, sitting down on a wooden chair, a very cold wooden chair.

"You're here," he said.

"Just got here," she said, and then mentally kicked herself. Nothing like sounding eager, like she'd run across the room, stumbling, to turn on the light so he would see it and call her. She didn't want him to call. She hated him. Or was supposed to.

How many times had they been through this? The passion, the betrayal, the breakup, the makeup. Like a circle, like the circular cycle of seasons. Summer, hot and slow, and then the explosive death of fall, and then the cold sulk of winter. Always the same. And always spring came again, the hope of heat, the promise of green life. Just like Keith. No matter what he did, what he did to kill what they had, he always came around, twirling hope and promise in his hands like shining knives, sparkling and dangerous.

He was dangerous to her, and he had proved it time after time, year after year. It was time to move on. Time to forget him. Time to stop running up to the lake and turning on that damned green light.

"Welcome back," he said, his voice a purr.

He said it as if he owned the lake, as if the whole place were his to bestow and his to rule. And maybe it was. He was the best at everything that mattered here: the best skier, the best swimmer, the best-looking, with the best car, the best boat. That had been important at seventeen, when the world seemed to revolve around such things. But she was older now, twenty, and in her third year at Duke. She ought to know better.

She had to know better. She couldn't get tangled up with him again.

"Thanks," she said, her voice tight with a hint of sarcasm. "How did your semester go?"

"Fine," he said. "Nailed Micro."

"That's great," she said, meaning it.

"When did you get back?"

"A few days ago," she said, wanting him to know that she hadn't rushed up here to see him, wanting him to see that she wasn't hungry for him, that she didn't need him, that this breakup was for real.

He was silent at that, but she could hear him breathing, hear the muffled curse he didn't try too hard to hide, hear him light up a cigarette.

"You're still smoking," she said.

"Yeah," he said on an exhale. "I start something, I don't quit it."

That was for her, a rebuke, a taunt that she'd given up on him. And she had. Some things were good to give up on. Smoking. Keith.

She didn't answer him. Let him sulk alone. She wasn't going to play this game anymore.

It wasn't like this with Jeff. Jeff was calm, rational, reasonable. All the things Keith wasn't. It might have been the best thing about Jeff, all the ways he wasn't like Keith.

Unfair and untrue. Jeff was gorgeous, taller and more muscular than Keith, which gave her a twisted sort of perverse satisfaction, since she knew Keith put a lot of hours into weight lifting to get the kind of cut that Jeff had effortlessly. Jeff was smart and kind and patient. He was the better guy. He was the right kind of guy. The perfect guy to fall in love with—a steady, reliable, predictable, soft-spoken guy. The kind of guy who kept his thing in his pants.

Another Keith comparison. She really had to stop comparing Jeff to Keith. It was wickedly unfair to Jeff, and he deserved better than that from her.

He was the guy any girl would want; she was more than halfway in love with him, falling in love with laughter that didn't have a price and with conversation that stayed polite. Keith was never polite. Keith was raw need, and all the need was his.

Except the need he inflamed in her.

Jeff didn't do that. She wouldn't let him get anywhere near enough to do that. Once burned, twice shy, and she'd been burned again and again by Keith. She should have learned to run from fire by now.

Should have.

"How long you up for?" he asked.

"The weekend," she said, letting thoughts of Jeff be pushed aside by the easy temptation of Keith's voice.

"You must be freezing your ass off," he said, laughing. He had a low, throaty laugh that sent shivers down to her knees.

"I am," she said, laughing with him.

"What you need is to get out of the house. Come snowmobiling with me. The ice is thick."

"I don't know," she said.

She didn't want to be alone with him. He was too dangerous to her resolve. She was *not* going to hook up with him again. She had Jeff, and Jeff was good news, while Keith was all trouble. Worse, Keith made trouble seem like fun.

"Come on, it'll be fun."

"Who else is going?" she asked, wondering why she bothered to ask.

Did it really matter who else was going? She didn't want to go. It was cold, it was dark, and it was cold. She'd never been a fan of cold. Anything below fifty degrees and she was shivering. It was way below fifty now. Trouble was, she'd loved this guy, once and over and over again. But that was done. She wasn't going to flake on Jeff.

Even though Jeff was out of state and would never know what she did or didn't do.

"Pete, Dave, maybe the Wall," he said. "You know. The guys."

"No girls?" she said, knowing the answer. There were never any girls. It was always Lindsay and the guys. Why make a thing about it now?

Because in the summer it was different. Open skies, open boats under the sun, lots of people around. Not like now. Nothing but massed cloud blocking out moon and stars, the bitter cold, and a hard wind in her face. And silence. No one around.

"It's just us, Lindsay," Keith said in an undertone. Oh, she loved his voice: husky, low, a throaty, velvety kind of sound that bounced against her skin and set it tingling. "I've missed you. I get hot and bothered every time I think about you."

"Don't think about me," she said, but she smiled. *Hot and bothered. Good.* Let him suffer a little. Couldn't do him anything but good.

"I tried," he said softly.

"I'll bet you did," she said, losing her smile. That was his problem. He couldn't keep it in his pants. Always running around on her, lying like he breathed, with every heartbeat, with every word. "Ask one of them to go with you. I'm staying home," she said, hanging up on him.

That felt good.

She rubbed her hands down her arms, rubbing some warmth into herself, rubbing out the anger that Keith always sparked in her. Young love, first love, and all that crap. She was older now, wiser, in college, on her own, twenty—too smart to get hooked up with him again. How many times would she have to repeat it before it sank in?

The phone rang, the sound bouncing off the pine walls of the cabin, slamming along the wide banks of window that were black against the night, hiding in the tall pitched ceiling of her parents' lakeside retreat. She picked up the receiver and then slammed it down.

Back off, Keith.

Why had she come up here? It was too cold and too isolated, all the summer crowds gone by

Labor Day, only the townies left and lots of cold emptiness. But it was still the lake, still her favorite place on earth, the place where she knew who she was, where she liked who she was. Not many places like that around.

College was great, too, of course. She loved it, loved her new life with new friends and a new guy. She was happy.

So why come up here? Who went to a small lake in Massachusetts in December, to a cabin that had a raised foundation and not a single roll of insulation? Well, that was the power of the lake; she wanted it anytime. Maybe this place was her first love and not Keith, who came part and parcel with it. He was a townie. He was always here, knew every back road, every trail, every boat. Every girl.

She threw that thought aside and went over and twisted the knob on the thermostat up until the plastic cracked in protest. They really needed to get this place winterized. Her parents hadn't updated a thing except the refrigerator since the late seventies, when they'd first bought the cabin as newlyweds. No microwave, no television, no dishwasher, an old white range with a metal tube for venting, a shower stall set against rough planking in the single bathroom.

It was rough. It wasn't one of those pretty cabins that were in all the home décor magazines. The closets were small, no air-conditioning, tiny floor heaters, banging screen doors, and a couch that had probably looked ragged when new, but it

11

was home in a way that their West Hartford home had never been. It was small, and cozy, and woody, and quiet. It was secluded and safe, nestled under a giant pine that arched over the roof and would probably take out the house if a good wind ever hit it just right. The porch was huge and spanned the width of the house on the lake side, and the water sparkled in the sun, sending up shimmers on the wooden ceiling all through the long summer days.

But it wasn't summer now. It was winter and it was dark and there was a good foot of snow on the ground from a solid Thanksgiving storm that hadn't melted much in two weeks. And the stupid heater couldn't bring the temperature in this drafty cabin up to fifty-five degrees in a week of trying.

Okay, so keep the old range and the old shower and the thin windows that let in every finger of frigid air; couldn't they just get some insulation shoved in under the foundation? Maybe a storm window or two? There wasn't even a cell signal up here. Primitive.

She eyed the old-style phone hanging on a strip of pine between the plate-glass window over the dining table and the door to the porch. Silent. He could have called again.

But she didn't want him to call. He was all trouble and she was past trouble, past wanting it, past needing the excitement of the ride he took her on every time she was with him. She was twenty. Old enough to know better, old enough to *want* better.

Okay, enough killing time; if that was the best the heater could do, she needed to eat something, and fast. She was shaking off calories with every shiver. Even if she started now, it would take at least thirty minutes for the oven to blast something frozen into something hot and steaming.

She should have stopped on the way and eaten something, but she'd been too eager, too hungry to get up here. Just like always. Her parents had wanted them all to ride together, but that would have meant waiting for them to get off work, and she hadn't wanted to wait. She never wanted to wait.

Back when she was in high school and the days were stretching out in warmth and sun, her mom would pick her up at school, the car loaded with food and clothes, and away they'd go, off to the lake for the weekend. She'd go waterskiing in a wet suit, hands frozen to the handle of the rope, the ice just melted. Out on the water, the joy of it after months away burst through the last of winter and the cold chop of spring water.

It had been the same today, though the boat was stored for winter, the dock pulled up and lying in a rectangular heap beneath the snow, the lake frozen hard and fast against the shore. But still, it was the lake, and she had needed to be here. Home from college in the south, where it was never this bone-numbingly cold, to her heart's home, this small cottage on the water under a pine.

She cracked open the freezer door, bracing

herself for the tingle of frigid air on her face. Nothing. The freezer was only slightly colder than the air in the cabin. Pathetic.

She surveyed the contents: four TV dinners, three frostbitten and half-dried ice-cream bars, and a can of orange juice. Not bad. She pulled out an ice-cream bar to survey the damage, carefully peeling the wrapper from it. A few good bites still left. She might have been freezing, but it was never the *wrong* time for ice cream. The TV dinners were all in good condition, a Salisbury steak, two chicken Alfredos, and sliced turkey. She pulled out the steak and one Alfredo, shoving the others back in. Let her dad have the pressed turkey; he'd eat anything.

She turned on the oven and waited for the heat to press against her skin. She put her gloves back on while she waited, taking another sweet bite of ice cream. A burst of wind slammed against the side of the cabin, causing it to shudder on its slender raised pillars of concrete. She took another bite and stared at the oven, willing it to give up some heat. It refused.

She pulled her cell phone out of her coat pocket. No signal. She sighed and took another bite; definitely a freezer burn aftertaste. She threw the rest of it into the plastic grocery bag her mom kept next to the sink to hold all the trash from the car trip up here. She hadn't had any car trash; she'd been in too much of a hurry to make any trash.

She gave up her vigilant stare into the white obstinance of the oven and walked over to the plate-glass window. It was colder here, the air pushing against the glass, seeping through it and around the caulking, finding its way in. She put her hand out, glove off, and touched it. It was like touching black ice, frozen beyond whiteness, lost to all but cold.

She put her glove back on and stared out. Her pale reflection showed ghostly against the sheen of glass, the lake beyond a field of ice and snow that could not show white, pressed down as it was by the oppressive hand of night. No moon, no stars, no light, all black cold and crunching frost. No life. No sound but the sporadic, angry wind.

The phone rang next to her head and she jumped an inch, her shoulders hunched against the assault.

"Hello?"

"Hi, honey," her mom said, breathless, frustrated, a bit worried. She heard all that. It was her mom. She knew all her moods and all her voices. "You made it okay?"

"Yeah," she answered, happier than she wanted to admit at hearing her mom's voice. She was twenty. Beyond that. Beyond that kind of need. "It's freezing up here, though. Where are you?"

"Stuck," her mom said. "There's an accident on 84, every lane blocked."

"That's awful," she said automatically. "What happened?"

"I don't know. It's way up ahead of us, but it seems bad. Fire trucks, ambulances—I think I counted eight police cars."

"Ten," her dad said distantly from his side of the car. He was driving. He always drove when the weather was bad. "Ask her if she's okay."

"I'm okay," she answered. "I'm just cold. Why can't we get some good heating up here?"

"If we used the cabin in the winter more . . ." her mom started to say.

"Well, I'm here, and you're coming, so we're using it."

"I'm getting off here," her dad said, his voice muffled. "This exit looks good."

"Where are you getting off?" she asked. She wanted to see them. The cold was oppressive, the dark a weight that pressed against her skin. Too alone, she was too alone, and the cabin and the lake were not as friendly in December as they were in July.

"We're getting off in Tolland to turn around," her mom said. "Are you okay there? We thought we'd try again in the morning, early. It's just such a mess now. You could come home if you don't want to stay. I think the southbound stretch is fine. Why don't you come home? We'll have hot chocolate waiting for you."

"You're not coming?" she said, struggling to get past that bit of information.

"Honey, we'd be sitting here all night and—"

"Tell her to come home," her dad said. "The winds are getting fierce and they're predicting sleet."

"Lindsay," her mother said, "how are the roads up there? Any trouble getting in?"

The gravel road down to the cabin was steep, perfect for a suicidal toboggan run. It hadn't been too bad getting down, but if it sleeted and then froze, only a Hummer could make it back up.

"Just tell her to come home," her dad said.

She was twenty, too old, too mature to need this kind of hugging care. The wind pushed hard and viciously against the walls of the cabin, bowing in the glass of the window where she could see her somber, distorted reflection. She wanted to go home. It was too cold, too alone here. Too dark and still and deep in cold, in silent, pressing, relentless cold.

A crack, a ripping, woody crack, and then a crash, muffled by snow and amplified by ice. Darkness. Silence.

"Mom?" she said into the silent phone. *"Mom?"*

She let the phone fall to hang in twisting silence upon its turning cord and went to the small side window, pushing back the summer-weight curtains. A limb from the pine had fallen, tangling with the suspended power lines, crushing the trunk of her BMW, boxing her in, shutting her into the dark.

The sound came first, a raw whine over the deep roar of power. An engine from out of the dark, sending its blast of noise over the ice, announcing its coming.

She ran to the picture window and looked out. A single light bouncing over the ridges in the ice-clasped lake, a snowmobile roaring toward her.

The only light in all that darkness, a cold light, alone and fragile, but still a light, and aimed right at her.

Her breath came out in white gasps of panic and hope. Pulling her coat tight around her, she wrenched open the porch door, which stuck with cold, and pushed the screen door against a pile of frozen snow on the threshold. It tumbled into the cabin to lie in a wet and bumpy pile on the worn wooden floor, but she was out, out into the darkness, hoping the snowmobile could see her dark form against the white of the cabin.

It slowed, searching, trailing back and forth, and then jumped forward in a loud burst of noise and light. Straight to her. She smiled in relief, her teeth chattering against the cold. She was cold, but she wasn't alone. Not anymore.

The snowmobile was just a long, dark shape in the night, only the single headlight marking it, showing its passage over the ice and onto the snowy bank. The buried dock loomed large for an instant, casting a long and deadly shadow to where she stood upon the porch, but then the light swerved, missing it, and the engine stopped. Silence fell down upon her like a down jacket, muffling her, wrapping her within its still embrace.

A figure parted from the machine, dressed in black, helmeted with a shaded full-face visor. Large black boots crunched over the snow, leaping over the steps to the porch with a single sliding step.

"Hi," he said, pulling off the visor that shielded his face. "You okay?"

Against every trace of better judgment and twenty-year-old maturity, she flew into his arms and wrapped herself around him. It was hard going, not unlike hugging the Michelin Man, but he still felt good, and it felt even better to have someone sharing the dark with her.

"I'm okay," she said, pressing her cold nose against his cheek. "The power just went out and my car's wrecked and I'm stranded here, but I'm okay."

"Your car's wrecked?" Keith said, pulling away from her and moving toward the open doorway. "What about your folks? Their car okay?"

"They're not here—traffic pileup on 84," she said, following him into the cabin. "And it's no use going in, since it's as cold in there as out here. Well, maybe not *as* cold."

"Not here, huh?" he said, turning to face her and pull her into the cabin, then shoving the door closed with a gloved hand. "Too bad."

She laughed just to look at him. Cornflower blue eyes with impossibly long, curled lashes. Dark blond hair, a jawline to cut your finger on, and the sexiest nose. Not many people could claim a sexy nose, but he could. And that voice, that seductive, throaty, velvety voice that he dragged over her skin like cashmere.

"Perv," she said. "It's twenty below, and we're past that anyway. We broke up, remember?"

"It's not even ten below, and you broke up with

me. I didn't break up with you. That's why I'm here. To talk. To get you back."

"To talk? Yeah, and when did we ever do much talking?"

"We did enough," he said, pulling off his gloves and wrapping her in his arms. He was so tall. She loved getting lost in his arms. "Cashmere?" he said, running his hands under her coat and over her sweater. "You knew I was coming. I can't keep my hands off you in cashmere."

She hadn't known he was coming, but she had hoped. Only to herself would she admit that. She couldn't fall into Keith again; he was nothing but heartbreak, and he lied about everything. But when he looked into her eyes, she believed everything he said. And he could get into her clothes like no man she'd ever known.

That had been the start of it. She'd gone out with him, a boat date on a June night on the lake, part of the dating ritual of the lake. She'd gone out with Keith because he was cute and persistent and she didn't have anything else to do. She was between boyfriends and just killing time with him. It wasn't ever going to be anything serious between them.

But it hadn't worked out that way. A pity date. Keith had been *that* close to a pity date, and then Keith had kissed her and she'd been lost. He'd literally kissed her blind. She hadn't known that was physically possible, but it was and he'd done it. He'd kissed her and then he'd found his way up her shirt and into her bra; a practiced twist of his fingers and her bra had been in his hand and then lying on the boat seat, a forgotten fragment of lace and elastic.

How long had it taken him? Ten minutes? She'd never been so completely *seduced* in her life. Ten minutes more and he was in her pants, her zipper cranked down and her breath heaving into his mouth, burning up with passion and lust and blind, hot need to touch and be touched. And then he'd said, "Now do me," and she'd blinked a few times like a sex zombie and found herself holding him in her hand, his pants unzipped and down around his thighs.

Well, that had been it. She'd gone farther with him in thirty minutes than she had with any other guy, ever. She was not an easy mark. Or she wasn't with anyone but him. She'd gotten herself re-arranged into her clothes while he got settled into his, kissing him like she couldn't live without his kiss on her skin the whole time, dazed and drugged on passion and on shock. He'd walked her up the dock, to the porch, said a proper good night to her parents, and she'd thought, *How did that happen?*

She was still thinking it.

"Look," she said, squirming out of his arms, "I happen to be freezing. Can we go to your house? I could call my parents from there."

"Yeah," he said, pulling off his helmet and holding it under his arm. His hair was plastered to his head, and when he shook it out it stood up in static-electric strands. He looked ridiculous and adorable and a little bit dangerous. "But what about your car? They're not coming and you can't go."

"What about *your* car?" she said, tightening her coat against the cold and against the seductive look in his eyes.

"Wrecked it last week. Wrapped it around a tree," he said.

"Your MG?" she said, coming to stand near him, laying her hands on his arms, running a hand through his hair, just touching him in any way she could, the MG a good excuse. "You loved that car."

"Yeah, and so did you," he purred.

She had. It was small and sexy and retro, and he'd looked amazing driving it, a cigarette dangling from his mouth, his hand on the stick, his eyes illuminated when he took a sharp drag of his cigarette. She didn't even smoke and hated the taste, the smell, the whole deal, but on him, it worked. Or at least, it worked on her. Hey, she'd seen *Rebel Without a Cause*. She was as James Dean nuts as anyone. Keith had that look, that sharp, vulnerable, sexy, dangerous thing that women just melted for.

Look how she'd melted on the upholstered seat of his boat.

"You okay? Did you get hurt?" she said, wrapping herself around him, pressing against his muffled heat. She was pathetic.

"Nope," he said, holding her to him. "Just the car. I was lucky, though. I was trapped inside it for an hour. They had to cut me out. If it had started burning . . . toast."

"Oh, Keith," she said, lifting her face for a kiss. He didn't disappoint her. In this, he never did.

Hot twirls of desire unwound and moved upward, downward, outward. Her heart fluttered before it kicked in and started hammering hard against her lungs, shortening her breath, tumbling her stomach from its spot to crash into her hips and flounder there. God, why? Every time. Every single time.

When they pulled apart, she said, "What happened? How did it happen?"

He shrugged and pulled out of her arms, turning his back to her. "I was drunk. Mad at you. Missing you. I just, ya know, wanted to die."

And, just like every time before, all soft feeling died. He always did this, this manipulation, this poor-pitiful-me thing that left her cold. Cold and angry. Did he really think she'd want to be with a guy who was suicidal? And a drunk driver? Yeah, how attractive.

"Too bad about the car," she said stiffly, grabbing up her cashmere scarf from her purse and tying it around her head. Her ears were about to fall off from the cold.

"Yeah, too bad," he said, spinning around to face her, his tone hard and his eyes angry. Just like always. Nothing ever changed, and never him.

"Your snowmobile still works," she said. "Think you can get me to your house without cracking it up?"

"My folks aren't home," he said softly, studying

her. "You still wanna go? All that heat. All those beds. All that 'alone'?"

Hell, no. They'd done that once before, last summer. His folks had been gone and they'd played on his bed all afternoon. If anyone could die of sex, she would have, right there. She'd been so wobbly when she left, he'd had to help her down the stairs to his dock. He hadn't taken the boat above five mph the whole long way back to her cabin; it had taken her that long to clear her vision and get her balance.

That was her problem. Keith had been her first, right there on the couch behind him, that ratty old couch that absorbed wet bathing suits and sand and semen and never complained or showed a mark. He was her first. He'd always be her first, and there was just no getting past it.

He was also her only. Jeff? Sorry, but no way was anyone else going to find his way into her pants. Been there. Too hard to walk away once passion had you by the throat. No way was she going to get tied to a guy again because he was good in bed and bad at everything else. Good in bed was great, as long as you never left bed. Life was more than that, and at twenty she knew it.

She wondered if Keith did. He still acted like good in bed was all he needed.

"No, I don't want that," she said, saying it all.

"I didn't think so," he said, his blue eyes soft with pain.

"I'm freezing here, though," she said, turning away from him, stamping her feet in her boots,

24

succeeding only in driving icy pain up through her shins.

"You've gone soft," he said, a smile in his voice. "Turning Southern, losing all your Yankee toughness."

"Oh, I'm still pretty tough," she said, ducking her head into her upturned collar, burying her cheeks against cashmere. "I never did like the cold. Why do you think I went to Duke? Nice climate. It was sixty degrees the day I left."

"And twenty-eight when you landed at Bradley."

"How did you know?" she said, turning in a whirl of surprise. "That was it exactly."

He ducked his face, sniffing against the cold, his nose turning red at the tip. "I called your mom. She told me when you were getting in. I went to the airport to see you."

"I didn't see you."

"I didn't come in. I waited in the car until you came out and then just drove home. I thought your parents had more right to you than I did."

But he had made a point of telling her, so she'd know that he had come, had cared, had kept his distance. Was she supposed to pity him or admire him? And he had lied again. Hadn't he just asked her on the phone when she'd come back from school? He'd known, but he'd lied, because lying was what he did best. Even better than bed.

"It was nice of you to come," she said quietly, falling back on good manners, unsure what to think.

"I just wanted to see you, Lindsay," he said. "Don't freak about it."

"Do I look like I'm freaking out? I'm freezing to death, that's all. I'll do it quietly, no freaking," she said, laughing at him and at herself. Young love, true love: total crap.

"You don't do anything quietly," he said, grinning at her. "Remember?"

"Shut up," she said, laughing.

She loved laughing with him. Never did much of that, though, since they were too busy fighting and making up. Too much passion between them. That was the trouble. Too much passion and not enough sense. He exhausted her.

"Come here," he said, with a macho motion of his head. It should have made her want to hit him. It made her want to melt.

"Yeah? I'm here," she said, not moving an inch. Thank God for bulky clothes. In the summer, when the only barrier was a wisp of cloth over her crotch and breasts, she was dead meat, ready for serving.

"Come on," he said, his voice a sexy snarl. "What can happen? I couldn't get out of this thing without a winch and a good ten-minute head start."

"Anything can happen," she said, moving across the wooden floor to him, her feet more eager than she was. "We both know that."

"Yeah, but that's only because I can't keep my hands off you," he said, pushing her scarf down to her neck, kissing her mouth, her cheek, her ear, nibbling, whispering. "Never could. Never even want to try. I love you, Lindsay. Let's make up."

Shivers of hot desire ran down her skin and

into her blood, melting her joints, liquefying bone until she could hardly stand. He was so good at this. So good.

"We're always making up. I'm sick of fighting," she said, running her hands through his hair, kissing his jaw and the line of his throat. Sharp line, coarse beard, smooth run of skin over flesh, the delicious smell of his skin teased by the acrid smell of tobacco; sexy. He was sexy, and she felt sexy with him. Jeff didn't do this to her. Not even close.

But she'd never let Jeff get this close.

"You fight with him? You make up like this with him?" he said, his hands roaming under her coat, under her sweater, his hands cold on her skin and then warming instantly as he took them into the fire of desire. His hands slipped around her back and shoulders, sliding her bra down to uncover her breasts.

Cold fingers on nipples: strangely exciting, instantly erotic. Trembling for him in seconds, wanting his hands everywhere, hot and aching, leaning into his kiss, like falling into fire, like swimming in lava, hot and thick. No thoughts but one: *More. More and more and more.*

"Who?" she said, unzipping his padded suit, her fingers cold on the heat of his neck. Unzipping, unzipping, the zipper went on forever, a long black line down past his crotch. Yes, the bulge of him that matched the hot void in her. A match, a perfect match. But only in this. It was when they talked that all the trouble came.

"Your college guy down there," he said, his voice harsh with anger and passion, a wild mix that she'd heard before. "You do this with him?"

She pushed him away with both hands, disgusted with him and with herself.

"Just . . . shut up, would you? I can't keep doing this," she said.

"Can't keep doing this with me?" he said, pulling her back into his arms. "I'll bet you can do it with him all night long."

"Would you just *shut up!*" she shouted, shoving him from her, pulling her sweater down, staring at him in panting, blind anger.

"No, I won't," he said. "I love you. I'm not going to lose you without a fight."

"You're losing me *because* you fight! I can't take all this fighting. It's over *nothing* half the time."

"But the other half is about something," he said, stalking her. "I'm not letting you go, Lindsay."

"Too late!" she yelled. "I'm gone!"

She turned and ran to her bedroom and grabbed a shoe off the shoe rack hung over the back of the door and hurled it at him. Summer shoes, a strappy, thin-soled sandal. Worthless as a weapon in a lovers' fight. He lifted a hand and pushed it aside. And kept coming. She threw another shoe. And another. She was a terrible shot. Nothing seemed to hit him. He looked enraged beyond bearing, but so was she. He always did this to her: hot desire and then hot anger. Never anything in the middle. Never any peace.

It wasn't like this with Jeff. Keith created his

own storms wherever he went. Or maybe he created them only with her. Maybe they were emotional poison to each other. Maybe with another woman, he was all calm reason and cool logic.

The idea made her sick.

She threw her last shoe, a flip-flop, and then he was on her, grabbing her by the wrists and shoving her onto the bed, his weight the only weapon he needed. He was taller and longer and stronger, but he was no angrier. She matched him there. He pressed her hands down and away, holding her down, his hips pressing against her splayed legs. And then his mouth came down, a hard and angry line that matched the cold crackle in his icy blue eyes.

A kiss, a hard, heavy, hot kiss that fanned both anger and passion until they merged and she didn't know or care which was which. He kissed her, his tongue—the very taste of him—a much-missed friend she welcomed with a sigh of longing. She heaved beneath him, relishing her confinement, his domination, his anger, and his passion. Let him punish her with passion. She wasn't afraid. She knew what he brought to her, and she wanted it.

She had always wanted it.

He had done this to her from the very start, the very first kiss, the very first touch. He wasn't the man she would have chosen, and she didn't choose him now. She didn't want Keith in her life; she didn't want the turmoil and the chaos, but whenever he touched her, she wanted him.

And so it went, on and on it went, though they had chosen colleges distant from each other, though their lives were moving relentlessly apart. Still they found each other and were like snarling, mating animals when they were together. Always finding cause to be together.

This was the hunger she had driven north to feed. This need for him, found within the cold beauty of the lake and all the memories of him that lived here, buried under snow and frost, burning to be free, firing her blood until she bubbled for him, gasping for release.

His mouth tore at hers, his teeth nipping at her, his tongue hot, invasive, his hands hard against her wrists, holding her to his will, capturing her will in his. Her breasts heaved up, brushing against his chest, her thin bra shoved askew.

"Touch me," she demanded against his mouth, gasping for air against his skin.

He let go of her hands slowly, testing her ferocity, and then he lifted her sweater up and pulled her bra down with rough hands, exposing her to his mouth and hands, taking her in his mouth, claiming her with his hands.

She bucked into his mouth, giving him her body, feeling her heart slipping through her grasp, her mind churned to mud beneath his touch. She did not trust him. She knew that. She could not forget it, though she wanted to. She gave him her body for the price of a kiss, but not her heart.

He fumbled with his zipper, hands to his crotch, and she lay panting beneath him, waiting for him to slide into her, plunging hard and deep, knowing it would feel right. Knowing that in the minutes after, when they had both cooled and her brain was working again, she would be buried in shame and desperation. The same ride. The same dark, dangerous ride.

Why couldn't she get off?

The sound of engines came to them from out in the cold dark. Multiple engines, many machines churning over the ice, whining in the cold.

"Shit," he said.

She could see the faint outline of him above her, a darker shape within the darkness. She heard his zipper and then felt his hands on her bra, pulling it down, pulling down her sweater, laying a hand on her stomach in a passionate caress.

"It's them. Pete and the guys," he said. "I told them I was coming here."

She sat up and pushed at her hair, shaking it out, hoping it didn't scream bed head. With his passion leashed, the room got suddenly colder, and she pulled her coat tight around her, buttoning it and feeling for her scarf.

She didn't say a word. What was there to say? Anything she said would make her sound stupid or angry or jealous, and she didn't want to be any of those things, or at least be thought any of those things. Every word with Keith was a potential weapon. He took offense at the smallest thing, and half the time she didn't even understand what it was they were fighting about.

But as he said, there was the other half when she knew exactly what they were fighting about.

"We're going to snowmobile in Brimfield State Forest. Come with us," he said, issuing the same invitation he had over the phone. "It'll be fun."

"It's pretty cold out," she said. The idea of snowmobiling in the strange darkness of a forest, in the bitter cold of December, was not a tempting thought. She wanted heat and a hot meal. And a car to get her to those things.

"Come on," he said as the angry drone of the snowmobiles got closer. The guys would be here any minute. They left the bedroom single file, heads down, as if ashamed of what had happened there. Not too far off, really. "It's better than sitting here in the dark."

"Yeah, I could be whipping through the dark at thirty miles an hour. That sounds great," she said. "Look, I've got to get out of here. Someplace with heat, food, and cars that run. That's Sturbridge. I can't stay here. Too cold."

Too alone. If she refused to go snowmobiling in Brimfield, Keith might leave her here alone, punishing her for not doing what he wanted. Definitely a possibility. Not an option she wanted to take. Alone for an hour or two while she waited for her parents to get here, that was okay. But now? With no power and no car? No way.

"So go," he said. The snowmobiles had stopped, one by one, outside on the ice. She could hear the muffled sound of male voices and the heavy squeak of snow being smashed beneath booted feet. They were on the porch. "Use your snowmobile to ride to Sturbridge."

"Ride on 84? I'll get hit by a car, the way my luck is running."

"No," he said as the door opened and a helmeted and fully outfitted man entered, followed by another, and another, tracking snow all over the floors. The room suddenly seemed full of masked men, but that was crazy. She knew these guys. She'd spent summers joking with them on boats and lounging around on docks, soaking up the sun. "Follow us to the state forest; it's a straight shot over to Sturbridge from there. I'll lead you there. No problem."

"Why do we have to go to the state forest first? Why not go straight to Sturbridge?" she asked.

"Come on, Lindsay," Keith said softly, dipping his head down so the guys wouldn't hear him. *As if.* They were only two feet behind him. "We set this up before. Come with us. It'll be fun."

"Unless you don't think you can keep up," Dave said, taking off his helmet.

She really hated Dave, a rat-faced kind of guy who was always at the back of the pack and so always looking real hard to shove someone behind him. Like her. He was small and blue-eyed and had a soft, mushy mouth. He reminded her of a cross between a rat and a skinny weasel and had the personality to match.

"Yeah," Pete said, his helmet off, his heavily waved brown hair untouched by the pressure of the helmet. "You've been riding on the lake. It's different to snowmobile in the woods. The track will be narrow with lots of turns. You could dump or crack up."

Definitely a challenge. She was used to it with these guys. She ran with them, because of Keith, and she competed with them in everything they did. And she did okay. She could keep up with them at skiing, boating, swimming, and snowmobiling. She wasn't a drinker, but her first time at drinking had been in a contest with these guys, and she was delighted to say that she had drunk Rat Dave under the dock and held her own with Pete and Keith.

It was her last time at drinking, too. It had been worth it, just to beat Dave. He'd tried to deny it the next day, but Pete and Keith had held him to the truth. He'd been outdrunk by a girl who weighed thirty pounds less than he did. He was a skinny little rat.

"Come or not, but let's get going," Wall said. His mom called him Wally, but no one else did. He didn't say much, just kind of smirked a lot. She didn't mind him much, and he didn't seem to mind her much.

"Isn't it illegal to ride through the state forest?" she asked, her final try at dissuading them.

"Yeah," said Dave with a stupid grin, "watch out or the park police will get you."

"I will," she said. "Now I just have to find the keys to the shed. I hope my snowmobile is gassed up."

Keith shot a look over her head to his friends.

"I'm sure it is," he said.

CHAPTER TWO

She was freezing. She was wearing all the appropriate gear, looked like she weighed about six hundred pounds, and she was rapidly freezing to death. It could have been worse. She could have been slowly freezing to death.

Keith took the key for the shed from her thickly gloved hand and worked the simple lock that held the dead bolt. It wasn't fancy, but the cabin was so remote, there wasn't much need for sophisticated anticrime equipment. The key turned easily in the lock; it was the dead bolt that was tough. It looked frozen in place, and Keith pulled hard on it to get it to slide over, opening up the barn-style shed door. Keith had helped her dad build this shed, just as Keith had convinced her parents to buy a snowmobile. Mr. Helpful. Did they know he had taken her virginity on the old couch her mom had nursed her on?

Probably not.

But they didn't like him much, for all his help-ful cheer and eager goodwill. Oh, her mom thought he was cute, could see his appeal, but her dad . . . he just watched Keith with a small smile pasted on his face and held his tongue. Whenever she'd ask about it, wanting everyone in the world to be in love with the guy she was in love with, her dad would just shrug and shake his head.

But it had been his idea that she look at col-leges away from New England.

She was happy at Duke. It gave her some dis-tance from Keith and from the weight of passion and obsession between them.

There'd been some distance at the start; he'd been a summer romance. A boy from the lake who could have no place in her *real* life in West Hartford. But somehow, life at the lake had be-come more real, more important than her other life, and Keith had found his way into her winters.

He had come to her senior prom, an unknown guy with magnetic sexual appeal who had charmed all her girlfriends and left them gasping and giggling in frustrated longing. He had come to football games, and once, in the dead of night, he had driven the fifty miles that separated them because she had called to say she needed him. She'd sneaked out of the house and met him at the end of the street and they'd made awkward and desperate love in the passenger seat of his MG.

The MG that he'd destroyed in a drunken fit of temper and self-pity.

Or maybe he'd just rear-ended some woman in a minivan in a parking lot. She'd never know. Just as she'd never know how many girls had crawled into his bed while they were in separate high schools. He came into her winters; she didn't go into his.

Duke had been a good choice. Once free of him, of the reach of his voice and his touch, she'd found her footing again. Life was calm, and she was logical and smart enough to make good choices. Jeff was a good choice. He was handsome and built and premed and her friends loved him.

Did she love him?

Maybe. She didn't know, but he was a good choice. No more bad choices. No more Keith, no matter what had just happened on her narrow bed in that pine-scented room. Or almost happened.

Keith walked cautiously into the black interior of the shed, shuffling his feet in the dark.

"You got the key?" he called out, his voice muffled by cold and dark and the high collar of his padded suit.

"Isn't it there?" she called back. "Oh. Right. It's in the junk drawer. I'll be right back."

The guys were waiting on the front porch, talking and laughing and gently slugging one another on the arm. *Typical.* She rifled through the drawer in the dark, feeling for the shape of the snowmobile key ring among all the other junk-crowded key rings in the drawer. Too much stuff on the key rings. What had seemed cute in her teens now seemed annoying. Every key ring had to be the size of a baseball. Her fingers brushed over the spare boat key with its small bright orange buoy, the spare house key on a simple brass ring with a brass tree silhouette hanging from it, a broken paring knife, a button, a pair of scissors, and a ton of old scraps of paper. In the very front, shoved in a corner, was the snowmobile key, the ring marked with a thick hunk of plastic in the shape of a ski.

She shoved the drawer closed with a huff of effort and a squeak of protest from the cold, dry wood and then shuffled her way out the back door to the shed, passing her broken car on the way. It didn't look *too* bad, but it would take some kind of machine to lift that pine branch off her car, and probably the phone guys would fight the electrical company over who would do it. Every agency claimed territorial rights over its own special wires.

"You got it?" Keith said, standing in the wide doorway of the shed.

"Yeah," she answered, handing him the key. "Listen, can't I just go to your house and use your phone? I got cut off from my mom and she'll worry."

"What about your cell phone?"

"There's never any reception here. Come on, I'm freezing."

"Yeah, I heard," he said, straddling the snowmobile and fitting the key in the ignition. "You want to back out, that's okay. It's just that"—he shrugged and turned to her, his voice wistful in the dark—"I want to be with you, that's all. I haven't seen you since August. Life's shit without you."

"I thought you liked Trinity," she said, trying to keep her distance from the net of his emotional need.

"It's okay," he said. "But you're not there."

"Don't do this," she said softly, shaking her head at him, warning herself that this was what he did best, tying her up, nailing her down. Nailing her, period.

"Don't do what?" he said, lifting his head, ready to fight. "I tell you that I miss you, that I love you, that my life sucks without you and I'm *doing* something? What the hell am I doing, Lindsay? *Loving you?* Is that it? Is that what has you all tied in a twist?"

"What's going on?" Dave called over the top of the pitched roof. "You guys going at it again? Let's *go.*"

"So can I go to your house or what?" she asked, weary beyond belief. She hadn't seen him since August. She'd forgotten how exhausting dealing with his never-ending emotional needs could be.

"My folks were going out to dinner. They're probably gone by now," he said stiffly. "You wanna go with us, come on. I'll take you to Sturbridge after."

"You know," she said, feeling anger rise in her, "it

would be kinda nice if you could, just this once, do something *I* need instead of what you want. I mean, I'm kinda in trouble here. I could use some help."

"Yeah, and it's always about what *you* need, and that hasn't changed in all the time we've been together. *You* need to go to Duke and so you go. *You* need to warm your cute ass and so I've got to put my night on hold."

"Look, could you stop it about Duke? You picked your school. I picked mine. You wanna go to Duke? Go!"

"I am," he said softly. "That is, if they'll take me. I put in for a transfer."

Shit.

"You don't look too happy about it," he said, standing up, his feet balanced on the runners. He towered over her.

"No, I'm just surprised," she said. "When do you start?"

What was she going to do about Jeff? How long would it take for Keith to find him? To mess things up with his lies?

They had broken up in August, when his college lay had shown up at the lake, ready for more and not too shy about saying it. And he'd been e-mailing her every week during school, whining about how much he missed her and how desperate he was for her. How much he *loved* her.

"It's not set yet. I don't know if the transfer will go through."

"Yeah. Right," she said, thinking, panicking. "But

40

won't you miss it here? I mean, being on the lake all the time?"

He might have been going to school in Hartford, but he was home on most weekends doing the guy thing: ice fishing, snowmobiling, skiing. At least he said that was what he was doing. He might actually be staying on campus and screwing everything in sight.

And he had every right. They had broken up in August. August 16, actually. Pathetic that she remembered the day.

"I miss you more," he said, his voice a weapon she had no defense against. His voice throbbed with need buried in velvet, a rough caress that urged her to relent, to submit, to forget her doubts and just believe. Believe every word he said. Believe every kiss and every caress. "I want us to have a chance."

"Come on!" Dave yelled from the front.

"Shut the fuck up!" Keith yelled in answer, making her jump in surprise.

"Stop swearing," she said, her automatic response. She hated swearing, the violence of it, the coarseness, just like she hated smoking. *Yeah, right. A real turnoff.*

If only.

"You gonna spank me?" he said, pulling her into his arms. She was buried in him, her face muffled against the black of his suit.

"You wish," she said, burrowing in, finding home in his arms, even if home wasn't happy and safe.

God, she was a mess around him. He *couldn't* come to Duke. She wouldn't stand a chance.

"You coming?" he said, reaching down to grab her butt.

Did she have a choice? She probably did, but she couldn't see it.

"Yeah," she said, checking her zippers. "Let's go."

She had no idea where she was. She was at the back of the pack, the sound of the motors the only sound in the darkness, the lights of the snowmobiles the only light, and that flashing erratically over snow and against tree trunks at thirty mph. She was following blindly, staying in the leaders' tracks, watching their lights bouncing against the night, determined not to be left behind.

It seemed pretty obvious that they wanted to leave her behind, which was nothing new.

Pete led them, Dave following, Wall next, and then Keith, just in front of her, looking back every now and then to watch her progress. It wasn't out of concern that she was in over her head or that she might be eager for this adventure in frozen joy to end. Oh, no, not that, because every time Keith looked back at her and saw her still there, he revved up his speed and they all lurched ahead. And so she throttled down and dug her booted feet into the runners, lowered her masked face behind the scanty windshield and matched them, mile after mile.

Her hands, frozen lumps of stinging pain, were starting to cramp.

But she couldn't stop and knew there would be no mercy for a girl who was cold.

She didn't know these woods. She couldn't find her way out if she let them get ahead of her. She knew most of the woods around the lake, had walked them and had dirt-biked the trails hidden behind the narrow roads, but that had been in summer and in daylight, and she had never ventured into the state forest. Why push against the law when there was so much to do within it? Guys, they never had any fun unless they were breaking something.

Her headlight showed a sudden clearing, a white break in the trees. The guys slowed and then stopped, and she stopped with them, hoping that this test of her toughness was at an end.

They spoke with their helmets on and their visors down; it was too cold to take anything off. They shouted to be heard, the sound of their voices reverberating behind their tinted plastic visors.

"You're doing good!" Keith called to her, gloved thumbs up.

"Thanks," she said, tightening her hands into fists, trying to revive her fingertips. Her toes were gone, lost in icy pain that only a fire could fix. Or a hot bath. A hot bath and then a fire and then hot chocolate and piles of downy blankets; that was how this night needed to end. Warm and huddled, safe and sleepy. "When are we heading back?"

Dave and Pete and Wall were talking to one another, their snowmobiles pulled into a loose triangle. Wall revved his motor and took off, his light disappearing quickly in the thick trees.

"Where's he going?" she asked Keith, who had stopped his snowmobile closer to hers.

"He had to go," Keith said.

"Yeah, well, it's been fun," she said, revving her engines just a bit, eager to be off as well. It was over, thank God.

"There's a good trail that takes you near the pond," Pete called, turning his machine. Pete knew all the trails for fifty miles. He was ROTC and determined to be tough. He'd always been that way, a pure competitor, pushing his body and angry when it didn't perform. He wouldn't let himself notice the cold; he'd take it as defeat. "Let's do it!"

"Let's not," she said, looking at Keith. Wall had left. Wasn't this over yet?

"One more," Keith said.

Of course. It would be too much to ask that he stand against what Pete wanted. Never mind that she was numb with cold and exhausted. He never stood with her, not when it meant standing against the guys. Why couldn't he ever put her first?

Oh, right, he could. When he needed to nail someone; then she popped up on his list.

"Tired, Lindsay?" Dave called out, snide laughter in his voice. Why did they hang with this guy? He was such a loser.

And who was she hanging with, and what did that make her?

"How far from here?" she said. Dave wasn't going to bully her into anything. Let Keith watch and learn.

"Not far," Pete called.

"We did it once on bikes," Keith said. "Good run."

Oh, well, *fine,* if they'd done it on dirt bikes, then why not on snowmobiles in the dark? The wind kicked up a notch, blasting fine needles of icy snow over them, hitting against the snowmobiles and making a pinging music, killing their vision for a minute.

"Let's go!" Dave said.

The engines roared from their throbbing idle and kicked hard sound into the bottomless night sky. She joined them, competition beating out sense. Whatever they did, she'd match them. Any game a guy could play, she could play with him, against him. If they wanted to ride around in the dark of winter, in a strange forest, illegally, then she'd ride with them.

But why play this game anymore? She wasn't like this, not at Duke. At Duke she was rational and reasonable. She felt no need to beat a bunch of guys at a game of their choosing. Then why did she do it?

Habit? She really wasn't herself, her new self, when she was with Keith. With Keith, she was seventeen again. Not a good thing, but she couldn't seem to stop herself from following, trying to keep up, trying to win a pissing contest when she didn't have either the equipment or the interest.

45

But she couldn't get to Sturbridge without them. She couldn't even find her way out of Brimfield Forest without them. As explanations went, it was weak, but it was true just the same.

They took off fast, the trail barely wide enough for the snowmobile to just make it. She scraped over a huge rock and the snowmobile tilted hard, but she didn't dump it. She shifted her weight and kept on, flinching automatically when a chunk of rock or mud flew at her from the back of Keith's Arctic Cat. Her hand eased off of the throttle for just a second as she took a hard right around a tree. The guys were another twenty-five feet ahead when she straightened out.

Faster. She had to go faster.

The trail was hard ups and downs, curving wickedly against massive trees, sliding through saplings that were coated in ice, running over brush and rock. Because she was last in line, the snow of the trail was thinner under her skis, the going rougher. If she scratched the paint on this thing, her dad would kill her.

If Keith didn't slow down and act like he knew her, she would kill *him*.

What was all this about, anyway? And why tonight? Wouldn't one night be as good as any other night for breaking the law?

Had Keith known she was coming up tonight? Her mom had told him about her arrival at the airport; maybe she had told him about their planned weekend up at the lake. Her mom *had* sort of fallen for Keith.

Anything in a skirt, that was his style, all the way.

Another ten feet lost in this weird race. She was losing sight of Pete completely; the roar of his machine was a weak and tinny whine that bounced around in the trees before hitting her ears. The lights of the other snowmobiles were narrow and fragile, spears of white in total blackness, bumping and shaking as if in death. Dwindling. Disappearing.

No holds barred now. She had to catch up. Cranking the throttle, she felt the machine jerk forward and she clamped tight on the seat with her knees as she pursued the tracks of the guys. Closer. Just a bit closer. They were going faster, too. She was going flat out, bouncing hard over the rough shape of the trail, flattening a sapling or two with her skis, her eyes dripping tears of cold, her breath a frozen thing that refused to leave her mouth, and still she couldn't catch them.

Fifty feet ahead.

She'd never forgive Keith.

Ditching her in the state forest. Nice.

And then her motor sputtered, choked, lurched, and died. Slowly, but completely. She didn't know if she was out of gas or had fouled the spark plugs; all she knew was that the snowmobile died a melodramatic death in the middle of Brimfield State Forest in the middle of the night in the middle of December.

The silence, the cold, stiff silence that surrounded her when her engine fell silent in that dark wood was so loud that it made her ears ring in alarm. For just a few moments more, she could hear the thin sound of snowmobiles driving away into the night, and then even that faint echo was gone.

And she was alone.

CHAPTER THREE

She was not going to freeze to death; it wasn't that cold and she hadn't been out in it that long. It only felt that way.

It really felt that way.

The night pressed against her like a hand. She stayed on the snowmobile, finding empty comfort in the promise of technology, the gleaming hope of noisy escape, but the snowmobile couldn't help her. It had taken her far into the forest, but if she wanted to get out, it would have to be on her own power.

Why had Keith done this? There was no answer that would make any sense to her, or give her any comfort, so she made herself stop thinking about it. Until the next sharp blast of wind kicked up snow and bent the trees to shrieking in the night. Then she thought of Keith again and her thoughts were as black as the sky.

Bastard.

She sat on the seat of the snowmobile, the freezing plastic radiating cold to her butt in less than a minute. She stood up. She looked at the snowmobile, sat down, and tried the key again. Nothing. Not the nothing of a dead battery, but the struggling nothing of an engine that wanted to burst to life, but couldn't.

Okay, okay, what to do? She got up again, putting the bulky key ring in her pocket out of habit and a vague sense that she shouldn't make it *that* easy for someone to steal her machine, and looked around. Looked around and looked around.

There was nothing to see, nothing but what she'd seen for the last hour: black night, churned-up snow, and a forest full of bare trees. It all looked the same and yet unfamiliar. She had never been in these woods. She didn't know the way out. She didn't know if Sturbridge was north, south, or east of her; it couldn't be west, because the state forest was west of Sturbridge and the lake, so she was sure she shouldn't go west. As if she knew which way was west. No moon, no stars, nothing but thick cloud pressing down on the tips of the skeletal treetops.

She wanted to stay with the snowmobile, her last and most powerful link to safety and civilization. If someone wanted to track her, following the ruts of the skis, they would find her more easily if she stayed with a nice, big, obvious machine lying in shining but spent glory in the midst of packed white snow. But did she want to be tracked?

Not by Keith and his band of idiots, she didn't.

Right, so stay out here all night, hiding, just to scare him straight? Who would she be punishing? Her feet, tormented by sharp, aching pains, told her exactly who she'd be punishing.

Okay, so the plan was . . . to stay with the machine and hope that Keith would come back and find her. She would let him rescue her. She could kill him later, when she was warm and dry and had her hands wrapped around a hot chocolate.

Right. So she was staying with the snowmobile. But she had to keep moving. She was too cold to just sit and let her blood freeze solid. Walking would keep her warm and pass the time.

She slogged through the heavy snow in a wide circle around her snowmobile, keeping her hands under her padded armpits, her chin down into the collar of her insulated suit. Her cashmere scarf was tied around her head, over her ears, the ends looped close to her throat, the helmet with its shaded visor covering the whole mess. She could hardly see with the visor on because it was heavily tinted to protect against sunshine and snow blindness, but she didn't care. It was keeping the wind off her face, and that was all that mattered.

It was very quiet. The only sound was of her own labored breathing, the crunch of snow under her boots, the pounding of her heart in her ears. No, it was more than just quiet. It was silent.

The deep silence of winter.
The heavy silence of snow.
The sharp silence of cold.

Nothing moved; nothing stirred. All the leaves were down, buried in white. Occasionally, a lump of snow would fall in a cracking tumble from a high branch, falling to a wet thud, merging invisibly with the deep cover of snow on the ground.

She loved the woods. Loved walking through them, loved sitting silent and still upon a log and watching the minute movements of nature all around her; the dance of the leaves in the wind, the determined march of insects, the reckless leap of squirrels. She knew all the trails around the cabin, walked through the woods barefoot almost every day, watching the movement of boats on the lake from a secluded, secret perch upon a hill, disappearing among the trees, breathing deeply of serenity.

But that was in summer. Those were woods she had learned, step by step, day by day. These woods, these cold, dark woods, she didn't know. A wood was beautiful only if you could find your way out of it.

The stillness of this cold wood pressed against her skin, malevolent and strange. She kept walking, comforted by motion, though her motion took her nowhere. Only endless circles in the snow. Endless, exhausted circles in the snow.

She was wearing herself out and going nowhere. *Stupid.* She had to get somewhere. She had to get *out.* She knew how to walk in woods.

She knew that a town or a house had to be some-where out there. There had to be a car or a phone or a portable heater. Maybe even all three.

She was leaving the snowmobile. It was useless to her, and in all the silence, she hadn't heard Keith's snowmobile coming back for her.

He really was a bastard.

With that thought firing her, she trudged off, fol-lowing the trail he had left.

"She's gone," Dave said, pulling off his helmet. "I knew she couldn't keep up."

Dave's hair, the color of stale beer, was plas-tered to his head in bands of sweat. He looked oddly excited, like a dog smelling a new asshole. That was Dave all over.

"She did okay for a while there. I almost dumped on that one turn, but she slid right over," Pete said. "It took longer than I thought it would."

Yeah, it had taken longer than he had thought, too. He tried to remember why had he done this.

"Too bad Wall bugged out," Dave said, laughing shrilly.

"Yeah," Keith said. "Guess he got bored with try-ing to ditch Lindsay. Dumb fuck, huh?"

"What are you pissed about?" Dave said. "You got what you wanted."

Yeah, and it was one messed-up idea. Sure, he wanted her to know what it felt like to get left, to need someone and have them not turn up, not even care enough to turn up. He hated her for that. She'd just left. Left like she was leaving nothing behind. Like he didn't matter worth shit.

"Jackoff," he mumbled to Dave as he pulled off his gloves and lit a cigarette. Damn, it was cold. Smelled like snow; sure was cloudy enough for it.

"You going back for her?" Pete asked, his brown eyes solemn. He'd hated this idea from the start, but that was Pete. He played hard but he didn't play rough. This was rough. She had to be scared shitless.

"In a bit," Keith said.

"It's too soon!" Dave said, taking a hit off of Keith's cigarette, lighting his own. Pete didn't smoke; he valued his body too much to mess with it.

"Shut the fuck up," Keith said, full of rage he didn't know how to handle. "This was your idea."

"Hey, I was only trying to help out," Dave said.

"Shut up," Pete said, turning from them to face the dark woods surrounding them. Their headlights lit up the night in a rough circle of light, leaving the enveloping woods in complete darkness. Only the tips of the trees soaring above them were visible.

"Yeah, help yourself into her pants by helping me out of 'em," Keith said, sure he was right the minute he spoke the words. "You've been hot for her for years."

"She's not my type," Dave said with cool arrogance.

"Like she'd ever look at you," Pete said, shaking his head and laughing.

"Only if she needed something to wipe her ass,"

Keith said, taking a deep pull off his cigarette, dismissing Dave with a look.

"Fuck you!" Dave said shrilly.

Yeah, that was Dave all over. Why had he ever listened to him? Because he was a dumb piece of shit who couldn't think straight without Lindsay around. He'd only gotten into her life because she'd been on a short rebound. He'd known it, known he was being used in dating games that made *Survivor* look like "It's a Small World," and he'd done what he had to do to keep her on a short, tight chain. If there was one thing he was good at, it was doing it right, and he'd done it right all over Lindsay's virginal ass.

So he'd ditched her in the woods to freeze her ass off. Yeah, she'd be real happy to have him around now. If he did go to Duke, she'd probably set fire to his car.

What car?

He really did have shit for brains.

"You going back?" Pete asked again, his breath coming out in a cloud of white.

Back to face Lindsay when she was spitting mad? He didn't want to. She could get real mad and hang on to it longer than anyone else he knew. Other girls, they fell down grinning, legs spread with an itch he could scratch even if they were mad, but not Lindsay. She had fire for a temper and could keep it blazing. Like she kept other things blazing.

Man, she was hot. He'd never known anything like it. They'd get together and things would just explode between them. He loved her, needed her. All he wanted was for her to need him just as much, and to admit that she loved him. Really loved him, no matter what he did.

Even ditching her in the snow in the middle of the state forest.

"Yeah, I'm going back," he said, flicking away his cigarette. "But not yet. Let her wait it out. She won't die of the cold."

Dave laughed.

She wasn't going to die of the cold. She wasn't going to die of the cold. She wasn't going to die of the cold.

It was a lovely marching chant. It would have helped if she believed it.

She'd been colder, but then she'd known a house was nearby, heat and a fire and hot food. Without the close anticipation of comfort, the cold just seemed to bite into her harder, with more teeth, latching on and sucking out all her heat.

She would never forgive Keith for this.

He was trying to manipulate her, just like he always did. She wasn't doing or acting or feeling exactly the way he wanted and so he'd push her around, manipulating circumstances to get the right reaction out of her.

He must want her to hate him forever, because that was what she was going to do.

It smelled like snow. She looked up at the sky, which was leaden and heavy. Nothing falling yet.

If it snowed hard, the guys' tracks would be covered over in a few minutes. She wasn't following their tracks to find Keith, but it might be that they'd left the forest and crossed a road. She needed to find a road, a nice plowed road that had lots of traffic. She'd thumb her way into Sturbridge or Southbridge or even Hartford. She had to get out of here. The weight of cold isolation was a load on her shoulders that threatened to knock her down.

The sudden vibration and cheery musical ring of her cell phone over her left breast almost *did* knock her down.

She yanked off her right glove and fumbled with the zipper of her suit. Two rings. She caught her fingers in the coiled length of her scarf. Three rings. She tried to find the inner pocket of her snowmobile suit, but her fingers were so numb she couldn't feel anything clearly. Four rings. She grabbed the slim phone with her fingertips and yanked it up and out . . . and into the snow, where it continued to vibrate and ring. Five rings. She pulled it out of the snow, her fingers burning with cold, and hit the receive button with her thumb.

"Hello?" she said breathlessly as she yanked off her helmet.

"Lindsay?" her dad's voice said, coming through the air in a weak electronic warble.

"Dad!" she said, crying and laughing at once. "I'm stuck! I'm—"

"Where are you? We made it to the cabin; the phone's out. We drove back to the overpass to get a signal. The snowmobile's gone. Did you take it? Your car's a mess, at least three thousand dollars in damage. Lindsay, where are you?"

"I'm in Brimfield State Forest and the snowmobile died and I'm alone. I'm lost, Dad," she said, tears taking over as she struggled to hold the phone in her icy hands. She couldn't feel a thing beyond the pain of cold.

"Alone? But there are tracks all over the place here," her dad said.

"I know," she said, sniffing hard and trying to be calm. It would be okay now. Her dad knew where she was. "But I'm alone now. Can you come get me?"

"Of course," he said firmly. "I'll find you. Do you know where you are?"

She started to laugh hysterically. "I'm lost, Dad. I don't know."

"Lindsay?" he said, his voice a blur of static. "Lindsay? I can't hear you, honey."

"Dad!" she said, shouting. "I'm lost in Brimfield Forest."

"Lindsay, I'm losing you. If you can hear me, stay with the snowmobile. Can you hear me? Stay with the snowmobile."

"Okay, Dad. Okay," she shouted into the static.

She felt it before she saw it: Sleet slid down the sky, slamming into the trees, the snow, the top of her head, pinging harshly as it struck. It wasn't snow she had smelled; it was sleet.

Sliding the phone back into her suit, readjusting her scarf and her glove, pushing the helmet back onto her head, Lindsay started walking back the way she had come, hurrying against the falling sleet that would turn the snow to mush, following her tracks for as long as they lasted.

The sound came first, as always. The harsh sound of machines roaring through the quiet heart of the woods, and then the lights, pinging off trees and into the endless shadows between them: Keith.

She had a little fight within herself for a moment or two, a bloody, silent battle with herself: stay where she was and be seen, or hide and let him ride by, searching fruitlessly for her now that he had played out his stupid game and was willing to pick her up?

It wasn't much of a battle.

Lindsay ran to the woods beyond the track and hid behind a large tree that was well shielded by flanking saplings. She didn't have to wait long. Three snowmobiles raced by, their lights bobbing against the dark, their riders hunched down behind the windshields, facing forward and nowhere else. He expected to find her crying in fear over the dead form of her snowmobile.

Not a chance.

Her dad knew where she was, and everything was going to be great. She didn't need Keith, and she couldn't wait for him to figure it out. With a grim smile of victory, Lindsay slipped back onto the trail, nice and fresh now from Keith's passing. *Thanks, Keith. Thanks a lot.*

* * *

"Thanks a lot, you shithead," Keith yelled at Dave.

"What? I held you down and made you?" Dave yelled back.

They stood around Lindsay's snowmobile, a dark, glistening form in the snow. The key was gone. So was Lindsay.

"Why would she leave her snowmobile?" Pete said. "Why didn't she keep following us?"

"She's mad, that's why," Dave said. "She's probably on the rag."

"Shut up," Keith said automatically. He should have told Dave to shut up when he first suggested this great plan for teaching Lindsay a lesson. "Okay," he breathed out, "why *would* she shut down her engine?"

"Maybe she didn't," Pete said. "Maybe it shut down on her."

"Shit," Keith said, reaching in his pocket for a cigarette. "But why not stay with it? She knew we'd come back."

"Sure she did," Pete said sarcastically.

"*Shit*," Keith said, taking a calming drag. "Now what?"

"Stay here," Dave said. "She'll come back."

"Why would she?" Pete asked.

"Look around, Brain-dead," Dave said with a snarl. "What else can she do?"

Get lost, Keith thought, throwing down his cigarette. *Get fucking lost.*

By the time she had decided to forgive Keith long enough for him to get her out of this cold, by the time she had followed the snowmobile tracks for another thirty minutes, by the time the sleet had stopped and begun freezing her wet clothes to her body, she knew she was lost.

She couldn't find her snowmobile. She couldn't find *anyone's* snowmobile. Sound and light carried far in the quiet of a winter's night, but there was no sound and no light calling out to her. She was alone in the woods and she had wandered off the track somehow.

She could hardly keep her legs moving, she was so cold. Her lungs didn't want to breathe in the frostbitten air. Her skin tingled and ached with every brush of wind and ice that touched her.

Where was her dad? Where was the help he'd promised? Even Keith would look good right now. She shouldn't have let anger make her decisions for her. She should have grabbed the first ride that came along, even if it meant sitting behind Keith. Hell, even if it meant sitting behind Dave.

Stupid. Twenty-year-old stupid, that was what her dad called it, though he smiled when he said it. But he meant it. It always made her pretty mad, but it seemed to fit right now. Twenty-year-old stupid.

She'd let a ride run right by her.

Yeah, that was stupid. The next ride she'd take, no matter who was driving. She was getting out of here no matter whom she had to bum a ride off of. Even the police would look good right now, and she'd pay whatever fine they laid on her. Whatever. She just had to get *out*.

She kept her head down and slogged on, one foot and then the other, making herself move, commanding herself to breathe. She had to keep moving. She had to get out of here. There was an end to this forest. Everything had a boundary; everything had an end. She just had to find this one.

She stopped and clumsily pulled out her cell phone, looking into the soft, warm glow of technology as it lit up in her hand. *NO NETWORK*. Great.

It was as she was carefully putting the phone back into her pocket that she caught the faint sound of an engine. Not a racing engine, but the slow, steady hum of a snowmobile running deliberately and cautiously over the icy forest floor. She listened hard, yanking off her helmet, pulling down her sheltering scarf to give all her attention to listening. Listening . . . Off to the right, down an embankment, she could hear it.

Lindsay shoved on her helmet and ran awkwardly, slowly, down the embankment, pushing aside the slender barrier of saplings and brush, clawing through the low branches of a pine, yanking in air in painful gulps, desperate, determined. Scared.

She fell down the last few yards, sliding on her butt, slowing her fall by dragging her hands behind her. Off to the right she could see lights, motion. Pulling herself to her feet, she waved her arms above her head, shouting, making any kind of human noise she could think of.

The light stopped. The engine dwindled to an idle.

Thank you, God.

She ran clumsily over to the snowmobile, already starting to laugh in relief, in joy, in safety and the promise of warmth.

The figure on the snowmobile turned to face her, his visor tinted black, his face a complete blank of plastic. He kept his hands on the throttle, his posture relaxed on the seat. His snowmobile was yellow and black and on the side it read *Blade.* She didn't know anyone who owned a Blade. At the moment, she could hardly have cared less.

"Thank you!" she said, pulling off her helmet. "Can you help me? I'm stranded and could use a ride to . . . well, to *anywhere,*" she said on a laugh.

He studied her for a moment while she gathered her breath in pants, calming the racing of her heart. It was okay now. Everything was going to be okay.

"Sure," he said, his voice a hollow rumble behind the visor. "Get on."

And she did. She was that determined to get out of the cold.

CHAPTER FOUR

"Are you sure she said Brimfield State Forest?" the state trooper asked.

"Yes, I'm sure," Todd Gray answered.

"But you said the signal was weak," the trooper said again, his expression carefully blank.

"Yes, but I heard her say Brimfield before we lost our connection," Lindsay's father answered, trying to keep his own face carefully emotionless, rationally calm. "My daughter is stranded in Brimfield State Forest. What can I expect you to do about it?" If his words were a little clipped and his tone a little sharp, he didn't think anyone could blame him for it.

"You are going to do something," Ellen said. "That's what you do, isn't it? Help people in trouble? My daughter needs help right now," she said stiffly, holding on to her panic with a frayed leash.

"We'll do everything we can, Mrs. Gray," he answered.

"And that is?" Todd said.

"And you're certain she's alone?" the trooper asked.

They stood in the warmly lit highway patrol office, the sound of cars speeding by seeming to mock the ponderous methods of the police. This man was fixated on the inconsequential while his daughter was lost in the forest in the dark of December.

"She said she was alone," Todd answered, grinding his teeth. He was fairly certain that this "professional" wouldn't help him at all if he let loose and knocked him to the ugly linoleum floor.

"But she didn't leave your cabin alone," the officer said.

"Look, she's alone now!" Jeff said from the rear, his throat tight with anger and fear. Todd looked back at the kid with a great deal of sympathy, but he waved him off, telling him to cool down with a motion of his hand.

As surprises went, this one had been a disaster. First, Lindsay had insisted on driving up alone. He was never crazy about that idea; he didn't like her spending any time with Keith. What they did together he never let himself think about, since he hadn't figured out how to stop it.

That was the trouble with having a daughter: From the minute she was born and he'd held her in his arms, he'd known he would never again have a moment's peace. He was a man and he'd fathered a girl. That was the problem. It was his job to protect her from every man in the world. Tough job. He had the feeling he hadn't handled it too well. Not where Keith Logan was concerned.

Looking back at Jeff Anderson, he still wasn't at peace. Oh, he seemed like a nice enough kid. Clean-looking, hardworking, doing well in school, and good to Lindsay, at least according to Lindsay. He didn't know how much faith to put in her judgment, since she'd gotten so tangled up with Keith.

Ellen, naturally, thought he was too hard on Keith. She maintained that he was a good kid, but that he was very vulnerable emotionally and had trouble handling his own emotions. The way he figured it, men just out of their teens had one emotion and they handled it one way: between a girl's legs. But that was just his opinion. It might have said more about him than it did about Keith.

But he didn't think so.

"Are you going out to look for her or what?" Jeff said to the cop, an outburst that did Todd's heart a lot of good. Jeff turned away and strode off a few feet and then marched back, his cheeks flushed in anger.

"Son," the cop said, his dark eyes supremely stern, "we'll do what we can. You folks just sit here for a minute while I see who's available. We had an accident down the road a ways and—"

"Yes, we saw it," Ellen said, trying to hurry him along.

"Could you describe your daughter for me, please?" he asked.

"Dark brown hair, brown eyes, five-four, a hundred and ten pounds," Todd answered with crisp authority.

"Beautiful," Ellen added softly.

The cop nodded and turned away, going down a coldly lit hall, then entering a door on the right.

There were three men in the room, and all of them looked up when he entered.

"There's a twenty-year-old female stranded in Brimfield State Forest," he said the minute the door was firmly closed behind him.

Three pairs of eyes looked up at him.

"Confirmed?"

"Yeah, as good as I can make out. She's in there. No way out but on foot."

The silence pressed against them, churning their blood, pumping their hearts to pounding.

"Shit."

"Just like Lisa Reed and John MacFarlane. Not a big forest. No reason for it."

"They're still dead, reasonable or not."

The three patrol officers stood as a body, pulling on their coats and hats, reaching for gloves that had been tossed on the wide, fake-wood table.

"What was she doing in the state forest on a night like this?"

"She's twenty. You want more explanation than that?"

"We've got to find her before he does," one of them said under his breath.

* * *

"Look, Mr. Gray, I could find her before they will. You've got that old Honda Enduro. It's cold enough. I could ride it in there, follow their tracks in. Find her."

Todd considered Jeff, already mentally denying this kid the right to seek out his daughter. It was *his* Enduro; he could ride it in the dark in a blizzard. More, it was *his* daughter out there. This kid didn't have any claim on her. If anyone was going to ride in and find Lindsay, it was going to be him. He trusted himself. He didn't trust Jeff Anderson, because when all was said and done, Jeff was just another man he was trying to keep off of his daughter.

"I think we should let the police handle it. They know what they're doing. They must do this all the time," Ellen said, slapping her gloves against her hand with nervous energy.

"But another pair of eyes couldn't hurt," Jeff said.

The kid was in a tough spot. He was practically a stranger, the college boyfriend who'd flown in for the weekend over Christmas break to surprise his girl. He was unknown to them and they unknown to him. Yet here he was, trying to politely push his way into the right to rescue Lindsay.

Not bad. He liked him better than Keith Logan already, though that wasn't much of a recommendation.

"If anyone goes, it'll be me," Todd said.

"With your knee?" Ellen said.

"It'll be fine. I know what I'm doing on that bike."

"It was on that bike that you blew it out the first time!" Ellen said, her patience stretched to breaking. Todd took her in his arms, burying her in a hug that she wouldn't settle into. All nerves, that was Ellen. All nerves powered by steely will. He loved her more every year he knew her.

"Mr. Gray," Jeff said in an urgent undertone as the police started to file out of a room down the hall, "it should be me. I race Enduros. I win. Nothing can stop me on that bike. Someone has to go who really *cares* about finding Lindsay. It needs to be me."

His eyes were intense, demanding, pleading. A sharp green gaze that pierced male ego with the truth. Jeff was right. He was younger, uninjured by time and age, fiercely in love, and better than good on an Enduro. He would find Lindsay because he believed he would. Sometimes that was all there was to success: the absolute belief that you would not fail.

"Mr. Gray?" the highway patrolman said. "We're sending out three men to search for your daughter. If you could show us on the map where your cabin is, we can narrow down the search for the entry point into the state forest."

"Sure," he said to the cop, nodding at Jeff, giving him his tacit permission.

Jeff in that instant looked like Gawain riding off through the snow to face the green knight, a man on a holy mission. A man who would not fail, Todd thought.

He prayed to God that he was right.

* * *

He knew he was right. The snowmobile tracks
had started off deep, when the snow was softer,
the air warmer. It was colder now, far colder. The
melt of the afternoon had frozen into a thin sheet
of firm crust as the temperature plummeted with
the coming of night. He could ride on this, could
get his speed up on the packed snowmobile trail.
He could even ride where there wasn't any trail;
as long as he kept his speed high enough, he
could just skim along on that firm crust, moving
too fast to break through. He loved Honda Enduros, the motorcycle that could face any hill,
any stream, any back trail. Mr. Gray had recently
replaced the knobby tires, even had the extra set
of lights for night riding. *Sweet.*

He turned on the gas, pushed down the choke,
twisted the throttle a bit, and jumped on the kick
starter. Nothing. Kicked it again. Nothing. His
heart froze. Damned Hondas—they were all hard
starters in the cold. A dozen frantic kicks later, the
Enduro sputtered weakly to life. Jeff nursed it in
idle for what seemed an eternity until it warmed
up, then roared up the road, his eyes on the old
tracks of the snowmobiles, jumbled, twisted upon
the snow, glistening under the ice. He was racing,
too fast for this kind of terrain, this kind of
weather, this moonless night, but if he slowed,
he'd get bogged down in the snow. And so he kept
his speed above thirty-five mph, speeding, sliding,
skimming over ice and snow, finding his way to
Lindsay.

He would find Lindsay.

He had to.

She hated this, hated the cold with a deep, driven fear of it. She was always cold. If it dipped below fifty-five degrees, she would slather herself in wool and still have chilled fingertips. She'd panic in this, the terror of being out in the cold, a cold that was steadily dropping as the night sped on, deepening, blackening as the blanket of clouds thickened and pressed down upon the earth, holding the cold against it. Pressing. Pushing. Until all warmth was blasted to memory. Until the bitter sting of cold was a hostile presence, intent and focused, seeking heat as prey, bleeding out warmth like blood upon the snow.

Jeff shook himself. *What a crock.* He should never have taken that Lit class. He was thinking like a damned poet. A psychotic poet.

It was only snow, and she hadn't been out in it that long. But she would hate being out in it, and that was enough to keep his gloved hand hard on the throttle. That, and the fact that she was lost. And Keith was the one who'd lost her. Who else? Who else would she go out in the cold for? Who else was low enough to ditch her?

Keith Logan, asshole of the millennium.

He knew all about Keith, about the history at the lake that Keith and Lindsay shared. It was because of Keith that Lindsay kept him at a distance, the shadow of Keith shimmering between them.

The shadow of sex.

That was what they shared; that was how Keith

held her to him, by chains of sex. It was working okay for him, too. It was a great way to tie a woman to you, and there wasn't a guy who didn't understand that, plus you got your rocks off. A total win. Except that he was going to break her free of Keith and get her for himself. He loved her. He wanted her. And he damned sure wasn't going to share her.

A branch whipped at his helmet, scraping, clawing at him as he raced by. He kept his eyes on the tracks in front of him and kept his head down, his shoulders down, his belly down; everything concentrated on finding Lindsay and saving her.

Saving her for himself.

It was only after she had her arms around her woodland savior, her helmeted chin bumping against his shoulder a few times as his Blade snowmobile raced through the forest, that she realized she didn't know who this guy was or where he was taking her.

She probably should get that worked out.

She tapped him on his shoulder and he turned his head slightly to show that he'd felt her nudge, giving her a bit more of his helmeted ear.

"Can you take me to Sturbridge?" she shouted.

He shook his head no.

No?

"Where are we going?" she shouted.

They had to be going somewhere. Somewhere warm. She craned her body forward and looked at his gas gauge. Full. They could be going to

Worcester with that much gas. He didn't answer her; he just twisted the throttle down and shot them forward into the dark.

A slither of fear and foreboding slipped down her spine like melting ice, slick and cold. She slid her hands from around his waist, clutching instead the grips under the seat, forcing her numbed and stinging hands to hold on. Forcing her numbed brain to think beyond the slap of cold against her skin, shooting its relentless way into her bones.

Who *was* this guy?

The trees whipped past in a blur of dark forms, blurring together to look like bars on a prison wall. Bars. Yeah, that was it. She was trapped, locked into place by a faceless man on a snowmobile doing forty-five mph in the depths of the forest. It was a state forest: no hunters, no cross-country skiers, no snowmobilers, unless they were there by stealth, ignoring the law. Like she'd been doing. Like this guy'd been doing. So she knew one thing about him: He was lawless.

She knew something else about him, too. He rode his machine through these woods like he was out on an open lake: fearless, fast, familiar. He knew these woods. He knew when to turn, when to shift his weight, when to slow for a sudden drop in terrain.

How many times had he ridden his Blade through these woods in the dark?

How many times had she? Zip. He had the advantage there. He had the advantage everywhere.

He had the snowmobile, the knowledge of the woods, and he had her.

But not for long.

She'd been working up to it in her thinking, in her careful plotting of what he brought to the table and what she brought—basically nothing—but she'd been working up to this and she was going to do it. She didn't have much choice. And she did have a few things going for her: She was small, she knew that Keith was out there somewhere, and her parents knew where she was, roughly. Three things in her favor. Three things that just might get her through.

She took a deep breath and looked ahead, around his black-clad shoulder. The trail climbed up just ahead, the trees thick and mostly pine. It was a great spot to work her plan.

The Blade whined a bit as it dug in, churning up the snow as it nosed up the incline. The man throttled down, giving it more power, lifting himself off his butt and leaning forward, urging the snowmobile onward. It was then that she slipped off the back, letting gravity and momentum take her, tumbling into the dark, away from the noise and the light of the snowmobile, away from the dark silence of the man to tumble into the dark and sheltered silence of the forest. Rolling, sliding, clawing over the snow, a dark form against acres of white, aiming for a shield of trees or rocks, crawling for cover.

Over the sound of her ragged breath, she heard the snowmobile slow to an idle, heard the gentle acceleration of a turn, heard the sharp, pointed sound of an engine aimed right at her. And held her breath. She pressed her small form against the snow, behind a downed oak that was soft with rot. If she stayed in the dark, he would not see her. If she stayed away from the single light of his machine, he would not find her.

He stopped the snowmobile right in front of her, the engine throbbing softly. With one hand he pulled off his helmet. She couldn't see his face; the light was behind him, and she was hiding behind the oak, too scared to breathe.

"You're scared, right?" he called out over the sound of the motor. "You should be. *Never* accept a ride from someone you don't know."

Yeah, point made.

"I'm with the parks service. My name is Mike Burns," he said, introducing himself. "I've been out looking for you, Ms. Gray. We've got five men out looking for you, three from the state police. Your dad, Todd Gray, told the police that you were out here."

Okay, so he had the facts. Maybe he was with the parks service. But somehow that didn't make her any less scared.

"Lindsay," he said calmly. "I know where you are. I can see where your body slid over the snow. Come on out. I'll take you to the ranger station and you can warm up. I'm sorry I scared you, but I wanted you to be scared for a minute. A little more caution on your part and you wouldn't be out here."

She lifted her head from behind the log and

could see that he was right; there was a slick, wide path of squashed snow that led from his headlight to her position. Okay, so he knew where she was. More, he knew *who* she was. Maybe she could trust him, but her heart was still hammering in her chest and she was still tense with fear.

And cold.

He had all the facts. He must be who he said he was.

She stood up slowly, her eyes on him the whole time. He just stood there. No aggressive moves; he just stood there, waiting for her. From behind her helmet, she asked, "What's my mom's name?"

"Ellen Gray," he said without pause.

"Okay, maybe I believe you," she grumbled, climbing back up the slope to him, slapping her outer pockets to make sure she still had her keys.

Still there. Hard to miss, she had so much junk on the ring: the plastic ski charm, a broken fragment of a green bead necklace her freshman roommate had brought her from Mardi Gras, the banged-up cylinder of Mace her dad insisted on, the tiny Swiss army penknife her mom insisted on, and the advertising logo of the shop where they'd bought the snowmobile in Sturbridge. It made a fat and uncomfortable wad in her pocket, and she'd half regretted taking it with her an hour after she'd left her dead snowmobile. She moved them to her inside pocket, just in case. If they fell out, at least they'd stay inside her suit. After all this, she wasn't going to lose them now.

He leaned forward as she got closer and offered her a hand. "I can see I did a good job of teaching you some caution," he said. She looked up as she put her hand in his and could see his face. Handsome, grinning, dark hair.

"They pay you extra for that?" she said, smiling, fear reluctantly easing itself from her to fall like snowflakes into the night.

"If only," he said, putting a hand to her waist as she slipped and lost her footing on an icy patch of snow. "You're not the only one to get lost out here this season."

His hand was big, just like he was. He had to be even taller than Jeff, and Jeff was six-two.

"I guess that makes me feel better," she said as she climbed onto the back of his snowmobile.

He put his helmet back on, hiding his face, closing off his eyes from hers. Lifting his leg over the seat, he sat down softly, his hands on the throttle.

"It shouldn't," he said, his muffled words making puffs of air that showed white against the night sky.

He followed the tracks, their bumpy ridges looking deep and shadowy in the slanting light of the Enduro. They ran pretty straight, following the trails in a jumble of tumbled snow that spoke of speed. They'd been racing pretty hard through here, forcing Lindsay to the back, probably, and then they'd left her. *Nice.* Only one kind of guy did that, the kind you beat into the ground with your fists and feet and left in a bubble of blood. He prayed for the chance to do just that.

If he needed any proof that there was a God in heaven, he got it.

They were standing in a loose circle, their snowmobiles churning exhaust into the night sky, their cigarettes sending smoke up in delicate mimicry. They turned, watching him come, their eyes cautious and their faces closed in suspicion. And guilt.

The Enduro throbbed over the snow, whining to get closer, to run them down, but Jeff kept it in check, controlled the raw rage that turned everything black and left only these three assholes in his vision. Yeah, he kept it under control. It might not even be them, might be three innocent guys out for a midnight run in the snow, three guys who'd never heard of Lindsay.

Right.

"Keith!" he called out, throttling down the Enduro. One of them jerked a bit and then tried to cover it by flicking his cigarette into the snow at his feet.

All the proof Jeff needed. He let his bike fall into the snow and attacked, his fist connecting with Keith's head, hitting him somewhere along the jaw, smashing his ear. Jeff could hear the sounds of shock, the scuffle of feet in snow, and then a blow to his back, a shove that lifted him momentarily into the air. He landed hard on the snow, and they held him down on his back, snarling at him. Jeff kicked out and caught one of them in the hip. A nice crunching thud.

"What the fuck are you doing, man?" Keith

yelled from above him, one of the pile who was holding him down.

"Saving Lindsay," Jeff spat out. "What the fuck are *you* doing? You get off on ditching girls in the dark?"

The two who'd been holding him down released him instantly. Keith, white-faced in the stark light of the headlights, straightened up more slowly. Jeff pushed him off and lunged to his feet, hands fisting, ready to kill.

"Who are you?" Keith asked.

"The guy who's gonna beat the shit out of you," Jeff answered.

"You go to Duke, right?" Keith said, his voice heavy and sullen with dark rage.

"Yeah," Jeff answered with a grim smile.

"Figures," Keith said.

Jeff landed one to Keith's face and heard a nice crunch as his nose flattened and then spewed blood. *Good.* Keith shoved him back with both hands to his chest and then rubbed a hand gingerly over his nose. His hand came away bloody. *Perfect.*

"Come on," Jeff urged, beckoning Keith closer with his gloved hands.

Keith looked at his friends. They looked at the snow at their feet, refusing to face him, refusing to help him.

"Need help?" Jeff taunted. "Sure you do. You can't even dump her in the woods by yourself."

"Fuck you!" Keith shouted, the blood from his nose gushing.

"Right," Jeff said dismissively.

"What about Lindsay?" one of the guys said. "How'd you know?"

Jeff looked them all over, his fists still clenched, his body ready for a fight, but then he let it go. This guy was right. It had to be about Lindsay, not his need to pummel something. Someone.

"Her dad got a call through to her. She told him where she was, that the snowmobile had conked on her. Her dad went to the state police."

"And so you're here on her dad's Enduro," the guy said. "Okay. We've been back over the trail we took, but she's left it, can't tell where. We've been east of here and south. You want to come with us while we head west?"

Jeff looked them over. They'd lost a girl in the woods. On purpose. They were pond scum. But they had snowmobiles and they knew these woods better than he did. Keith's nose had settled down; he'd put a wad of snow to it. He looked at Keith, at his swollen nose, at how he was babying it, and felt the urge to kill rise up in him again, stronger than before.

"You go west," Jeff said to the only guy with a brain in this pack of assholes. "I'll go north."

"It gets wilder to the north, not as many trails," the guy said, holding his gaze. He had dark eyes, steady and earnest. Maybe he wasn't a complete asshole.

"I'll take north. You never know," he said, shrugging.

"Okay," the guy said. "My name's Pete."

"Jeff," he answered, acknowledging him, which was major, considering what had happened.

Without another word, the guys each got on their machines and blasted off into the night, looking for Lindsay.

"So where are we going?" she shouted over the roar of the engine, her arms looped loosely around his waist.

"A shack we've set up. Get you warm first, then take you in to your folks," he said over his shoulder.

Warm. That would be good. Her hands and feet were totally gone now, just lumps of bone wrapped in icy skin, no feeling, no tingling, just weight that she moved around by will.

"Where are my parents?"

"At the highway patrol on 84."

The highway patrol. How far could that be? Couldn't they just go there first and last? She really wanted to see her parents. She should have been embarrassed at how much she wanted to see her parents, to be with them, to feel their arms around her and hear her mom scold her for being such an idiot. She should have been embarrassed, but she wasn't.

She wanted her mom.

"How far are we from the highway patrol?"

"The shack is closer," he said as he sped the snowmobile over a patch of flat land bounded by black trees. The snow here was covered in tracks, the brown of dirt showing through in ragged spots. "Let's get you warm. You need to get your body temperature up."

Warm. She couldn't seem to turn from that and couldn't really see the need to try. Okay, she'd get warm first and then go to her parents. They were safe at the highway patrol, and she was safe with the parks service guy. It was okay. It was all going to be okay.

Except that she was a little jumpy. Her blood skipped around like falling icicles in her veins, cold and sharp and slippery. She couldn't settle, couldn't rest. She didn't feel safe at all.

Must be that stupid joke he'd pulled back there. She was still rattled from it. Guys could be such jerks, even parks service guys.

Even Jeff could be a jerk sometimes, and he was pretty great overall. But he sure could get himself in a twist over nothing. Well, maybe it wasn't over nothing. He knew about Keith and he wasn't happy about it. Who was? She sure wasn't. Keith had her roped up and she couldn't seem to break free. It was the sex. She couldn't break free of the sex.

Oh, she hadn't told Jeff that she was screwing around with Keith; she wasn't that stupid, and it *was* screwing around. It wasn't making love or being intimate or any of the other ways people liked to describe it. With Keith, it was screwing. Maybe even fucking. Yeah, he fucked her. He fucked her and fucked her over again and again. *Nice.*

God, she made herself sick. She was pathetic.

Of all the things she'd dreamed for herself, being a girl who got fucked wasn't one of them.

At least Jeff was nice about it. It was a sure bet that he knew she was having occasional sex with someone, and he knew it wasn't him. The nice thing was that he never got ugly about it. Some guys did. They made you feel that for the price of a date you owed them your body. As if. She was worth more than a movie and a slice of pizza.

Oh, yeah, she was tough. What had Keith ever done for her, besides screwing with her head and breaking her heart?

Okay, enough about Keith. Keith was history. Jeff—maybe Jeff—was the future. He was a nice guy.

A nice guy. Maybe too nice. Maybe she just wasn't ever going to get hot for a nice guy. Maybe she was going to spend her life dragging from one Keith to another. Maybe she was only interested in the bad guys out there.

Maybe they'd do an *Oprah* on it and she could figure it out.

In the meantime, getting warm had to be her first priority. She'd get warm, she'd get with her parents, she'd go home to West Hartford, and she'd call Jeff. She didn't know what she'd say to him, since she felt as guilty as the cheating girl-friend she was, but she'd call him. She needed to hear his voice, needed the safe nest he always made for her with his words. He was so calm, always and ever calm, and he was always so reasonable. Nothing at all like Keith. Jeff would never have ditched her, would never have lied to her, would never have slid his way into her pants on their first date. Jeff had too much class, too much restraint, and she liked that about him.

Although, sometimes . . . sometimes late at night as he walked her to her dorm from a library date, she wondered if maybe Jeff might be a bit too cool, too controlled, and when she was feeling very down she couldn't help thinking that maybe he was just cool with her. Toward her. That he didn't act like a guy in love.

He didn't act like Keith, and that was all she knew about what a guy in love did, not that Keith was a great example of anything. In fact, Keith was about the worst example of everything. Still, one thing about Keith: He sure had a lot of heat. There was nothing as exciting as a guy who got all hot and out of control, losing it because he had it bad for you.

Yeah, and then he ditched you in the woods because he was a brain-dead bastard.

She really had to get a grip. Keith was history—dangerous, turbulent history. Jeff was the future. Maybe. A nice, safe, predictable future.

That was crap. Jeff wasn't the future. Jeff was *now,* for as long as she wanted him to be *now.* Or for as long as he wanted her. He might be calm and nice, but she didn't have him locked in place. He hadn't taken a blood oath of undying love for her or anything.

No, Keith had done that, and look how much *that* meant.

"There it is," Mike said, jerking her out of her thoughts.

She looked over his shoulder. It really *was* a shack. Old timbers, irregularly cut, some painted, some peeling, some varnished, made up the walls. The roof, which had a shallow pitch, looked like it had tar-paper shingles poking out from a weight of snow. It had a bowed door that looked water-damaged and a single square window on the side. It looked like an old ice-fishing shack that someone had pulled off the lake and hoisted onto concrete blocks in the middle of the woods. Couldn't the parks service do better than this? There really must have been some major budget cuts in one administration or another. Did this place even have heat?

Now, *there* was a question that mattered.

"Does it have heat?" she said as he maneuvered the snowmobile over a small hill and stopped it in front of the door.

"Yeah," he said. "There's a gas-powered heater."

"Great," she said as he cut the motor. "I can't wait."

Mike waited for her to climb off the back and then he stood and faced her.

"Neither can I," he said, lifting his helmet off. He wasn't smiling. He looked kind of intense, maybe even mad. Lindsay shook off the thought. *Stupid.* What did he have to be mad about? His job was to rescue people. He was probably just cold.

"How long before it heats up?" she said. She was standing shin-deep in snow. It had been a long time since anyone had been up here; there weren't any tracks but theirs.

"Not long," he said, staring down at her.

"Great," she said again more softly. It was kind of weird, the way he kept staring at her.

He smiled then, a crooked smile that took up only half his face, like the other half was frozen in indecision. Or cold. He used a key from the same ring that had his snowmobile key on it and opened the lock on the door, a padlock hanging from a chain. Couldn't the budget even stand a real locking doorknob?

"You weren't kidding when you said it was a shack," she said as he pushed open the door, a spray of snow following him in. It was black inside, and the smell of cold, stale air pushed free of the darkness to merge with the cold bite of fresh December air. "This isn't your main . . . post, is it? It doesn't seem very state-of-the-art."

He lit a kerosene lantern and the room was suddenly lit by the golden glow of light. It seemed warmer instantly.

"Kerosene? Do they still sell that?" she said, moving into the room. She couldn't seem to stop talking. He was so quiet. Very strange guy. Well, there was probably something strange about anyone who spent most of his time alone in the woods. Bigfoot came to mind. Swamp Thing. Creature from the Black Lagoon.

She was losing it. Her brain cells were probably freezing solid.

"So where's the heater?" she asked.

"Right here, and I'm lighting it up," he said. "It's so small in here that you'll feel the warmth almost right away."

"Great," she said. Again. "Do you have a radio or something? I want my parents to know I'm okay."

"Does your cell phone work?" he asked from his side of the tiny room. It was a shack, no other word for it: a ratty bed with a pile of fleece blankets in bright colors, a warped and gouged wooden desk under the black window with a metal stool pulled up for a chair, a plastic-coated map of Brimfield State Forest on the wall behind the heater with some little colored pins sticking out of it at various points.

Colored pins, two of them . . . what did they mark?

"Does it?" he asked again, taking off his gloves and laying them on the desk, inside his upturned helmet.

Right. The cell phone. She pulled her gaze from the mystery of the pins and made herself take off her gloves. The air in the shack wasn't much warmer than the air in a deep freeze. At least it wasn't windy. She pulled off her helmet and put it at her feet, keeping herself and all her stuff in a tight grouping. She was too cold to move much, to walk around, to make herself at home . . . to walk closer to the heater where Mike was standing.

Or that was what she told herself. Okay, so he was a little weird. At least he'd brought her someplace warm. Or someplace that *could* be warm.

She looked down into her cell phone, keeping

his feet in her line of vision. He wasn't moving. Neither was she.

Maybe they were both a little weird.

"No signal," she said, looking up from his feet, up the long line of his body to his face. He was nice-looking. Dark haired, rugged, great eyes, but something was *off* with this guy. Something about him made her edgy, and she was too tired to fight against her instincts and dredge up good manners. "So are you going to radio or what? I want my parents to know I'm okay."

"Are you okay?" he said softly, like a whisper of ice.

Wrong. He'd said it wrong somehow, the inflection of his words off, and every instinct shouted a warning. The cold surrounding his words banged hard against her bones, trying to break them. Trying to break her. But she wasn't going to be broken that quickly.

"I'm great," she said, slipping her gloveless hands into her pockets, sliding her fingers around, searching silently for her snowmobile keys. "I'm ready to go."

"I thought you wanted to get warm?" he said, unzipping his snowmobile suit in one long motion, that crazy half smile mocking her.

The keys weren't in her outer pockets. She'd put them in one of the inner pockets for safety. For safety . . . that was almost funny now.

"I'm warm enough," she said coldly, unzipping the front of her suit to her breasts, proving it. Giving her access to the inner pockets of her snowmobile suit. No way to casually reach into those pockets without him knowing it, unless . . .

She put her bare hands under her armpits, warm against the cashmere, its soft elegance discordantly out of tune with this shack and this man. He was danger. He was threat. He was harm. All her instincts from that first wild impulse to throw herself away from him had been right. The need to escape the cold had confused her, pain calling more stridently than danger. But no more. Now she saw the real danger. It was him. He was worse than cold.

"There," she said, pressing her hands against her torso, shifting them down to the pockets that nestled against her ribs, "much better. Let's go."

"Not yet," he said, taking a step toward her. "I just found you."

She had the keys. Right breast pocket, which meant she would have them in her left hand. Not good. She was right-handed, almost useless with the left.

"That's your job, right?" she said, backing a step away from him, keeping the door behind her.

"I'm good at it," he said, his smile unfreezing, moving over his whole face. This was something that made him happy, relaxed. He was proud. Make him talk about it while she fumbled with the key ring.

"I guess so," she said, trying for a smile and failing. "What's with the pins?"

"My finds," he said. "I told you. I'm good at it." He walked to the desk and took a pin from a shot glass in the drawer. "This will be your pin. Brown, like your eyes. You're cute, ya know? Yeah, sure ya know. Girls always know when they're cute."

"Well, uh, thanks," she said, flipping open the lock on the can of Mace that hung from her key ring. *Thanks, Dad, for being overprotective and putting Mace on every key ring in the house.* "Where do you put the pin?"

"What?" he said, turning to face her.

He was huge. His neck was massive. He was wearing a zippered fleece shirt under his snowmobile suit, and the zipper was down. Dark hair crept upward from his chest to strangle his throat. *If only.*

She had to get it right. The Mace was small, one long shot of it, and she had to hit his eyes and nose. One shot. She couldn't miss, even left-handed. There was no time to switch to her right. There was no time for anything.

"What do the pins mark?" She was trying for casually interested. She sounded squeaky and panicked. "Where lost? Where found?"

"Where I find them," he said. "I've found two so far, and now you. That's three. The last one was during the last snow. People get lost in the snow. They don't know what they're doing. They don't belong out here."

"Yeah," she said, staring at him, knowing that fear and horror were growing in her eyes and unable to stop them. "I guess you're right. Good thing you're out here to save them. But that's what you get paid for, right?"

"I'm a volunteer," he said. "I do this because it's what I'm supposed to do. I'm good at it."

"You are," she said. "You are good at it."

So he wasn't with the parks service, at least not officially. Did that make it better or worse? Did anyone know about him? Did anyone know about *her?*

"But you shouldn't have been out there," he said, carefully putting the brown pin that marked *her* in his map. She'd been way up on the northwest side, close to nothing, the Mass Pike ten miles farther north.

While his back was turned, she tried to lift out her keys and move them to her right hand. They clinked together like a wind chime and he turned abruptly. She kept them in her left hand, staring back into his eyes.

He looked almost normal. That was the thing that kept throwing her. Almost normal. Almost.

"What was that? What do you have?" he asked, moving swiftly.

"Nothing," she blurted. "Nothing. My keys."

"Keys to what?" he said.

She had to do it now. If he got much closer, he'd be too close, his body pressing against her, backing her against the door. She wouldn't be able to move. She had to do it. Now.

Now.

With grace born of need, she pulled the Mace free, feeling with her fingertips for the front, pressing her thumb on the top as she held it up to his face. It came out in a stream, thin and wobbly.

92

The liquid hit him in the chin, the cheek. . . . God, she had to focus; she had to get it right, had to aim. *The eyes, aim for the eyes, the nose. God, help.*

Help.

It hit his eyes. First his right and then across the bridge of his nose and to his left eye. A solid hit of Mace into the soft, blood-rich membranes of his eyes. His hands went up, hiding, but she was able to slide a stream of pain past his hands and into the soft tissue of his nose. He dropped down to his knees, a dead weight of agony, moaning, crying. Helpless.

Whirling, she turned to the flimsy door and yanked it open. The scent of snow was bracing, the cold fist of night refreshing after the heated fear of the shack. There were worse things than cold.

Her victory was short-lived. She was still lost. Still without a machine to take her out. Her keys were truly useless now, and his were out of reach; she wouldn't go near him again.

She had to get out. That was the important thing. She had to get away from him. How long did the effects of Mace last? How long before he found her again? He had the means and he had the will. Maybe more so now. Now he had good cause to hate her.

"Bitch!" he cried out, rubbing at his eyes; his face was marked in red bands of pain. "I'll find you again. I can always find you."

She didn't answer him. Could he even see her?

She should have paid more attention when her dad was telling her about the effectiveness of Mace. All she'd remembered was to aim for the eyes. But how long did it last? How long before he came for her?

It didn't matter. She had to get out. That was all there was to think about. And she'd found *him* last time; he hadn't found her. That wouldn't happen again.

As quietly as she could, she left the shack and walked across the snow until she was out of sight of the shack. She'd left her helmet and gloves behind, but it couldn't be helped. She wasn't going to walk past him to get them; he might have swung his arm around and caught her, holding her there until the Mace wore off. No way was she going to risk that.

She ran in the tracks of his snowmobile, hoping to hide her footprints in the rumpled snow. It wasn't a bad idea, but she knew that he'd know what she'd done when he didn't see any other tracks. How easy was it going to be for him to track his own trail? *Stupid snow.* She hated the stuff.

She kept her hands tucked up in the sleeves of her suit and tightened the scarf around her head. She ran through the snow. Ran and ran until it hurt to breathe. Until she was dizzy. Until she had to stop, crying in her frustration. Crying in fear.

It was when she was wiping her nose with the end of her scarf that she heard the sound of a motor in the distance.

CHAPTER FIVE

He'd followed her tracks, scuffed and shuffled snowmobile tread, footsteps wiping away the clean line of skis and cleated snowmobile track. The mark of footsteps, so hard to hide in the sweep of snow, had led him. He had her. He'd found her.

He'd known he would.

She didn't belong out here, that was obvious, and what didn't belong had to be removed. That was all. It was very simple. He would keep the woods clean, untouched, unfouled; that was his job, and he did it without pay.

He loved his job.

He was good at it.

He'd already removed two. It had been easy, and he had enjoyed it. He got better at it each time, too. He had a skill for removal. Some might even say it was a talent.

Maybe Lindsay would even say it. She seemed smart enough to recognize talent when she saw it. She'd been smart enough to hide a cylinder of Mace in her pocket. His eyes and throat still burned with it.

He hadn't expected it, but he wasn't too upset about it. An animal cornered would strike. That was all. Simple.

But he could strike, too.

Simple.

His Blade rumbled over the snow, his eyes on the jumble of tracks she'd tried to hide, but couldn't. He'd found her. In minutes, he'd have her.

Hide. She had to hide. He was too close for her to run. The sound of him coming through the night was like ghostly vapor, like the icy touch of frost as it rose into the air. Like death.

This was beyond rape. He wanted to kill her. She'd felt it, heard it in his voice, seen the shadow of it in his strange eyes: death. The promise of death, held within his hands like a gift.

Bigfoot? He was Freddy Krueger, a nightmare from out of the dark.

But she wasn't going to be one of the stupid, screaming movie girls who got killed too fast and too easily. Her Mace was gone and she was on foot, but she wasn't going to scream, calling him to her. She was going to hide. And pray. Pray that the night would never end, that the rising sun wouldn't reveal her to him. Pray that the snow would melt and that she could walk trackless on frozen earth. Pray that she'd survive.

Beyond the sound, growing, loud, harsh in the deep dark of the hours before dawn, she could see the light of machinery. Man-made light, harsh and white and slicing through the dark. But not all-encompassing. Man-made light was thin and focused; she could hide from a beam of light, if she could hide her tracks. She had to hide her tracks. But she'd tried and he'd found her anyway.

Try harder.

Survive.

The trail she was on was the one *he'd* made. No good. She had to leave this trail; it would only take her to where she'd been, where she'd first found him. No point going there again.

She began to run once more, ignoring the pain of locked muscles and the cold slice of frozen air as it knifed its way into her lungs. The trail ran straight for fifty yards in front of her, banked close by trees before hooking right and up a steep hill covered in dense young pine. She could fall down that hill, sliding her way into the trees and into the dark, leaving the trail and finding a way that no snowmobile could follow.

Forty yards to the hill.

The whine of the Blade followed her, mocking her. She couldn't outrun a machine, especially a machine made for snow.

But snowmobiles couldn't go around tight-packed trees; they couldn't bend or twist or squeeze through spaces less than a foot wide. But she could.

Thirty yards.

The noise became deafening, like the roar of the sea, only sharper, thinner, menacing. With the noise came the prick of light piercing the dark like a blade, searching her out, stripping her bare of the protection of night.

Twenty yards.

Her feet were like concrete blocks, shifting the snow, pushing it from her, heavy and clumsy. She wasn't running; she was shuffling, panicked, exhausted, cold in her bones and in her blood. Only her fear was hot.

Ten yards.

The light found her, sliding across her tracks, slicing into her legs. The light, cold and white and thin, caught her in its glare. Caught.

No, not caught. Not taken. Only found. But that could change. The hill was before her; a sharp left and she was sliding down the hill, her feet slipping, her hands grasping as saplings brushed her clothes and dumped their slender weight of snow onto the trail she made, covering her tracks, helping her to hide.

Run.

Hide.

The snowmobile stopped somewhere above her, the engine throbbing against the cold. She didn't look back. Her face would show white against the night, and she was all in black, her dark scarf helping to hide her against the black of wet tree trunks and the depth of night. She slipped into the darkness, holding her breath. It was like diving into the lake in summer, holding her breath, pulling herself along with handholds of cold mud.

Staying under. Staying quiet. Disappearing.

It would work. It had to work.

The light, cutting into the darkness above her, turned away, taking the sound of the motor with it. The darkness was complete, the silence growing as the snowmobile moved away over the snow, leaving her in peace.

Peace? Not yet. She had to keep moving. She wasn't safe. She wasn't out of the woods.

She giggled weakly at her stupid joke. Her dad always said that, his voice serious, his eyes serious. *You're not out of the woods yet, Lindsay.*

I know, Dad. I know.

She wasn't out of the woods yet. Not yet, but she would be. She didn't know which way she was going, but if she kept walking, she had to end up *somewhere.* Even somewhere was better than being here.

Staying low, walking carefully down the incline, her knees creaking in protest, she made her way down the rest of the hill. It leveled off slowly, the baby pines giving way to larger oaks and maples, opening up wide paths of snow beneath the trees.

Opening the way for machines.

She needed steeply pitched ground and dense undergrowth, not this open space, but she had to keep walking. She couldn't just stay in the thicket of pine; he'd find her, even if he had to get off his machine. He'd find her, and she couldn't let him find her. She had to get away, and that meant she had to keep walking. If she was quiet, if she stayed close to the dark mass of tree trunks, he might not find her.

She slowed, looking around her nervously as her feet churned to a halt, her back pressed against an old and towering oak. It dominated the space, hiding her well, letting her snuggle against the rough bark, letting her rest.

Rest? She couldn't rest. And the trouble with big trees was that they pushed out all smaller competition. The oak she had chosen as haven had swept all clear beneath its far-spreading branches, leaving a wide band of revealing snow at its rooted feet and forcing the nearest tree to stand thirty feet off. Not a good place for her. A snowmobile could come here easily.

But there was no snowmobile now, no sound of machinery hammering against the silence. She didn't have to be quiet and careful now. He was gone, for now, and it was her chance to run and put some distance between them. He had lost her trail and he might not find it again. She had found *him* the first time. Why couldn't she remember that?

Okay, get going, keep moving, and move fast.

She gave the oak a pat of farewell and forced her feet to run through the woods.

How many heartbeats was it before she slowed

to a fast walk? Ten? Fifty? She was exhausted and hungry; her body had nothing left to burn. She should have eaten more than three bites of ice cream for dinner.

Well, while she was thinking of all the things she should have done, she should have locked Keith out when he came jumping up her porch steps. This was all his fault.

The silence pulled at her, unrelenting and heavy, forcing her to hear herself. Forcing her to see herself. She wasn't seventeen anymore, and twenty really was old enough to see the truth.

It wasn't Keith's fault. She'd made choices, right from the start when he'd first kissed her that long-ago summer and right up to tonight. Her choices. Her consequences.

Time to grow up, Lindsay. Time to own up.

The sound of an engine tore at the night, ripping all introspection from her to lie dead upon the snow.

He'd found her.

That was her first and only thought, and it sent energy soaring into her muscles so that she ran with raw heat across the snow, searching for deep cover, dense wood, plunging valleys to bury herself within. Anything to get away from the relentless pursuit of man and machine.

The ground stayed defiantly flat.

Lights tore into the sanctuary of darkness that shrouded her. Lights and roaring noise and the sound of a male voice raised in full-throated victory. The light shone like a crystal path, lighting her way when she wanted the dark, showing the frantic movements of her body as she lunged forward, her shadow long and weak against the snow.

Not like this, God. Don't let me die like this.

And then the light multiplied. In front of her another light spilled out across the snow, white, blinding. It bounced into her eyes as it sped toward her, washing her in light. Leaving her no escape at all.

Two? Were there two of them?

She veered hard to the right, searching for her hill. She'd climb up it if she had to, clawing her way to the top, anything to delay being taken by Mike again. She wouldn't go with him willingly this time. She still had her keys. She'd mark him, blind him with the hard scrape of jagged metal and the bite of her tiny penknife, leaving a red DNA trail for someone to follow.

"Lindsay!"

She turned at the shout, at the sudden quiet of an engine idling. She knew that voice.

"Jeff?"

Long legs straddled a motorbike. Long arms lifted off a dark helmet. And then she saw him. Jeff. Dark-haired, green-eyed, tall, wonderful Jeff.

"Oh, God," she breathed, laughing and crying. "Thank you. Thank you!" she shouted, running across the snow, slipping, laughing hysterically.

She threw herself against him, wrapping her arms around him. He was freezing, his face frozen, his nose running, but he held her hard against him, balancing her and the bike and himself. It was over. She was safe, held in arms of safety, wrapped in rescue.

"What are you doing here?" she panted.

"Surprise," he said softly, smiling down at her. Why had she ever thought safety was boring? The world was dangerous enough to make safety very alluring.

And then the sound of a snowmobile pushed into her safety, breaking it into shards in seconds. That second light had not disappeared. No, it was coming—and coming for her.

"It's him," she said against Jeff's cheek. "Let's go. We have to go!"

"Who is it?" he said. "What happened? You're more than cold. You're scared."

"It's the guy," she said, pulling at his arm. "The guy with the pins. Look, we have to go!"

The snowmobile was upon them. It was Mike. She'd known it. She'd known it, known it, known it. He might kill them both. He might still get her, get Jeff. He might be armed. He might do *anything*.

She slid her hand into her pocket and felt for her key ring, slipping the metal keys between her fingers so that they pointed outward, fashioning a quick weapon, opening her little Swiss Army knife, leafing out the blade, the nail file, and the tiny scissors. Not a bad weapon. Better than nothing.

"I see you found her," Mike said, sitting on his snowmobile, letting the engine softly idle as he pulled off his helmet and hung it on the right handlebar. "Did you track her or just get lucky?"

"Both," Jeff said, moving Lindsay slightly behind him.

Lindsay was shaking in his arms, pulling at him in silent panic, trying to get him to move. But he didn't move. Who *was* this guy?

"I tracked her," he said.

"Good for you," Jeff answered stiffly. "Who are you?"

"I'm the tracker," he said with a heavy shrug. "People get lost. I find them."

"You good at it?" Jeff said, distantly aware of Lindsay's tugging, but keeping his attention focused on the tracker. Something was off about him.

"I found Lindsay," he said with a smile. "Twice."

"I found *you* the first time!" Lindsay spat out between angry shivers. "Let's *go!*" she said to Jeff, yanking on his arm.

He turned to look down at her, at the desperation, anger, and fear that merged in the depths of her dark eyes. This was more than being cold, more than being lost, more than being scared. This was raw terror.

"Okay," he said to her softly before turning his gaze to the tracker. "I'll take her home."

The tracker had left his snowmobile and swept silently closer to the Enduro, which Jeff still straddled, Lindsay pressed against his hip in silent need. She was no longer shivering; she was staring at the quiet approach of the tracker and she was as still as a frozen lake, calm and white and impenetrable.

She was ready for a fight, and her eyes were all for the tracker.

Just as the tracker's eyes were all for her.

That decided it.

In one motion he took his helmet, grasping it by the chin strap, and let the bike fall into the snow, stepping free of it. In that same motion he stood between Lindsay and the tracker, the heavy helmet the best weapon he had, and not a bad one at that.

"Back off," he said softly, his words rising as mist into the night.

"But I found her," the tracker said. He was a big guy, bulky, and Rottweiler determined.

"But I've got her," Jeff said. "And I'm keeping her."

"I found her," the tracker said again, his eyes going to Lindsay somewhere behind Jeff.

There was nothing more to think about, nothing more to say. Jeff swung his helmet and knocked the tracker on the side of the head with it. It hit with a heavy, satisfying thud, and then the tracker was down in the snow. Out. Something long and dark rolled from his unclenched hand: a hunting knife, oiled and sharp.

"Come *on*," Lindsay panted.

He turned. She was trying to lift the Enduro and get it upright. It was a heavy bike for her, and cold muscles would only make it seem heavier.

Funny, but he wasn't cold at all anymore. He was hot with fight and blood, feeling more alive than he ever had in his life.

He gave the tracker one last look. Out. Then he lifted up the bike and held it by the handlebars. Lindsay stood at the tailpipe, her hands on the seat. They looked at each other over the length of the motorbike and then she smiled, a great, blinding smile that made him feel even better than he had.

"You're pretty good with a helmet," she said, teasing him. "I didn't know you had it in you, tough guy."

He loved that about her; she was always teasing him and getting him to laugh. He hadn't laughed much until he'd met her. Premed was nothing to laugh about.

"Dirt-biking is a tough sport," he said with a shrug. "I hold my own."

"I guess so," she said with a soft snort of laughter. "I guess you're pretty good at a lot of things, huh?"

"Kind of slow to figure that out, aren't you?" he said, teasing her back, lifting his leg to straddle the bike, shifting forward to give her room behind him on the narrow seat as he kicked it to life. The engine started right up, hot to go.

She slid on behind him, wrapping her arms around his waist, nuzzling her face against his back like a cat eager to purr.

"I'm figuring out a lot of things. A long walk in the woods will do that; lots of time to think," she said.

"Yeah? Like what?" he said, handing the helmet back to her.

"No," she said, pushing the helmet toward him, "you keep it. You might need it again."

"Nah, he's out," Jeff said, looking toward the still figure of the tracker. "What was with that guy? He didn't hurt you, did he?"

"No," she said softly, inching closer to him. "But he would have. Thanks," she whispered.

"Anytime," he said as he throttled the bike up, getting them both away from the tracker in the snow. He still had to go fast or risk breaking through a thin spot in the icy crust. "Hang on," he called back as the sound of the motor grew to kill the quiet of the night.

Her arms clasped him harder, her legs tightening around his hips. "I am," she yelled into his ear. And then, so softly he almost didn't hear her, she said, "I will."

STILL OF THE NIGHT

by Dee Davis

CHAPTER ONE

New York City

"I'll be home for Christmas. . . ."

Judy Garland crooned in surround-sound, and Jenny Fitzgerald resisted the urge to throw something. She'd wanted to get rid of her husband. That much was true. But not in a permanent sort of way.

All she'd wanted was a divorce, and now Connor was dead.

He'd never be home for Christmas again. Which made the carol all that much more of a twisted joke. Stifling a sob, Jenny threw the pants she was folding onto the bed, her gaze dropping to the envelope on the nightstand.

The divorce decree.

All it needed was a signature and it was final. Only, Connor hadn't bothered to open the enve-

111

lope, and it seemed that widowhood made the point moot. Jenny grabbed the envelope and stuffed it into her purse, not sure why exactly she did so, except that she didn't want it mocking her.

"How about a break?" Sandy Markham appeared in the doorway, her face purposefully cheerful. "I found some wine." She held up a bottle, her expression turning apologetic.

Sandy had been Jenny's best friend since first grade. She'd helped Jenny toilet-paper Connor's house in the sixth grade, found her a date when Connor's family moved just before junior prom, celebrated their reunion in college, been maid of honor at their wedding, supported Jenny when she'd decided to leave Connor, and, two days ago, she'd stood beside her at his memorial service.

A lifetime of memories all tied to a dead man.

"Wine would be good." Jenny folded another shirt and laid it in the box marked ST. ANN'S.

Sandy walked into the room, setting the bottle on the bureau. "Are you sure you should be doing this? I mean, there isn't any hurry. Surely you could wait until—"

"Until what? I'm stronger?" Jenny crossed her arms over her chest, hugging herself.

"Oh, honey." Sandy frowned. "I didn't mean it like that. I just hate to see you so upset."

Jenny shrugged, picking up another shirt. "It's got to be done. Mr. Bowman's let me out of the lease, but that means the apartment has to be empty by January."

"So at least wait until after Christmas. Or hire someone to do it."

"I will hire someone. I just wanted to go through his personal things. I can't . . ." She sat down on the bed, burying her face in her hands, then pulled up, forcing a smile. "I can't stand the idea of anyone else going through them."

Sandy wrapped an arm around her. "I understand. But we don't have to do it all in one day. Right?"

Jenny nodded, emotionally drained. "I guess I just thought doing something would make me feel better. Accept the reality of it all. I mean, after six years as a cop's wife, you'd think I'd be used to the idea of death."

"Death as an abstract is a lot easier to conceptualize than the real thing." Sandy sighed. "Besides, this isn't just any death. It's Connor."

And that said it all, really. Connor Fitzgerald had been an integral part of her life, and even their impending divorce hadn't erased the memories. No matter what he'd done, Jenny still cared. His death only punctuated that fact.

"I must have imagined something like this happening at least a million times," she said. "It's part of what drove us apart, I guess."

"Yeah, that and Amy Whitaker." The minute the words were out Sandy ducked her head, her face white with regret. "I shouldn't have said that."

"Why not?" Jenny asked, her insides threatening to fuse together. "It's true."

"Yeah, but I shouldn't have brought it up. As

usual, my mouth just engaged before my brain." Sandy offered a weak smile. "For what it's worth, I still really have trouble with the idea. I mean, he was so in love with you. Anyone could see that. Even afterwards—" She broke off, obviously at a loss for words.

"Sometimes love just isn't enough." Jenny shrugged, pretending a nonchalance she didn't feel. "Besides, Amy was just the tip of the iceberg. Being with Connor was never easy, and his working Vice just made it that much harder. He was gone all the time, and he couldn't talk about his work. It just got more and more difficult to connect." She fought against old feelings of failure, pushing them aside with a sigh. "Anyway, none of it matters anymore. Connor is gone. And the past has to become just that—the past."

"I think that's the problem," Sandy said, her gaze concerned. "It isn't over. Not really. Too much was left unsettled between the two of you. And that's what's making it so hard to accept that he's gone."

"Maybe you're right." Jenny stood up, wiping her hands on her jeans. "You know, I keep expecting him to come through that door and yell at me for going through his things. Crazy, huh?"

"No. Not at all. In fact, I suspect it's absolutely normal. But that doesn't make it any easier." Sandy's smile was sad. "Hey, why don't we go out for a while, have something to eat, and then we'll come back here and tackle the rest?"

"No." Jenny shook her head, squaring her shoulders. "Let's just get it done." She reached for a sweater, trying to ignore the familiar smell of Hugo Boss. "I will have that glass of wine, though. There's a screw pull in the second drawer by the sink."

Sandy grabbed the bottle and headed for the kitchen. As soon as she was out of sight, Jenny sank back onto the bed, her thoughts in turmoil. She'd hoped that with the memorial service behind her, she'd at least feel a sense of relief. Instead, the pain seemed only to intensify. Repression was what her psychiatrist would call it.

Heartbreak seemed a better word.

She'd known Connor almost her whole life. Loved him. Hated him. Loved him again. And then she'd left him. But she hadn't managed to get him out of her heart. That had simply been beyond her abilities.

Now he was gone, and she was, as usual, left behind.

What she needed was closure. Only she wasn't going to get it. At least, not in a way that she could live with.

The doorbell and the phone rang at the same time, and Jenny dove across the bed. She wasn't really up to talking, but better answering the phone than the door. She'd let Sandy handle that.

She fumbled with the receiver, losing her grip on it once, then finally managed to put it to her ear. As she said hello, she heard the murmur of voices in the foyer. When it rained, it poured.

For a minute the other end of the line was

silent. Long enough that Jenny started to put the receiver back in the cradle, but the sound of static made her stop, her heart pounding in her ears.

"Get out of there." The voice was low, almost inaudible. "Now."

The line went dead, followed by a popping noise. Jenny glanced automatically at the window, listening for further sounds from the traffic below, her beleaguered brain finally confirming that the noise had come from the direction of her living room.

She started to call out, but some inner voice held her silent, and she moved toward the bedroom door, holding her breath. The hallway was empty, but she could still hear voices. Masculine voices.

She waited for Sandy to say something, the skin on her arms crawling with gooseflesh, but Sandy was silent; only the men's voices carried down the hall. As if they'd been cued, the words from the telephone caller echoed through her brain.

Get out. . . . Get out. . . . Get out. . . .

But she couldn't leave her best friend.

Edging forward, she was careful to stay tight against the wall, telling herself that there was a perfectly logical explanation to everything. Still, better to be careful. She reached the end of the hall and stopped. Any farther and she risked being seen. Better to assess the situation first.

Connor's voice sounded in her ear, almost as if he were there giving her instructions. Sucking in a fortifying breath, she risked a peek around the corner. Two strangers stood in front of the breakfast bar. One of them was holding a gun. Feeling as if she were watching a movie, or some surreal reenactment of a crime, Jenny's eyes fell to the floor.

Sandy was lying in a pool of blood, eyes wide—sightless.

Jenny clutched the wall for support, a scream rising in her throat. With a force of will she hadn't realized she possessed, she clenched her jaw, swallowing the sound. Noise was her enemy.

Moving back, she tried to combine speed with stealth, but she managed only to trip on the rug, her hands hitting the wall with enough force to sound like a cannon. She knelt on the floor, holding her breath, praying for everything she was worth.

A minute passed, and then another, and when no one entered the hallway she began to crawl back to the bedroom. Her mind was already planning an escape route. All she had to do was make the window and the fire escape and run like hell.

It was doable. Despite the fact that Connor had always teased her about her lack of common sense, she had a good head on her shoulders, and with that and a little luck she'd get out of this alive. She hoped.

"It's not in here," one of the men called to the other, his footsteps sounding absurdly loud against the parquet floor. "I'm gonna check the other room."

Terror held Jenny frozen for a moment, her

mind refusing to acknowledge that danger was approaching. A new appreciation for deer caught in headlights flashed through her brain. Then the terror bit into her, her adrenaline rushed, and she sprang to her feet, scrambling for the bedroom.

She skirted the bed, grabbing her purse in the process, her hip slamming into the bedside table. Ignoring the pain, she slung the purse onto her shoulder, commando style, and reached up to flip the lock on the window, praying that it would open silently.

Behind her, she could hear the man's footsteps in the hallway. Just seconds to go until he rounded the corner. Cursing her lack of strength and the fact that they'd never had the window repaired, she worked to jerk it upward, feeling it give inch by inch. Slowly. Too slowly.

"What the hell?"

Despite herself, Jenny shot a look over her shoulder. The man in the doorway was reaching for his gun. Grabbing a pillow, she swung back to the window, hitting it with the full force of her hand. Even with the protection of fiberfill she could feel the shattering glass, shards of it cutting her arm.

A hiss and more shattered glass got her moving again. The stranger had shot at her! She pushed her body through the window, pillow first. She landed on the fire escape with a clatter of metal and broken glass, and rolled to her feet, another bullet ricocheting off the railing.

With panic born of terror, Jenny sprinted across the landing to the ladder, her feet finding purchase as her brain struggled to find sense among madness. She swung around the ladder onto the next landing, and heard the gunman hitting the grating above her. Slamming herself back against the brick wall, she edged forward. Another bullet hit the exposed metal rail.

Frozen as she was, the sound of her pursuer sent Jenny into motion again. She slid down the next ladder, her feet hardly hitting the rungs, and dashed across the third landing, pushing a potted tree over in an attempt to slow her enemy. As the third ladder disappeared behind her and she rounded the corner to start the fourth, she heard the man above give a muffled curse.

Score one for the deer.

The fifth landing was the last, the sliding ladder leading to the ground her final means of escape. She swung onto it, waiting for her weight to send it toward the ground, but nothing happened. Holding tightly to the sides, she jumped, wishing for once that she weighed more than a hundred and ten pounds. The ladder refused to budge, the telltale signs of rust mocking her actions. She glanced across at the darkened window of the second-floor apartment. The window was shut tightly against the frigid air, the closed blinds making it look even more forbidding.

Still, it was her only chance.

She moved to step back onto the landing just as the gunman rounded the corner, his expression deadly, the gleam of his gun in the lamplight even more so.

119

Stifling a scream, Jenny clambered back onto the ladder and pushed downward for everything she was worth. The damn thing refused to move, and the man above her drew closer, his mouth cracking into a smile.

He leveled his gun, and Jenny considered jumping. The pavement below might hurt, but at least it offered a thread of hope. She leaned out from the ladder, her weight shifting as she prepared to leap.

She heard the report of the gun and an accompanying groan. For a moment she thought it was her own; then she realized the sound came from the ladder. Her movement, or maybe serendipity, had loosened the rust, and she slid noisily toward the ground—her assailant's latest bullet hitting nothing but air.

In seconds she was on the ground and running up Fifty-eighth toward Third Avenue and the Christmas crowds. If the man followed her there, it was unlikely he'd be able to shoot. All she had to do was lose herself in the people.

The street was unusually quiet, and her footsteps echoed in her ears, accompanied by the tympanic sound of her assailant's heavier tread. Not daring to look back, she ran on, zigging back and forth across the sidewalk like a drunk, some latent memory about escaping gunfire urging her on. Connor's voice was again playing in her head.

Run, Jenny. Run.

She staggered onto Third, her breath coming in ragged gasps. One block more and she'd be at

Bloomingdale's. The crowd was already streaming around her, protecting her as they jostled along, unaware of her plight.

It was tempting to grab a stranger and ask for help, but adrenaline kept Jenny moving. There was safety in distance, and that was what mattered right now. Once she was safe, she could call for help.

The light changed and the crowd surged across the street. Jenny moved with it, the sounds of New York at Christmas assailing her from all sides, taunting her with the reality that amid the supposed joy of the season, her life was unraveling. Her husband and best friend were dead. And somewhere behind her, a man with a gun wanted her dead, too.

She pushed through the door of Bloomingdale's and past the army of women spraying perfume. Just a few steps more and she'd be at the elevator.

Her mind fixed on the safety of the fourth-floor ladies' bathroom. It was always crowded, but particularly at Christmas. There was safety in crowds; that much she was certain of. And the bathroom would be even better. No man, not even a gunman, would dare to follow her there. Not into a crowd.

She slid inside the elevator, pressing her back against the wall, waiting as harried shoppers pushed forward to fill the metal box. A tall man in black was the last on, and her heart accelerated, panic threatening again. But her brain intervened with the knowledge that it wasn't the same man. This one was taller and thinner. He wasn't the one.

Sagging against the wall, she stared at the lights that changed from floor to floor until the doors dinged open on four. Two older women moved forward, and Jenny used them to block her, as she scooted out of the elevator, well out of sight of the man in black.

Better safe than sorry.

She sprinted toward the restroom, already fumbling in her purse for her cell phone. A woman at the head of the line must have mistaken her panic for bladder pain, because she offered the stall she was about to enter with a wave of her hand.

Jenny didn't stop to thank her. She slid inside, bolted the shuttered door, and sank down onto the toilet seat, hot tears filling her eyes. With shaking fingers, she opened her cell phone and dialed Andy's number.

Connor's partner would know what to do.

CHAPTER TWO

"What the hell happened?" Nico Furello slammed his hand down on the table, the pounding pulse in his temple almost deafening. "You were supposed to retrieve a package, not blow away half of the Upper East Side."

"So I killed a broad." Reggie Anzio wasn't the brightest bulb on the tree, but he'd been useful on more than one occasion. Unfortunately, this wasn't one of them. "It's not like it's the first time."

"That woman could very well be the wife of a Vice cop. You got any idea the kind of heat that could bring down on us?"

"No more than some motormouth claiming she'd seen us," Reggie said.

"Well, that logic only holds water if the motormouth was the only witness." Nico glared at his minion, his mind already trying to sort out the repercussions.

"I tried to kill the other one, too." Reggie shrugged. "She just got lucky."

"I got a make on the stiff." Sammy Lacuzo walked into the room, flashing a photograph. "Sandra Markham. She was friends with the ex."

Nico's stomach twisted. There was going to be hell to pay for this. "And the one that got away?"

"Jenny Fitzgerald." Sammy spat the name out like a curse. Which wasn't far from the truth. Thanks to Reggie's ineptitude, the woman was now a liability. And at the moment Nico had too damn many of them.

"How good a look did she get?"

Reggie winced but stayed silent, his gaze shooting to Sammy.

"She could definitely make him," Sammy said.

"It was dark. . . ." Reggie trailed off, uncomfortably shifting from one foot to the other.

"I don't want to hear your excuses." Nico ground his teeth together in an attempt to contain his anger. "The fact of the matter is that you killed one woman and left another as a witness. And to top it off, you failed to find Fitzgerald's proof."

Reggie was a large man, but that didn't stop him from backing up. "We tossed the place. There wasn't nothing there."

Nico nodded, his hands curling into fists. "That doesn't mean it doesn't exist. And now, thanks to you, someone knows we're looking. What about you?" Nico turned to Sammy. "Did she see you?"

Sammy shook his head. "Maybe from behind.

124

But I'm not even sure about that. I never went in the bedroom."

"And the body's been disposed of, right?"

"Let's just say it's not going to see daylight anytime in the foreseeable future." Sammy smiled.

Nico nodded, his mind already formulating a solution to his problem. At least, to the most immediate one. "All right, then, we clean up the mess." Nico's gaze met Sammy's, and the other man nodded, his blue eyes devoid of emotion.

Reggie shot a look at Nico and then Sammy, backed up another step, and raised his hands in supplication. "I ain't a liability."

"Unfortunately, Reggie, that just isn't true." Nico sighed and shifted to the left, allowing Sammy a clean shot. It was over in less than a second; Reggie dropped to the floor, his eyes still wide in surprise.

Sammy holstered his piece and stepped over the body. "I'll make sure he disappears. It's not like anyone will miss him."

Nico nodded, his mind already turning to other problems. Bigger ones. They had to find out what, if anything, Fitzgerald had on them; and, even more urgently, they had to find his girl. At least she'd be identifying a dead man. But that wouldn't necessarily be enough.

Nico and his father didn't always agree on things. The old man was too fucking old school. Playing by rules that no longer existed. No drug dealing. No beef with cops. Hell, Nico was in bed with them! It was a new era and, despite his old man, or maybe because of him, Nico intended to create his own playbook. To make good on his own terms.

But there was one thing he and his old man agreed on: Damage control was everything.

Reggie's link to the family wasn't obvious, but with digging, the connection would be made. And Nico couldn't have that happen. Not if he wanted to stay alive.

Which meant Jenny Fitzgerald had to die.

The diner was like about a thousand others in New York: a counter and tables crammed into less space than a walk-in closet. The waiter had tried to give her a table in the window, but the last thing Jenny wanted was to be exposed.

Instead, she was sitting in the rear of the restaurant, back to the wall, waiting for Andy. She'd wanted to meet at the station, but Andy hadn't wanted her on the street. He'd said it would be easier to meet somewhere close to Bloomingdale's. They'd agreed to meet at this diner.

Jenny's hand shook as she lifted a glass of water, and she quickly put it back on the table, pretending instead to study the menu. She'd already checked out the sparse inhabitants of the diner—mostly shoppers sitting amid packages, enjoying some time off their feet.

Considering everything she'd been through in the past few hours, she was handling it all reasonably well. At least, better than most middle school

English teachers would. Of course, most of them didn't have a husband in Vice. *Ex-husband*, her mind automatically corrected, and she swallowed a bubble of hysteria.

Maybe she wasn't handling it so well after all.

"I'm sorry it took me so long." Andy Proctor slid into the booth across from her, his handsome face creased with worry. He had been Connor's partner for the past four years, and his friend for even longer. For all practical purposes he was family.

Andy had been the one to tell her about Connor's death, to explain about the explosion, and to make her see that, despite the fact that there was no body, Connor was gone. There had been DNA evidence. And the reality was, no one could have survived that fire.

Despite his friendship with Connor, Andy had remained her friend after the separation, shooting straight with her about Connor's involvement with Amy Whitaker, a uniform in their precinct. It had hurt to hear the truth, but it had also helped Jenny maintain her resolve.

She sighed and smiled weakly, grateful when Andy covered her hand with his. "Did you check out the apartment?"

"Yeah." He squeezed her hand, his expression hardening. "Sandy is dead. One shot to the head. Looks like the guy knew what he was doing."

"There were two of them."

Andy frowned. "Did you get a good look at them?"

127

"Only one." Jenny shivered, closing her eyes. "The other guy had his back to me, and the living room wall blocked my view. I'm sorry."

"There's nothing to be sorry about. I'm just glad you managed to get out of there. And if you can ID one of them, that'll at least give us a place to start."

"Do you want me to come look at mug shots or something?" Jenny shivered again, and Andy tightened his hold on her hand.

"That won't be necessary. At least not now. Let us do our job first. There's forensics and canvassing and all sorts of things that have to happen. What you need right now is to rest."

"But what if someone is following me?" She pulled away from Andy, wrapping her arms around herself. "I mean, the guy knows I saw him."

"My guess is that they're long gone. There's no reason to believe they were after *you*."

Jenny nodded her head, but the voice in her head was singing a different tune. There was something deliberate about everything that had happened. "I can't help but feel that this was more than a robbery. I mean, they knocked. That isn't usual, is it?"

"No." Andy shrugged. "But sometimes it's the most direct route to money."

"And Sandy let them in. It couldn't have been more than a few seconds before they killed her." Jenny shuddered, her mind obligingly trotting out a picture of Sandy's lifeless body.

Andy's eyes searched her face, his gaze interested. "Was there any indication they wanted something else?"

"Maybe." She ran a trembling hand through her hair. "I don't know. One of them said something like, 'It's not here.' "

"And you think the 'it' was specific?" A shadow crossed Andy's face, his features hardening.

"It could have been." She studied his expression, trying to figure out what it was that frightened her. "Is there something you're not telling me?"

Andy stared down at his hands, clearly debating.

"Andy?" She reached over to cover his hands with hers. "What is it? What aren't you telling me?"

He looked up, his eyes dark with an emotion she couldn't identify. "It's about Connor."

The sentence came from left field, and Jenny felt her eyes widen in surprise. "You think this was about him?"

"I think it's possible." Andy looked as if he wanted to sink through the floor.

"Tell me," Jenny demanded, sucking in a breath, not certain she really wanted to hear.

"I didn't want you to know." Andy sighed, looking suddenly tired. "I thought with Connor dead, maybe I could keep it from you."

"Keep *what* from me?" Jenny felt as if the world were spiraling out of control. Or maybe her mind was finally accepting the reality of everything that had happened. Either way, her stomach was threatening revolt.

"Connor was working both sides of the game, Jenny." Andy sat back, his face creased in apology.

"What the hell are you talking about?" She wasn't sure what she expected to hear, but this wasn't it. Connor Fitzgerald might have made some mistakes along the way, he might have even dallied with another woman, but there was no way in hell he'd ever cross the line of the law. Even when he'd worked undercover he'd been able to compartmentalize it. Connor was one of the good guys, and Jenny was willing to swear that on everything she held holy. "There's absolutely no way, Andy. You know that as well as I do."

Her words were vaguely reminiscent of the ones she'd spouted the day Andy had confirmed Connor's infidelity. And the irony wasn't lost on her. But she still wasn't going to believe him. At least not without something concrete.

"I wouldn't have believed it." Andy shook his head. "But it's the truth, Jenny. I have proof."

"What kind of proof?"

"Tapes and video. I even witnessed some of it. IAD had been investigating for almost six months before they called me in. And I was like you—skeptical and furious. But there was no refuting the evidence, Jenny. None."

"I don't know what to think."

"Look, after Connor was killed, the department decided to drop the case. There really wasn't any point in persecuting a dead man. So I figured you'd never need to know."

"But the explosion"—Jenny struggled with the thoughts crowding through her mind—"was an accident. I talked to the investigators myself." He'd supposedly been killed while on a stakeout.

"That's what they wanted you to think. With Connor dead, it was just easier."

"So you're saying it wasn't an accident?"

"I don't think so." Andy shook his head. "Connor told me he was meeting with a snitch. But I talked with the guy after the fact, and he swears he hadn't talked to Connor in months. And frankly, Jenny, I believe him."

"So maybe there was another reason he was in that warehouse?"

"We'll never know for sure. But the men he was mixed up with . . ." Andy paused, his gaze holding hers. "One of them owned the warehouse."

"So why isn't someone trying to nail them for Connor's murder?" All her troubles faded at the thought that some lowlife had killed her husband and was getting away with it.

"There was a cursory investigation. Very much under the table. But the evidence was inconclusive, and considering what we had on Connor, it was decided that more harm would come from making anything public. The case was closed, and the explosion was ruled an accident."

"The blue wall in action again." She tried, but couldn't keep the sarcasm from her voice. This part of the job was what Jenny detested. And it had played a significant role in the demise of her marriage.

"Like it or not, Jenny, you know how it works."

"Yeah, I do. Bury it deep and maybe no one will smell the stink."

Andy raised his hands in a shrug. "Connor made his bed. Considering what I've seen, he's lucky he went out like he did."

"You don't mean that. Nothing, not even prison, could possibly be worse than death."

"You haven't seen what I've seen, Jenny. Besides, a bad cop doesn't stand a chance in hell in the joint. If the inmates don't get him for being a cop, the guards will for being a *bad* cop. I'd rather be blown to bits, believe me."

She stared at Connor's partner, wondering suddenly if she'd ever known him. If she'd ever known Connor. "Did you ever confront him with any of this?"

"No." Andy shook his head, this time with regret. "At first I didn't want to face it. Later, I wasn't allowed to say anything."

"But he was your friend."

"And it killed me to keep this from him. Believe me, it did. But he'd changed, Jenny. You had to have seen that yourself."

There was truth in that. Truth she couldn't ignore. "Six months ago?"

"Probably more than that, but that's when it first appeared on the radar."

Six months ago Connor *had* changed. He'd always kept his own counsel, but to some degree Jenny had always felt a part of his world. Then suddenly, like a door slamming in the wind, he'd locked her out. At the time she hadn't understood. Later, when she'd found out about Amy Whitaker, she'd assumed that was the explanation. But maybe Andy was right. Maybe there had been something more.

"You should have told me."

"I thought I was doing the right thing."

"And now?"

"Now I figure you're better off with the truth. I have every reason to believe that this was nothing more than a random robbery. But if someone was looking for something specifically related to Connor, you have a right to know."

It was all too much to process, the information slamming through her brain like steel-reinforced dominoes. "If someone was after something, maybe they found it."

"Maybe." Andy didn't look convinced. "But based on what you said, they were still looking when you ran. Did you take anything from the apartment with you?"

The thought sent panic racing through her. "No. Nothing." She frowned, trying to think. "I grabbed my purse, that's all."

"And you ran."

"Yeah. Out onto the fire escape." She tipped back her head, trying not to cry. Tears weren't going to help anyone at this point. "He fired at me, and then started to follow. It all happened so fast."

"You did the right thing." Andy's words were meant to be comforting, but Jenny didn't feel any better. "And I honestly don't believe you have anything more to worry about. Even if someone was there trying to find something in the apartment, the fact is that you and Connor were separated. Anything that touched him couldn't possibly have touched you. Whoever is behind this—if anyone is behind anything—will know that."

"But I saw one of them. Surely that's not something they can ignore. I mean, they killed Sandy. . . ."

"It'll be okay. I'm here now. I won't let anything happen to you."

She wished she could believe him, but nothing seemed certain anymore. She'd thought she'd known her husband, but now his friend—*her* friend—was sitting here describing a stranger. A stranger who'd played with fire and lost. And as a direct result, Sandy Markham was dead.

"Oh, God, Andy, I just left her there."

"She was dead, Jenny." His effort to comfort was immediate, but it didn't ease the pain working its way through her gut. "If you'd gone to her, you'd be dead too." He reached for her hands again. "I wish I could make it all go away. But I can't. What I can do is make sure these bastards pay for what they've done."

Jenny nodded, the tears pooling in her eyes. "For Sandy."

"No, Jen." Andy shook his head, his gaze intense. "For you."

She swallowed, then pulled her hands away, uncomfortable with the intimacy in his voice. "So what do I do now?"

"Why don't you go home?" Andy said. "You're still living at your parents' house, right?"

She'd inherited the house in Cold Spring when her mother died. It had been a sanctuary after the separation, a safe place where her failed marriage could be forgotten—at least for a little while.

"You think it's safe?"

"Yeah. I mean, there's no reason to believe these guys would be able to connect you to Cold Spring. Even if they did, I've already notified the authorities up there and explained the situation. They're going to keep the house under surveillance. And I'll come up as soon as I can. I just need to finish up with things here."

"What about a statement?"

"I've got enough for a preliminary statement just from what you've told me here and on the phone. We can do the actual paperwork tomorrow."

She nodded, emotion still roller-coastering through her. "What about Sandy's mom? I should call her. Tell her what ha-happened." She choked on the words, the idea twisting in her mind.

"Don't worry about it. I've already sent uniforms. You can talk to her when you're ready, but there's no need to do it tonight." He pulled out his wallet and threw a couple of bills on the table. "Why don't you let me take you to the train station?"

Jenny swallowed her tears, squaring her shoulders. "I'll be fine on my own. It's not that far to

135

Grand Central. I'll just take a taxi." She checked her watch. "If I hurry I should be able to catch the next train." Home and a bath suddenly sounded really good. She just wanted to be away from the city. Somewhere she felt safe. Somewhere she could think things through.

Andy, however, didn't look convinced.

"You said I'm perfectly safe. And it's a lot more important for you to get to the bottom of this. I won't really be able to rest easy until those guys are behind bars, you know."

"Yeah. I do." Andy frowned. "It's just that I really hate the idea of leaving you on your own."

"You won't be. Grand Central is full of people. And you already said that no one is chasing me. I'll be fine. Really."

They got up and walked out of the diner. The cold wind whipping down Lexington reminded Jenny she didn't have a coat.

"You're freezing. Take this." Andy shrugged out of his leather jacket and draped it around her shoulders.

She pulled the coat around her, grateful for its warmth. Andy hailed a cab and, miracle of miracles, one stopped almost immediately. Andy gave the driver instructions, then opened the back door. His hand stopped Jenny as she started to slip inside.

"I'll be out there as quickly as I can. In the meantime, don't contact anyone. Just stay put, and call me immediately if anything seems off or out of place."

Jenny nodded. She attempted a smile, but the result was more of a lopsided grimace. "I'll be okay. And I'll call if I need anything. You just find out who killed Sandy."

She slid onto the cab's vinyl seat, the door slamming firmly behind her. As the taxi pulled away, she turned to look back. Andy was already striding down the street, talking urgently with someone on his cell phone.

Her brain clicked, a memory surfacing, and she realized she hadn't mentioned the phone call at the apartment. Leaning back against the seat, she closed her eyes, the voice echoing through her mind. It teased her with its familiarity.

Get out . . . get out. . . .

And Jenny wondered if she'd truly forgotten to tell Andy, or if maybe she'd held on to the information for reasons of her own.

CHAPTER THREE

The train was only about half-full. Jenny had purposely chosen a fairly crowded car, preferring the company of strangers. However, she drew the line at sharing a seat, and so she sat next to the window with Andy's jacket occupying the space next to her.

The night flashed by with only occasional bursts of bright light, the Hudson River illuminated by a soft swath of moonlight. There was a hunter's moon. Jenny shuddered, the thought hitting too close to home.

No one in the car seemed the slightest bit interested in her, but she couldn't help watching them. Most weren't suspect, either women or kids. Not that women or kids couldn't be involved, but Jenny figured if anyone was following her, it was most likely one or both of the men who had been in Connor's apartment. There was a lone male at the head of the car, but he was older and balding, and he hadn't looked up from his newspaper since boarding the train.

So, for the moment at least, she felt safe. Sort of.

Andy's revelations were still eating at her. Loyalty to Connor, no matter their marital situation, was warring with the facts as Andy had laid them out. Cops went bad all the time. Especially when they did undercover work. The temptation was often more than they could handle. But not Connor. If he'd been going to cross the line, he'd have done it a long time ago.

And he hadn't.

Which meant that there had to have been something else, some motivating factor that explained his actions. Either that, or Andy was wrong. But Andy had mentioned IAD, and that gave the story a thread of legitimacy Jenny couldn't ignore. Closing her eyes, she felt the swaying of the train as it slowed. Two more stops and she'd be home.

The train lurched to a stop, and the woman in front of her got up to leave, gathering sacks full of Christmas gifts, the red and green wrapping paper sending a wave of longing through Jenny. Christmastime had always been her favorite part of the year. It was a time of joy and celebration.

Until last year—when she'd been left to celebrate alone.

Perhaps it had been the stress of the season, or maybe the burdens had finally become too great, but the joy had gone out of not only the season but the marriage. And when Connor had chosen work over home and hearth yet again, Jenny had had enough. She'd asked him to leave, a fit of anger making her judgment less than solid. If she'd only held her tongue, let him stay, maybe none of the rest would have followed. Maybe he wouldn't have turned to someone else. Maybe she'd still have a husband.

And maybe, just maybe, he'd still be alive.

She knew somewhere in the sensible recesses of her mind that she wasn't alone in what had transpired; that her actions, although emotional, had been reasonable. Besides, if Connor had wanted to make amends he could have. But he hadn't.

And now he was gone. Nothing was going to change that fact. Not blaming herself, and not wishing for do-overs. Reality was here on this train, and the sooner she accepted that, the sooner she could go on with her life.

Assuming she made it through the night.

Pulling her thoughts away from the past, she searched the train again, surprised to find that a number of new people had entered. A man and his son now sat directly in front of her; an elderly woman flanked her in the seat across the aisle.

She twisted slightly to view the back of the car. Two teenagers were necking three seats back, their obvious attraction blocking out all other distractions. Behind them a man was reading a magazine, the cover blocking his face.

Jenny shivered, something about him seeming familiar. Turning to face front again, she couldn't stop the feeling that the man was watching her, his eyes boring into the back of her head, but when she turned surreptitiously to check, his face was still hidden behind the magazine.

She swallowed her fear and purposefully sucked in a deep breath. The motion was intended to calm her, but it didn't. So with a sigh of resolution, she stood up and made her way to the front of the car, not daring to look behind her.

She pushed through the doors and across the platform connecting cars, and on into the next coach. This one was more sparsely populated. An elderly gentleman slept with his head against the window, and two toddlers played with Barbies next to a harried-looking mother.

Jenny walked to the front of the car and slid into an open seat, this time on the side opposite the river. Trees and rocks whizzed past as the train picked up speed, and slowly Jenny's breathing returned to normal.

For all she knew Andy had already apprehended the killer. Maybe it was all over.

Then she shook her head at her flight of fantasy. If Andy had any news, he'd have called her. She reached for her purse, thinking that maybe she should call him, but managed only to knock it out into the aisle.

Obviously, she was more spooked than she wanted to admit. With a sigh, she reached over to retrieve her bag, and her gaze fell automatically on the back of the car as she straightened. The man with the magazine had moved.

She couldn't be absolutely certain, of course. But she'd swear it was the same magazine. And the same hands holding it. Like before, his face was hidden behind the magazine pages, but Jenny shivered nevertheless, her mind filling in the features of the man who'd killed Sandy.

The train slowed, pulling into Cold Spring, but Jenny knew she couldn't get off. She couldn't possibly lead the man to her home. Besides, the tunnel between the station and the town would be dark and deserted at this time of night. It had scared her as a kid. Heck, it had even worried her a bit as an adult. Now, with real reason for fear, she knew that it would be foolhardy to try.

Instead, she'd call Andy and stay on the train.

Careful not to look behind her, she walked out of the car as if she were going to detrain. Moments stretching like hours, she waited until she heard the hiss of the train starting again, then dashed through the doors into the next compartment. Without looking right or left, she continued forward through three more cars until she reached one that was almost completely full.

She sat down on the edge of a three-seater already occupied by an elderly woman and what was probably her daughter. The two of them smiled at her, and Jenny smiled back automatically, grateful for the company.

Surely she'd be safe now until they reached Poughkeepsie.

The conductor appeared at the front of the car, working his way back toward her seat, and Jenny fumbled with her wallet, extracting enough money for the additional fare. It was tempting to tell the conductor that she thought she was being followed, but since the magazine man had not appeared in this car, she felt foolish raising a ruckus about something that might very well have been her imagination.

Instead she paid the conductor, and with another smile at the two ladies next to her, pulled out her cell phone to call Andy. She punched in the numbers and waited as the phone rang and rang. Finally an automated voice announced that she was being transferred to voice mail. With a sinking stomach, she left a message saying only that she was detouring to Poughkeepsie.

The two women had ceased chattering and were eyeing her with interest, and Jenny again had the urge to share her fears; but the thought of Sandy dead on the floor stopped her. No sense in getting anyone else involved.

After a quick check to be sure that the magazine man hadn't followed her, she leaned back against the seat and closed her eyes, letting the gentle sway of the train soothe her mind. All she had to do was get out at the busy Poughkeepsie station and stick with the crowds until she could get hold of Andy.

Maybe he was already on his way to Cold Spring.

The idea cheered her immensely, and she breathed easily for the first time since Connor's apartment. All she had to do was keep her wits about her and hang tight. Andy would take care of things. Connor had trusted him.

And quite possibly betrayed him.

Andy and Connor had worked together from the moment they'd been assigned to Vice. The two seemed the perfect team. But looks could be deceiving. Jenny knew that better than most.

When she and Connor had split up, no one had been able to believe it. They'd been the perfect couple. The one that everyone had wanted to emulate. But that had been a lie, too. And maybe Connor's secrets had played a bigger part than she'd realized.

She shook her head against the vinyl train seat, her mind still refusing to believe that Connor had turned. There had to be something more. Something even Andy wouldn't know. But of course there was no way to find out for certain. The only one who could have told her the truth was Connor. And he was dead.

The train loudspeaker crackled to life, the conductor announcing Poughkeepsie—the end of the line. Jenny gathered her things, turning to pull on Andy's jacket, and her heart stutter-stepped as she recognized the magazine man. He was back, this time only a few seats away.

Her mind scrambled for a plan of action. She ought to be safe in the crowds, but the idea of sharing any space at all with this guy was more than a little frightening. Complete escape was a much more comforting option.

She chewed on her lip, trying to come up with

something solid, some way to get away. And again, as if he were sitting next to her, Jenny heard Connor's voice in her head.

Five-second slip.

It was a game they'd played in high school, one of those adolescent larks that served to stimulate adrenaline. The train to Poughkeepsie pulled in at the same time that its sister train pulled out, heading back to New York. If one exited the right car at the right time, it was possible to get off one and onto the other before it pulled away.

Jenny had been horrible at the game, never quite managing the proper sequence to guarantee success. At last, Connor had helped her. He'd wrapped an arm around her shoulder, and with his breath warm against her cheek, he'd pushed her off at just the right moment, still holding her hand as they'd dashed across the platform and through the closing doors on the other side.

The exhilaration had come not only from her success, but from Connor's nearness, the feeling that the two of them were one against the world. Jenny felt tears rising, and she angrily dashed them away. There was no sense in letting emotion hold sway. It would only get in the way of keeping her safe.

Resolute in her decision, Jenny stood up and made her way to the back of the car, passing the man with the magazine along the way. He didn't look up from the pages, but she was fairly certain he tensed, and seen from this angle, he seemed familiar—not the man who'd held the gun. But maybe he was the other one.

She couldn't be certain, and she wasn't about to take a chance.

She hadn't done the five-second slip in years. Heavens, she wasn't even certain the trains would be running the same, but it seemed worth a try. If she made it, she'd buy herself some time. Maybe she'd even throw the man off altogether. There was no reason to believe he knew where she was headed.

Anyway, once she was on familiar ground at Cold Spring she'd feel better. The police were going to be watching over her, and Andy was no doubt on the way. All she had to do was pull off the maneuver and everything would be fine.

She started to count train cars, knowing that it was crucial she find the right one. The overlap had to be almost perfectly lined up. A straight shot across the platform was her only chance. Finally she stopped, certain now that she had the right place. Behind her, she could see the magazine man making his way through the car, his gaze searching, his face tight with determination.

At least now she was certain of the truth. The man wasn't a figment of her overworked imagination. He was after her. And she had no doubt what the end result would be.

The train lurched as it pulled into the station, and the man stumbled, giving Jenny a few seconds' lead. The doors slid open, and she stepped out, already sprinting across the platform. The other train beckoned, its car door still tantalizingly open.

She counted under her breath, hitting midway on three. A porter with a cart of luggage moved across her path, and Jenny's heart rate ratcheted up a notch, but she swung to the right, missing the man by inches. He shouted at her, but she didn't dare stop, leaping the final few feet between the platform and the train. The doors were already beginning to slide shut.

She barked her shin on the edge of the door, but made it, the blissful hiss of the closing doors sending shivers of relief flashing through her. She could still see magazine man. He was standing on the platform searching the crowd, trying to pick her out among the other holiday revelers.

She smiled and waved a fist in the air.

Turning, she made her way into the car and slid into a seat, her heart still pumping with the rush. The moon still shone over the Hudson, its silvery rays rippling across the black water. Jenny closed her eyes, forcing herself to relax. At least for the moment, she was safe.

Score two for the deer.

"This was supposed to have been a simple retrieval. CYA all the way." Nico Furello clenched the edge of his desk as he tried to control his temper. "Instead, we've got two dead people, a woman on the run, and no fucking information."

"Two dead?" Andy Proctor frowned. "Who besides Sandy Markham?"

"Reggie was a liability." Nico shrugged. "The Fitzgerald woman saw him."

"Jesus, Nico, there's going to be a trail of blood a mile long."

"No way. We disposed of Reggie, and Sammy took care of the Markham woman." He watched Andy for signs that the man was regretting his choice of allegiance. It had been a risk bringing him in in the first place—a necessary one, but still a risk. Add to that the man's nosy partner, and the problems had increased tenfold.

But at least Connor Fitzgerald was no longer a threat.

"I assume the bodies went the same way?" Andy lifted his eyes to meet Nico's, and Nico was relieved to see the gaze was steady. "No one's going to find them?"

"No fucking way. Which means we're in the clear as soon as we take care of Jenny Fitzgerald." Nico sat down, not certain whether he was relieved or just exhausted. In the past month, his carefully laid scheme had nearly unraveled. He'd worked long and hard to make a move away from his father. To set up his own line of distribution. And if he failed—if his father discovered what he'd been up to—well, there'd be more than hell to pay. His life wouldn't be worth a nickel. Anthony Furello would see to that. Nobody crossed the old man, not even his firstborn.

"You talked to her. How much do you think she knows?" Nico asked after a moment.

"Not much." Andy shook his head. "She was

scared to death, but she didn't have any idea what was really going on."

"So what'd you tell her?"

"That Connor was on the take, and that maybe someone from his past was searching for something."

"You think that's wise?"

"I think she needed something more than 'it was a robbery.' And we've been planning to pin things on him anyway. I don't see that his being dead need alter that."

Nico studied the cop, wondering what flaw in his character allowed him to betray his partner. In Nico's world people were betrayed all the time, but never without provocation. There was a code, and though most people wouldn't condone it or even understand it, it existed. In his father's case, maybe it was a little outdated.

But Andy Proctor obviously had no such code.

Nico sighed. Whatever the man's motives, they weren't something he was going to lose sleep over. As long as Andy Proctor remained useful, he'd stay alive. If things changed, so be it. It wasn't as if Nico owed him anything.

The phone rang, and Nico reached for it, checking caller ID to see who it was. "So, Sammy, tell me something good."

"Not gonna happen." Sammy's voice held a note of frustration.

"You lost her." Nico met Andy's gaze across the desk, shaking his head.

"Yeah. Bitch just vanished. One minute I had

her, and the next she was just gone. No idea what the hell happened."

"You've searched the area?"

"Twice. She ain't here, believe me." Sammy blew out a sigh. "What do you want me to do?"

"Hang tight. I'm with Proctor. Let me see what he thinks and then I'll call you back with instructions."

There was silence on the other end of the phone, and finally a grunt of acceptance. Nico replaced the phone in the cradle, his face tightening with anger. "He lost her."

"So I gathered." Andy nodded, his face dark with anger. "What I don't understand is how the hell it happened. I told you she was heading for Cold Spring."

"She was on the train." Nico shrugged, the action doing nothing to relieve the pounding in his temples. "But there wasn't an opportunity to accomplish anything. Too many people. Sammy followed her, but she must have made him, because she stayed on the train until the end of the line."

"So what? She's at large in Poughkeepsie?"

"Sammy says she gave him the slip."

"Christ, Nico, can't you handle anything?"

"Watch your mouth." Nico stood up, furious, his hand closing around the piece he carried. "You'd do well to remember who you're dealing with."

"Daddy's little boy?" Andy spat. "Give me a break, Nico. Your father isn't going to back you up in any of this. Not considering the fact that you've been undercutting him for the past couple of years."

151

"This isn't my fault! I wasn't the one who set fire to that warehouse."

"Neither was I." Andy was standing now, too. He and Nico were almost nose-to-nose across the desk.

"Well, *someone* was behind it," Nico barked, his anger deflating as quickly as it had come.

"Maybe not. The investigation didn't turn up anything suspicious. I think Connor was just in the wrong place at the wrong time."

"Which served us well. Assuming we find out what he had on us."

Andy shrugged. He asked, "Have you considered the fact that maybe Connor was bluffing?"

"The man didn't seem the bluffing type." Nico sank back into his chair, his head pounding so loudly he half expected Andy to comment on it. "You double-checked the apartment, right?"

"Yeah," Andy said. "It was clean."

"You think maybe the wife has it?"

"No way." Andy shook his head. "She and Connor were on the outs. She's innocent in all of this."

"No one is innocent, my friend." Nico forced a smile. "And even if she were, that doesn't reduce her as a liability. She can still talk. And believe me, the last thing we want right now is your colleagues asking questions."

"So what do you want from me?" Andy asked, spreading his hands wide.

"I want to know where she's going."

Andy paused a moment, a flash of regret in his eyes.

"You got feelings for this woman?" Nico's disgust mixed with annoyance. It was always something.

"No." Andy's expression hardened. "I don't. I want her dead as much as you do. And despite her making Sammy, I still say she'll go to Cold Spring. That's where we agreed to meet. So she'll think it's safe."

Nico studied the cop, then shook his head. "Fine. I'll send Sammy. What's the address?"

Andy wrote it on a piece of paper and slid it across the desk. "I promise you she'll be there."

"Oh, I know she will." Nico smiled. "Because you're going to make sure of it." He picked up the phone and handed it over. "I never leave anything to chance."

CHAPTER FOUR

The town was quiet, snow banked against curbs and drifted against houses. The moonlight danced against white mounds, bringing them to life with iridescent sparkles. Nature's jewelry. Normally Jenny would have taken her time, let the cold air fill her lungs, clearing her head and her heart. But not tonight.

Tonight, she watched every shadow for signs of movement, sticking close to the other couple who had exited the train at Cold Spring. No one else was in sight, and the couple didn't appear to be in any hurry to get home. They stopped every block or so to kiss, laughing against the cold, filled obviously with more than just the spirit of the season.

Despite herself, Jenny smiled.

Main Street was illuminated with the glow of Christmas decorations and streetlamps, store windows decked with a variety of seasonal gaiety. It wasn't New York City, but it was home, and it embraced her just as it had for the last twenty-odd years.

The couple turned onto Stone Street, leaving Jenny alone, and she shivered, pulling Andy's jacket closer around her. There was nothing to be afraid of, she told herself; but she wasn't sure her legs had gotten the message. Her knees were threatening to turn to Jell-O. Just two more blocks and she'd be home, in light and familiarity.

Also, Andy would be here soon. And until then, he'd arranged for someone to watch over her. There was comfort here, although at the moment it felt a bit hollow.

Jenny turned onto Garden Street and was relieved to see the taillights of a patrol car up ahead. Andy had obviously kept his promise. A little more relaxed, Jenny made her way up the road and across her icy driveway.

The yellow Victorian was over a hundred years old, and it had been in her family for three generations. Her mother had closed in the porch, which to Jenny's mind ruined the lines of the house, but it did offer a year-round enclosure instead of one that could be used only for the few months that summer descended.

Once inside the weatherproof door, she stopped to relock it, this time with the dead bolt. No sense in taking chances. From there it was only a few steps into the main hallway, the glow of the overhead light immediately dispelling some of her gloom.

After taking off Andy's jacket and hanging it on the hall tree, she headed for the kitchen, dumping her purse on the counter. What she needed was a drink, but instead she'd settle for a nice cup of Earl Grey. And then maybe a book. Anything to keep her mind occupied.

She filled the kettle, lit the ancient range, then walked over to check the answering machine. No messages. Whatever Andy was doing, it obviously didn't leave time to check in. With a sigh, she moved back to the counter and her purse, and extracted her cell phone. There most likely wouldn't be a message, since she'd had the thing with her the whole time, but she couldn't help checking.

She flipped the little phone open, surprised and relieved to see that there was indeed a message. Pressing the proper code, she waited as her voice mail rang and an androgynous voice affirmed that she had one message.

Andy.

Just the sound of his voice made her feel better. According to the message, everything had been taken care of in New York. Sandy's parents had been notified, and CSU was hard at work on the apartment. The plan was to finish things up as soon as he could and then get to Cold Spring. In the meantime, the Cold Spring PD would be on the watch for anything unusual.

Jenny checked her watch against the time of the voice mail. The call had come in about half an hour ago. She had obviously been too involved with trying to evade her shadower to hear the ring.

She started to call him back, to tell him about the man on the train, then hesitated. He was busy, and she was safe. Maybe it would be best just to wait for him here. Surely there was no way the man on the train could find her now. She'd lost him. And, at least for the time being, that ought to leave her in the clear.

Ought to being the operative words.

With a sigh, she dialed the number.

Andy answered on the second ring. "Proctor."

"Andy." She breathed his name as if it were salvation. Then again, maybe it was. "It's Jenny."

"Are you all right?" His deep voice vibrated with concern. "When you didn't answer, I was worried."

"With good cause, actually. There was someone following me on the train."

"Are you sure?" His tone sounded skeptical. All cop. It reminded Jenny of Connor.

"Yes. At least, I think so. I changed cars several times and so did he. And when I was leaving the train at Poughkeepsie, he was right behind me."

"How did you get away?" The concern was back.

"An old trick of Connor's. Something we used to do when we were kids. I slipped onto another train before he could figure out what I was doing."

"Any chance he followed you?"

She shook her head, realized she was on the phone, and responded verbally. "No. There were only a few seconds—no way could he have made the train, too."

"So you're at home now?"

She felt a bit like she was being grilled, but under the circumstances she supposed it was called for. "Yeah. Just got here. Everything's fine. I even saw a police cruiser go by a few minutes ago. Thanks for that."

There was a pause; then the phone crackled. "I'm glad you're safe."

"Should I come back to the city?" It was the last thing she wanted to do, really, but the idea of having company appealed greatly.

"Absolutely not. There's nothing you can do here anyway. Just sit tight and I'll get there as soon as I can. I've arranged for you to give your statement in the morning, there in Cold Spring. So basically you just need to hang on. Can you do that?"

"I think so." She sighed, the events of the day suddenly crowding in on her, threatening her composure. "Do you . . . do you think that someone is still trying to find me? I mean, is there any way he could find out where I live?"

"I won't lie to you. It's certainly possible. But it will take time to track you down. And I expect to be there in an hour. It's going to be okay, Jenny. I'll take care of you. I promise."

There was something in his tone that sent a shiver running through Jenny. It had been the same in the diner when he'd tried to hold her hand. Maybe it was just that he and Connor had been so close. Anything between her and Andy would be a betrayal of sorts. Truth was, anything with anyone would feel that way.

There were some commitments that just couldn't be broken, and despite Connor's infidelity and the not insignificant fact that he was dead, she still felt tied to him. Maybe someday it would be different—or then again, maybe not.

"Jenny, you there?" Andy's tone was sharp, its urgency pulling her out of her thoughts.

"Yeah. Sorry. I'm just exhausted."

"Go see if you can get some rest, and I'll be there before you know it."

"All right." She nodded to reinforce her statement, trying to convince herself that his words were true. "There's a key beneath the big rock behind the house. You can let yourself in. And, Andy . . ." She stared down at her hands, trying to hang on to her bravado. "Thanks for taking care of this."

"It's what I do, Jen." His laughter was warm, but again she felt a tremble of unease. No one but Connor ever called her Jen.

Andy disconnected, and she stood there holding the phone, staring out the window at nothing in particular. The moon had set, and the shrubbery looked dark and ominous as it shifted in the wind.

Jenny put her phone back into her purse, and reached up to close the curtains. No sense setting herself up for a scare. After pulling a cup and saucer from the breakfront, she poured the tea and carried it back into the living room.

She really ought to call Sandy's parents, but the idea held little appeal. She wasn't sure exactly what she would tell them. And they had her number. Besides, it was late. A glance at the clock confirmed the fact, and she sank gratefully into the oversize armchair by the fireplace. Tomorrow. She'd call tomorrow.

She thought briefly about lighting a fire, but discarded the idea, as it would mean going outside for wood. Maybe when Andy came. The Christmas tree stared at her forlornly, lights dark, but she couldn't bring herself to turn them on. Holiday cheer seemed a mockery in light of all that had happened.

She sipped her tea, almost scalding her tongue. Muffling a curse, she set it on the table, instead picking up the book she'd been reading. *The Gabriel Hounds*. That was just what she needed— big, bad dogs to watch over her. Unfortunately, all she had was a cat. An absent one, she realized. Putting the book down, she called Asa's name. But there was no answering meow.

Asa was an indoor cat, which meant she had to be somewhere in the house. A fixture since Jenny was in college, the black feline was slow and old, but certainly not deaf. And usually the moment Jenny walked in the door, Asa was there clamoring for dinner or lunch or maybe just an in-between-meal snack. Which went a long way toward explaining her less than svelte appearance.

"Asa," Jenny called, heading for the stairs. Usually, the cat, when not nose-deep in cat chow, could be found on Jenny's bed. The beast, it seemed, was the only one completely satisfied with Connor's defection. He hadn't allowed her on the bed, and once he was gone, she'd had full access—occasionally even sleeping on what had been his pillow.

At the top of the landing, Jenny reached for the light switch, but nothing happened. The bulb in the hall light had obviously chosen a most inopportune time to burn out. A faint mewing sound came from somewhere in the dark, and Jenny called out again. "Asa? Where are you?"

The cat meowed again, her voice muffled by something.

Jenny smiled. Asa's second-favorite spot was the laundry hamper. In the apartment in New York, the hamper had been built into a cabinet—which had caused much consternation for both cat and owner the first time Asa had inadvertently been shut inside.

Now the hamper was an open basket in the bathroom, but occasionally the door got closed, and Asa was obviously stuck.

"I'm coming, sweetie," Jenny called, feeling her way along the passageway. When she reached her bedroom, she stopped to turn on the light, surprised again when nothing happened. Fear pushed its way to the forefront of her brain, for the moment killing rational thought.

She backed up a step, already turning to run, when she heard the steady whisper of the ceiling fan. Biting back a bubble of hysteria, she reached for the switch again, this time hitting the right one. Soft lamplight filled the room, banishing the shadows to the corners.

Her cat yowled again, and Jenny turned back to the hallway and the bathroom up ahead. The light from the bedroom made the passage navigable, and she quickly closed the distance, reaching out to open the door. Before she could pull it completely open, the cat screeched something awful, and launched herself at Jenny through the narrow opening, her weight sending them both crashing back against the far wall and to the ground.

"Easy, Asa." Jenny gasped, holding the struggling cat, her heart pounding a rhythm to beat the band. "You're safe now."

Calmed by her owner's voice, Asa stepped out of Jenny's lap and began nonchalantly cleaning her fur. The cat was clearly determined to put the incident behind her. Jenny pushed to her feet, and started for the stairs again, and the feline preceded her, her entire attention now centered on the probability of a midnight snack.

As she passed her bedroom, a flicker of something in the mirror made Jenny stop, her gaze searching the room for anything amiss. Everything seemed in order, and the whoosh of the ceiling fan and the soft whistle of the wind outside were the only sounds. Jenny shook her head and turned to leave, wondering how long she was going to jump at shadows.

Forever, a voice whispered.

But her common sense told her that this too would pass.

At the bottom of the stairs, Asa waited impatiently, her plumed tail waving in agitation.

"Hold your horses, kitty. I'm coming." Jenny descended the stairs and turned the corner into the living room, surprised when Asa didn't follow. Instead, the cat stayed at the foot of the stairs, tail whipping back and forth.

Jenny sucked in a breath and turned to survey the room. It was exactly as she'd left it, the Mary Stewart book and her now-tepid tea still laid out on the table.

"What's with you tonight?" she hissed at her cat, her anger more of a reaction than anything. "This is *not* the night for you to go ballistic on me."

Ignoring the animal, she walked over to the chair and picked up her teacup. Maybe a refresher would be a good thing. Something to calm her nerves. She glanced at her watch. Only thirty-five minutes after when she'd last looked. Which meant Andy wasn't due for another twenty minutes at least.

She headed for the kitchen, stopping when the cat spat ferociously, the skin along Jenny's neck and arms prickling in response. "What?" She turned to face Asa, her anger this time defensive. "What is it?"

The cat, of course, remained silent, a flicking tail the only sign of her unhappiness. Something was clearly bothering her, though, and for once, Jenny was not inclined to ignore that.

Still, there was nothing in the living room, and the rest of the house was silent.

As if to refute the thought, a floorboard creaked. Jenny whirled to face the front door, her brain registering the direction of the sound only after the fact. The noise had come from the kitchen.

She swung back around, noting that the cat had conveniently disappeared. No support from that quarter. Jenny waited, staring at the little hallway that linked the kitchen to the living room, her heart beating in a staccato rhythm against her ribs.

Damn it all to hell.

Not given to outbursts, internally or externally, Jenny squared her shoulders, then inched forward until her back was to the wall. At least there was a sense of security in the action. She wasn't sure what exactly she should do next, but her mind was singing out that the phone was only a few paces away.

Unfortunately, it was in the direction of the creaking floorboard.

But the truth was that this was an old house, and it creaked a lot. And there hadn't been a second creak. Maybe she'd just let the cat scare her again.

Or maybe there *was* a stranger in the house.

Jenny bit her lip, screwing up her courage. There was another phone upstairs, but at the moment it seemed miles away. All she had to do was inch forward, grab the cordless receiver, and run like hell.

She sucked in a breath, counted to three, and

made the dash, the cold, hard plastic of the phone signaling success. There was another squeak of a floorboard, this one accompanied by the soft tread of a shoe. Jenny sprinted toward the stairs, clutching the phone, but before she could reach the bottom rung, a hand closed around her arm, jerking her back, forcing her to turn around.

"I'm afraid it's too late for that." It was the man from the train—the magazine man—and his face was blank of emotion, the gun in his hand dark and deadly.

"Who are you?" she breathed, already knowing the answer but praying for time. Praying for some inspiration for escape.

"Doesn't matter," the man said, his voice as lifeless as his eyes. He shrugged. "That was a nice move you pulled at the train station."

"Five-second slip," she answered as if he cared, as if it mattered, knowing decidedly that it did not. In a few more seconds, nothing was going to matter.

Magazine Man nodded, evidently intent on pretending that they were having a casual conversation. Maybe that was the way he dealt with murder. It was an odd thought, but strangely apropos.

"Did you kill Sandy?" Again, she wasn't sure why she asked, except perhaps as another desperate ploy for time.

"No," Magazine Man said, shaking his head. "That was Reggie. You saw him."

"And that's why you're chasing me."

His smile was more like a caricature than a real

expression, giving his face a slightly demonic expression. Which was certainly fitting under the circumstances. Jenny realized he'd dropped her arm, and she took a step backward, her hands out in front of her as if she could ward off the bullet. Everything seemed to be happening in slow motion, her brain trying to convince her to run, her body frozen to the spot.

Magazine Man lifted his thumb and a bullet slid into the chamber of his gun.

This time, it seemed like the deer was going to lose.

Jenny moved again, her back pressed against the balustrade. There was no way out. None at all. At least she would see Connor again. There was something positive in that. Hysteria filled her throat, and she swallowed a bubble of laughter.

Death, it seemed, was not without humor.

A hiss of a bullet signaled the beginning of the end, and Jenny waited for the pain. But there was nothing—only a look of surprise on Magazine Man's face as he sank to the ground, a bloody flower blossoming on his forehead.

Jenny spun around, hands still raised in defense. The eyes that met hers were familiar. Intimately familiar.

"Connor?"

She fought for breath, her mind spinning, his arms closing around her just before she hit the floor.

CHAPTER FIVE

Jenny opened her eyes, half expecting to see the wallpaper in her bedroom. A dream was about the only thing she could come up with to explain the past few hours. Instead, what she saw were the concerned dark green irises of her husband's Irish eyes.

"You're dead." As statements went it was certainly to the point, but considering the man leaning over her was very much alive, it seemed a bit on the absurd side.

His left eyebrow rose in amusement, and Jenny felt tears as she reached up to trace the line of his face. "Oh, my God," she whispered, awe combining with emotion so powerful it threatened to overwhelm her.

"It's not *that* amazing," Connor said, his deep voice enfolding her like a well-worn blanket. "Just a little matter of properly placed DNA evidence."

Leave it to her husband to reduce resurrection to some kind of Crime Scene Unit hijinks. "I was at your memorial service!"

"Where there wasn't a body." His right eyebrow rose to join the left.

Body. The word brought back a flash of memory. "Magazine Man." She struggled to a sitting position, her head reeling. "Is he dead?"

"Very." Connor helped her up, his arm warm around her waist. "Are you all right?"

It was a stupid question. Or maybe just an automatic one. "I'm okay. Just a little surprised." *There* was an understatement. Her heart was beating so fast she thought it might spin right out of her body.

"Then we need to get out of here."

Jenny's gaze met Connor's, a myriad of questions ripping through her brain, but he shook his head. "There'll be time for that later," he said.

She pulled in a breath, steadying her nerves. After all, she'd made it this far. "What about the police? Shouldn't we contact them?"

"Not yet." Connor reached for her hands. "For right now, you're just going to have to trust me. Can you do that, Jen?"

It should have been harder. She should have at least needed time to think. Considering everything that had happened, he wasn't exactly trustworthy. But apparently her heart didn't agree, and her brain wasn't really up to the protest. "All right." She nodded to underscore the words. "What do we do?"

"We get the hell out of here."

"What about him?" She angled her head toward the body.

"Leave him. If they send someone else, it'll be a warning."

"English teacher packs a piece?" Jenny quashed a bubble of laughter with a sigh. "They're not going to believe I did this."

"I don't see why not. You were married to a cop."

His use of the past tense hit her hard. Not that it mattered at the moment. "Let me get my purse." It was a stupid, feminine thing to say, as if her purse could protect her in some way from the madness that had become her life. But there was sanity in normalcy, and at the moment she needed all she could get.

Connor nodded, turning to the balustrade, and carefully wiped off any fingerprints.

Covering his tracks. Jenny shivered despite herself, Andy's accusations echoing through her head. But still, she couldn't bring herself to run. After all, Connor had saved her life. If nothing else, that bought him the chance for explanation.

She made her way to the kitchen and grabbed her purse, surprised to find that the room looked normal. No broken glass, no upset furniture—there was nothing at all to indicate Magazine Man had broken in.

Returning to the living room, she found Connor standing by the door, holding Andy's coat. His brows were drawn together in a ferocious frown. "What are you doing with this?"

"Andy loaned it to me." She shrugged, not yet willing to share anything more. "I'll take mine." She reached around him, ignoring the sparks that danced along her skin when her hand brushed his, and pulled a parka down off the hook.

It was gaily festooned with a Santa Clause pin, her grandmother's. Christmas seemed a long way from this place—this time—the little pin twinkling absurdly in the light.

"You ready?" Connor was standing at the window now, peering out through the blinds at the street. His face looked hard in the light. A stranger. Jenny shivered again.

"Yeah." She slid into her coat and hitched her purse onto her shoulder. "You want to take my car?"

Connor shook his head. "Too obvious. There's no telling who's watching. I've got a rental parked around the corner. We'll go through the kitchen."

Jenny followed him through the house, watching his back, lines of tension radiating through his shoulders. Whatever was happening, the game was real and the stakes were obviously lethal.

They slipped out the back door and into the yard, Connor being careful to walk in the dead man's footprints through the snow.

"He *didn't* break in." Jenny frowned as the realization hit her.

Connor stopped walking. "Maybe you left the door unlocked."

"Or maybe *you* did." She stopped, hands on hips. "Maybe this is exactly the way you wanted things to play out."

"Come on, Jen, you really think I set this up so that you'd have to run away with me?" Irritation flashed across his face. "Think about it. It doesn't even make sense."

She supposed in some ways it didn't. But, still . . . "Maybe you didn't set it up, but you had to get into the house somehow."

"I have a key." He held up the silver key ring she'd given him Christmas before last.

"So maybe you forgot to lock it."

"No." He reached for her arm, urging her onward. "I came through the front and went upstairs. I just wanted to be certain you were all right."

She thought about Asa as she allowed Connor to pull her along. "*You* put the cat in the bathroom."

"She's too damn noisy."

"So, what—you were just going to watch over me and then leave?"

"Something like that." He sounded so nonchalant, she wanted to scream.

"But you let me think you were dead!" Her voice rose, and Connor lifted a finger to his lips.

"Keep it down. The last thing we need right now is nosy neighbors."

"Right," she mumbled, lowering her voice. "They might do something terrible, like contact the police."

He yanked her around to face him. "Jen, you have no idea what you're involved in here." His anger met hers, then diminished, regret coloring his expression. "Look, I told you I'd explain things once we're safely out of here. But right now we're sitting ducks, and I don't know about you, but I don't fancy getting my ass shot off standing in the driveway arguing."

It was a valid point. Jenny started to move again, her hands jammed into her pockets, her mind spinning through a million different possibilities. Surprisingly, though, none of them involved Connor on the wrong side of the law. Whatever was happening, she was certain that he wasn't to blame.

An odd feeling, surely, to have for a man who'd left her for another woman.

But then again, Jenny was beginning to wonder if anything was really as it had seemed. Everything had turned decidedly topsy-turvy. Like Alice down the rabbit hole. Only, Jenny hadn't landed in Wonderland. This was much more like *A Nightmare on Elm Street*. And to survive, she had to trust someone.

Despite everything, that person was her husband. Ex-husband. *Whatever*.

The place wasn't much more than a flophouse, a studio apartment that rented by the week, but it granted the anonymity Connor had needed. And, truth be told, he had never intended to bring Jen here. Unfortunately, he hadn't had a choice. He'd needed to get her out of Cold Spring, and the city was the best place to disappear.

It wouldn't be long before someone put two and two together and realized Jen had had help disposing of Sammy Lacuzo. And from there, the leap might be made to him. It wasn't a sure thing, but it seemed a signal that time was running out.

Jen had been amazing: Following him almost without question. Allowing him to take control of the situation in a way she'd never have done before. She'd also managed to give Sammy Lacuzo the slip at least once. That was something not too many people could brag about.

He felt an absurd sense of pride and reached out to touch her, only to withdraw his hand. She'd fallen asleep in the car, and roused only briefly when they'd arrived. He'd carried her up the stairs and laid her on his bed, his body celebrating the familiar smell and feel of her.

But now wasn't the time for a reunion. Hell, considering the water under the bridge, there might never again be a time. His heart twisted at the thought. He'd loved her as long as he could remember. She was a part of him. But that very fact had made it imperative that he leave her behind.

Not that it had done much good. They'd found her anyway.

He clenched a fist. His killing Lacuzo had been motivated by his need to protect Jen, but there'd been a certain sense of pleasure as well. A sense of wrong righted. But Lacuzo was just the tip of the iceberg, and before this was over, Connor intended to melt the lot. By whatever means necessary.

"Connor?" Sleepy blue eyes met his, a faint look

of wonder spreading across Jen's face. "Is it really you?" She reached up to touch him, the same way she had before. Only, this time, there was no fear in her face. Only joy, and something else, something he was almost afraid to give a name.

"It's me," he said, covering her hand with his own. "I'm sorry I had to lie to you."

She shook her head, her gaze soft. "You wouldn't have done it if it hadn't been absolutely necessary."

Her faith in him was humbling.

His gaze locked with hers, desire coloring every part of his being. It had been so long. He leaned down, cupping her chin, lifting her face to meet his kiss. Her eyes widened a little in surprise, but she didn't pull away, and he reveled in the feel of her mouth.

Her hands closed around his head, her fingers in his hair, pulling him closer. There was an urgency in her touch, as if she was afraid he'd disappear. He felt a moment's guilt at all that he'd put her through, but his need for her was stronger, so he took what she offered, his tongue tangling with hers, their movements fraught with years of familiarity.

The kiss deepened as he stroked the side of her face. This was home, in the soul-deep sense of things. It was the place he belonged. He shifted so that he could kiss the soft spot beneath her ear, felt her shiver in response, then trailed kisses down her neck to the hollow at the base of her throat.

She moved beneath him and he lifted his head, his gaze locking with hers. Maybe she was having second thoughts. Not only was there the marital gulf between them; there were the events of the last few hours. Two people dead.

Connor was more than aware of the fact that people reacted to death in different ways. Sometimes they sought proof of life in intimacy. And he couldn't stand the idea of taking advantage of Jen in any way.

He searched her face for signs of regret, but saw none. Instead, her eyes had darkened with need, and her smile was tentative but true. With a groan he bent his head, taking possession of her lips again, his hands hungrily roaming the contours of her body, the touch of her skin against his beyond enticing.

He had wanted this woman for as long as he could remember. And despite the things that stood between them, he wanted her now. There would be truths to face. Perhaps things that ultimately could never be put right. But all that mattered now was that she was here and that she wanted him, too.

It was an elemental reaction, probably not wise, and certainly not based on logic. But passion was dictated by headier things than logic, and just for the moment he wanted only to lose himself inside Jenny, to escape from the world that surrounded him day in and day out, to lose himself in the one thing he knew was pure.

Her love.

He stroked the curve of her breast, popping buttons and pushing away her sweater so that he could feel the soft texture of her nipple beading at his touch. He rolled it between his fingers, then brushed it with the pad of his thumb, loving the way she pushed against him, urging him on, begging for more, his name uttered with guttural abandon. Joy in its purest form.

He took her other breast in his mouth, sucking, drinking. Refilling the part of him that was parched and dry. He stroked her with his tongue, the taste of her sweet against his lips; then, with a groan, he crushed her to him, his mouth seeking hers, their dueling, thrusting tongues a promise of things to come.

Giddy with passion, they undressed each other, feasting with their hands and eyes, delighting in each revelation as if they were first-time lovers. But, then again, perhaps in some way they were. A rebirth of sorts. A second chance.

He shook his head at his own folly, knowing that there was no such thing.

Choices were made, and one had to live by them. Still, for just this moment, he allowed himself to pretend, to lose his heart to the magic of her hands and lips. Her fingers circled his penis, and he groaned with pleasure as she stroked him, squeezing gently as she moved. Following her rhythm, his fingers found her soft pulsing heat, their joint pleasure threatening to shatter him.

In and out, up and down, stroking, kissing, building and building until he reached the point of no return. And, certain that he could take no more, he pulled away, his gaze meeting hers, his heart reflected there as surely as if he had handed it to her. She rolled onto her back, her legs open, waiting. With a groan of anticipation and desire, he slid inside her, her moist heat surrounding him, urging him onward.

Together they began to move, each knowing the dance by heart. They rocked slowly at first, savoring the moment—the *connection*—then gradually began to move faster, each stroke bringing them tantalizingly closer to the edge of the precipice.

Tension built between them like a delicately strung wire, pulling tighter and tighter, pleasure and pain mixing as one, need driving every movement. Jen reached up to grab the railings of the headboard, arching her back, pulling him deeper. Balanced on his elbows, he yielded to her demand, the pounding of his heart echoing the motion.

Higher and higher they climbed, locked into a cataclysmic spiral that threatened to unman him. With one last plunge they fell from the edge, their bodies linked, their spirits fusing as one, the explosion of crystalline color rocking through Connor with an intensity that satiated and starved him all at one time.

It was everything and yet it was nothing.

And then Jen smiled, and his world filled with light.

At least for a moment, Connor Fitzgerald had come home.

CHAPTER SIX

Jenny stood by the window, looking out onto the quiet street below. Even in the middle of the night, there were always people out in the city. A couple, the woman of questionable profession, stood arguing on the corner, and a homeless man shifted in his pile of boxes on the shadowed stoop of a boarded-up building.

The ugly side of New York.

Still, even here there was hope. The colored lights of a Christmas tree blinked on and off behind the gauzy curtains of an apartment across the way. The windows of another were decorated with cutouts of Santa and his sleigh.

A half-forgotten memory filled her head. Her first Christmas with Connor. No money. And a Charlie Brown Christmas tree. She'd made the ornaments, painting and glittering cardboard rendings of snowmen, candy canes, and stars. It had seemed so easy then. Simple. One step at a time—never a look ahead, and never a look behind. Believing that love would be enough to carry them through.

But it hadn't worked that way. Instead, they were here. Separated by betrayal and lies, and yet connected by so much more.

Somewhere in the darkness, a bell rang. A Christmas bell. Because no matter the state of the world, or her own personal crisis, Christmas was coming. Soon the world would wake up and rejoice.

No one cared that she and Connor were lost in some sort of nightmarish hell. That her best friend was dead. That the world had twisted in on itself, leaving nothing behind that made any sense.

She leaned against the icy windowpane, feeling the wind that whistled around the edges. What kind of joy was she supposed to be feeling? She was alone in a fleabag apartment with a man who for all his familiarity was a total stranger.

And she'd slept with him. Reconnected in a way that couldn't be healthy.

She glanced at the bed, at the man sleeping there, his hand thrown above his head, his hair flopped across his face, and her heart swelled. She loved him. God help her, despite everything she still loved him. He was so much a part of her that anything less would surely destroy her.

And yet, he had left her. Walked away without looking back. Found solace in another woman's arms, and if Andy was to be believed . . .

She turned back to the window, watching as

the snow swirled through the air. The arguing couple was gone, the homeless man quiet in his lair. The Christmas tree had gone dark, and Jenny shivered, wrapping her arms around her middle, feeling suddenly alone.

So much had been lost.

But there's always hope, a voice seemed to whisper; and above her, the clouds parted for an instant, a star blinking in the night. *There's always hope.*

Then, just as quickly, the clouds moved again and obliterated the light. Or maybe the star had never been there at all.

"I never slept with her, Jen."

Jenny whirled around, her gaze colliding with Connor's. "But you told me—"

"I didn't tell you anything." He sat up, swinging around to sit on the edge of the bed. "You accused me, and I didn't deny it. But that doesn't change the fact that I never betrayed you. At least, not like that."

Confusion and anger flooded through her, her mind trying to sort out the meaning of his words. "Why would you have wanted me to believe something like that?" She took a step forward, then back again, the movement a reflection of her twisting insides.

"I didn't want to hurt you, Jen." He lifted a hand, then dropped it. "It's just that your accusation presented the perfect way out."

"Of our marriage." Her stomach sank into her feet, her heart ripped in two all over again.

183

"No." He stood up, his voice harsh. "I didn't want to end our marriage. That was all you. But then things started heating up"—he paused, considering his words—"at work."

"And so you pretended to have an affair." She backed up again, feeling the windowsill against her hip.

"I let you believe what you thought was true."

He moved toward her, but she held up a hand to stop him. "Andy saw you."

Connor's jaw tightened, and his face hardened with an emotion she wasn't certain she could identify. "Andy had his own reasons for what he did. But it had nothing to do with the truth. I never slept with Amy Whitaker. Hell, I never even touched her."

Jenny nodded. It seemed like the thing to do. But her mind was still having trouble grasping the truth. "So you're saying that you purposefully let me believe that you were having an affair because of problems at work." She was repeating things, but maybe if she said them often enough, she'd find the logic.

"Look, I wanted to keep you safe from people like the man in your living room."

The dead man. The issue of infidelity suddenly seemed trifling.

"Then Andy was right. You're on the take." The words were out before she had a chance to think about them, and when she saw the hurt flit across his face she immediately wished them back. "I shouldn't have said that."

"You have every right. I haven't exactly given you a load of reasons to believe in me of late." There was truth in his words, but still she regretted the fact that she'd hurt him.

"No." She shook her head. "I just said that because I'm confused. I didn't believe Andy when he told me, and I don't believe him now. Whatever is going on, whatever has driven you to these lengths, I refuse to believe it has anything to do with you breaking the law."

"Thanks for that." His smile was faint, held a hint of self-reproach.

"Connor, the issue has never been about me trusting you. It's about you trusting me." She tipped back her head, her frustration cresting. "If you'd confided in me instead of pushing me away, then none of this would have happened."

"I told you. I wanted to keep you safe." He shrugged, his face contorted with stubborn pride.

"Well, it didn't work, did it? They came after me just the same. All you did was throw away your marriage for some sense of misbegotten machismo." She clenched her fists, fighting for control. "We're supposed to have been *partners*, Connor. And that means sharing. The good and the bad. I knew what you did for a living when I married you. Come on, Connor, you've been living on the edge all your life. *I* know that, because *I* was there. It's part of why I love you. And you seriously sell me short when you treat me like some sort of porcelain princess you can keep on a shelf by the bed."

She stopped, tears filling her eyes, then added, "I love you. And I want to help you. But I can't do anything if you shut me out. That's why I walked away from the marriage. And I can't come back until you learn that I can be trusted, too."

She turned to face the window again, surprised to find that the sun had come up, its pale rays giving the gray winter clouds a faintly pinkish cast.

"I'm sorry, Jen." Connor's voice rumbled against her ear, stirring the hair around her face. His strong arms encircled her, and despite her doubt, she leaned back into his strength.

"I know." She sighed. "But it doesn't fix things between us."

"So . . . it's over?" He sounded so despondent, like a little boy.

"I didn't say that." She turned to face him, still within the circle of his arms. "It's just going to take time, and commitment, and a lot of things you're not going to like very much. But if it's important enough—"

He covered her lips with a finger. "It is. Believe it. If there's a chance, then whatever it takes, I'll do it." He bent his head to kiss her, but she shook her head, stepping away.

"Then let's start with the truth about what's happening here. Until we get to the bottom of this, there's not much sense in planning for the future. You know?"

"Fair enough." He moved to sit on the edge of the bed. "I'll tell you everything I know. But first I want to know about your conversation with Andy."

The question took her by surprise. "I'm not sure that it matters."

"It matters a lot," Connor said, his face gone strangely still. "You said he told you I'm on the take." He grimaced. "When did he tell you that?"

"Yesterday. I called him as soon as I got out of the apartment. From the bathroom at Bloomingdale's."

Connor smiled.

"It seemed safe." She knew she sounded defensive, but there was nothing she could do about it. "I told him about Sandy, and the killers. And he promised to get Homicide over there immediately. Then I told him I'd meet him at the station, and he said it would be easier for me if we met somewhere else." She stopped, frowning. "I didn't really like the idea, but I figured he knew what was best."

Connor was glowering, the muscle in his jaw working. "Go on."

"So I met him at a diner on Lex. I gave him the details of what happened, and he assured me that the police were on the job."

"He specifically said that?"

Again the question seemed strange, but she answered anyway. "Yes. He mentioned canvassing and forensics. And then, later, on the phone, he assured me that officers were contacting Sandy's family. All I had to do was go home and wait for him there."

"And that didn't strike you as odd?"

"I'm not sure what you mean. He said I could

give a statement in the morning. It seemed reasonable. Of course, I wasn't exactly clearheaded."

"I see." He nodded, but didn't add anything to clarify.

She blew out a breath. "Look, if we're going to do this together, you can't just say something like that without explanation. I need to know what you're thinking. So explain to me what you see."

His gaze was somber. "Andy was lying, Jen. He never called anyone in. I was there. At the apartment."

Realization hit with the impact of a falling elevator. "You called me."

He nodded. "I was on my way to the apartment when I saw a couple of Nico's henchmen heading into the building. I turned to go, figuring I'd wait and follow them when they came out. But then I saw the light in the window."

"But you didn't know it was me."

"Who else could it have been?" He shrugged. "Besides, you and Sandy both walked in front of the window a couple of times. I warned you about keeping the drapes shut."

There was a sense of familiarity in his admonition, and, despite the gravity of the conversation, she smiled. "So you called."

"A voice from the grave." His expression was wry, but his eyes remained serious. "I just thought, if I could warn you before they got there . . ." He stopped, staring down at his hands. "I should have come up. Maybe I would have been able to do something."

"No." She shook her head to reinforce her words. "You'd have been too late. The phone rang at the same time as the doorbell. There was no time. And if you hadn't called, I've no doubt I'd have been dead, too."

"I was there, you know, watching you on the fire escape. But the guy was too far up for me to get a good shot. I've never been so frightened in all my life. But when he hit the ground, I managed to distract him long enough for you to get away."

"How?"

"I knocked over some garbage cans. It bought you time. By the time he got past, you were out of sight."

"So you saved me again."

"No, Jen." He lifted his head to meet her gaze. "You saved yourself. I was really proud of you."

Again, she felt a swell of unfamiliar emotion: pleasure mixed with pain. Everything was so confused. "You said that Andy was lying. How do you know that?"

"Because when I went to the apartment it was empty."

"But Sandy's body was there," she insisted, trying to make sense of this latest turn of events.

"No, Jen. It wasn't."

"But I saw her lying there." She frowned, confusion warring with anger. "It wasn't my imagination."

"Of course not." His eyes were filled with regret. "I never meant to imply that. Look, I had to wait to go up there. First to make sure you got away safely, and then to see what Mutt and Jeff were up to."

"You said they were Nico's henchmen. Did you recognize them?"

"Yeah. Sammy Lacuzo and Reggie Anzio. Sammy's the guy we left at the foot of your stairs. Reggie's the one from the fire escape. Anyway, Reggie went back inside, and about fifteen minutes later the two of them emerged carrying a large duffel."

"Sandy." Jenny hardly dared to breathe.

"Yeah. I started to follow them, but I wanted to get a good look at the apartment first. There was something I needed. Something important. Look, what matters is that I was there at least forty minutes—more than enough time for the police to have arrived. No one came. And even if they had, there wouldn't have been anything to find. The place had been sanitized."

"So that means that Andy—" She broke off, unable to finish the thought. Andy was Connor's friend. Her friend. "Why would he lie to me?" She sank down on the bed beside Connor, grateful when he took her hand.

"Because *he's* the one on the take, Jen. Not me. I've known about it for a while. But I didn't have any proof."

"Is that why you faked your death? To get away from Andy?"

"Not entirely. Although I guess it was part of it. Maybe this will be easier to understand if I start at the beginning."

She nodded, waiting, not certain she really

wanted to hear it, but determined to honor his decision to share his world with her.

"For years now we've been trying to infiltrate Anthony Furello's organization. To set it up so that we can take him down. But getting the old man's trust is next to impossible. The closest we were able to manage was to establish a relationship with his son, Nico."

"When was this?"

"The summer before you and I broke up."

She nodded, saying nothing, but it explained a lot.

"It started out just me, working undercover for Nico. Then, when I felt like I'd gained his trust, I brought in Andy. The idea was that with two of us on board, there was a better chance that one of us could wind up with something on the old man."

"But it didn't work." It was a statement, not a question, but she needed to say something. To keep herself grounded in reality.

"At first it was working fine. Nico basically ran errands for the old man, and sometimes he'd trust them to me. But then things changed. Nico decided he'd be better with his own piece of the action. He approached his father, but Anthony turned him down. So Nico decided if he couldn't get a share the easy way, he'd slice it off in bits and pieces."

"He was stealing from his father?"

"In a manner of speaking." Connor nodded. "At

first it was just petty stuff. A grand here or there. But then Nico decided to use the old man's connections to start a little drug trafficking."

"And you and Andy were in the thick of it."

"Yeah." He nodded again. "Not exactly something you want to bring home to the dinner table."

"It's what you do, Connor. Not who you are."

"Sometimes it's not so clear, Jen." His fingers tightened on hers. "Anyway, the job was going nowhere fast. The further Nico delved into his own business, the farther he moved from his father. And since Anthony was the primary goal, it seemed pointless to continue the work. I was the ranking officer on the case, so I made the decision to walk, but Andy didn't want to. At the time, I just thought he was obsessed with getting the old man. And he was my friend, so I told him we'd wait. But something felt off."

"Andy was working with Nico."

Connor nodded. "It took me a while to find proof. And even then, I didn't want to believe it. But he was definitely in league with Nico."

"It couldn't have just been part of his undercover role?" She wasn't sure why she asked the question—some misguided attempt to clear Andy, she supposed.

"No. I'd have known about it if it was. Anyway, I started doing a little of my own investigating, and found out that Andy'd given me up. Nico was just waiting for the right time to take me out."

"So why didn't you go back to your department with the information?"

"Two reasons. First off, I was pretty sure Nico and Andy had set me up to take the fall should the shit ever hit the fan. Second, I wasn't—still am not—certain how high up the ladder the conspiracy goes. But I'm fairly sure it's not just Andy. So what I needed was solid proof, something that tied Andy to Nico, and Nico to the drugs. And I needed time to figure out who else in the department was involved."

"But you didn't have time, because this Nico person was gunning for you."

"Yeah."

"And this was around last Christmas, I'm betting."

He frowned, studying her face.

"I'm not stupid, Connor. That's when you really started to put distance between us. You didn't want me caught in the cross fire."

"Fat lot of good it did."

She allowed herself a small smile. "We've already covered that. New chapter, remember?"

"Right." He sighed. "So I worked like hell to try to get things together, but Andy was getting more and more suspicious."

"So why didn't he try to cut you in on the action? I mean, you were friends."

"He knew better. God, if I had a dollar for every time I pontificated on that very fact. No, he knew I wasn't going to be tempted by money. The only way he was going to come out of this in one piece is if I was taken out of the equation. And if I got blamed for any fallout."

"So you beat him to the punch."

"Exactly." He shot her an admiring look. "I figured that with me dead, there'd be plenty of time to gather the information I needed. Of course, it meant hurting the people I loved. But then, I'd already done a pretty good job of that."

"So why not add death to the picture?" She tried for a light tone, but missed by a mile.

He tilted her chin with a finger, his eyes dark with regret. "I love you, Jen. You have to know that I'd never have hurt you like that if I hadn't thought it absolutely necessary."

She nodded, not sure if she really believed it was necessary, but she wanted to believe. And despite the difference, it was enough—for now. "So how did you do it? They found DNA at the scene."

"You can't work undercover with the kind of lowlifes I do without picking up a few pointers here and there. A couple years back, I worked with an arsonist. Suffice it to say, I learned some of the tricks of the trade."

"And so you were dead."

"And everyone's problems were solved. So to speak. I waited to see if maybe Andy would use the opportunity to frame me, but with me out of the picture his motive to do so evidently evaporated and it was business as usual."

"Except that you were watching."

"Exactly. And gathering information. I had almost everything I needed. But then Nico's father started sniffing around Nico's business. The old man isn't opposed to much of anything when it comes to making money. But he's old-school when it comes to drugs. And he won't tolerate any trafficking done under the umbrella of his organization."

"And Nico had been doing just that."

"Yeah. So suddenly Nico is paranoid as hell and looking for a way to cover his tracks. He confronts Andy about me. And the two of them start to worry that maybe I left something behind. Something that would incriminate them."

"That's why they were searching the apartment."

Connor nodded.

"Was there anything?"

"Unfortunately there was. A disk. It was a compilation of documents and recordings. Not enough to sink the ship, but enough to put a sizable hole in it."

"And enough to kill for." Jenny shuddered. "And now they've got it."

"Would appear so. When I went up there, I couldn't find it."

"Where was it?"

Connor ducked his head, his cheeks turning red. "I, ah, sealed it in the envelope the divorce papers came in."

"Oh, my God." She pulled her hand away, standing up to reach for her purse.

"Jen, I'm sorry. I know it seems like I trivialized the matter; it's just that it seemed like a safe place."

"It's not that, Connor, honestly." She laughed, the sound high-pitched, not at all natural. "You see, I've got it." She pulled the battered envelope from her purse with a flourish. "I've had it all along. I'm not sure why I took it, really. It was just sitting there, mocking me. And Judy Garland was on the radio, and . . ." She sank back onto the bed, suddenly exhausted.

His arms closed around her in an instant, and he pulled her close. "It's all right, sweetheart, let it out. You've been through a hell of a lot."

"No," she mumbled, pulling away, holding out the envelope. "There's no time for that. We've got to do something with this." She held his gaze, sucking in air as if it were in short supply. "It's time for those bastards to pay."

Connor's eyes went wide, and then he laughed, the sound freeing in a way she couldn't explain. He took the envelope, then reached for her hands, his gaze warm with approval. "I love you, Jenny Fitzgerald. Whatever happens, never doubt that."

She nodded, reveling in the fact that, at least for the moment, they were in this together. Just the two of them against the world, and that was the way she always wanted it to be. "So what do we do now?"

Connor's jaw tightened, his expression hardening. "We set a trap."

CHAPTER SEVEN

Andy Proctor shifted his weight uncomfortably from one foot to the other, and Nico smiled. He might not agree with everything his father preached, but he sure as hell knew a thing about how to sweat the help. He needed Andy—for now. But there was no sense letting the man get cocky.

"So what the hell happened out there?" he asked. "I thought you said taking the girl out would be easy. To date, she's cost me two good men."

"Word on the street is that Reggie had some-thing to do with Sammy's death."

"Yeah, right." Nico snorted, then sobered. "But maybe that plays into our hands. Though it doesn't solve our problem."

"Jenny."

Nico shrugged. "I just call it the way I see it. And we still have a liability."

Andy's face paled, and Nico contained a smile. God, he loved power. "So did you know this broad could use a gun?"

"No." Andy shook his head, staring down at his shoes. "As far as I remember, she hates guns. But Connor was a thorough kind of guy. Maybe he taught her."

Nico reached into a drawer and pulled out a satin bag of cocaine. "I've known Sammy since I was a kid. I'm not going to sit by and watch his killer walk. I want the bitch dead. But first we got to take care of Sammy. If he's found now, we got a lot of explaining to do." He waited, watching the cop, despising him for the flicker of fear in his eyes. "You got the body out of the house?"

"Yeah."

"So all that's left is to get rid of the girl."

"And to find Connor's proof."

Nico pulled out a mirror, dropped a pinch of coke, and made three neat little lines. "Whatever Fitzgerald had, it won't surface once everyone is dead." He raised the mirror, positioned a straw, and inhaled, the tightness in his head immediately easing. "So we handle the girl and we're home free."

"Except that she's disappeared." Andy was frowning at the cocaine, his disapproval evident. Not that Nico gave a rat's ass what the bastard thought. He wasn't the one playing both sides of the field. "It worries me that she hasn't called."

"You call her?"

"Of course. I've left about ten messages."

"Maybe Sammy got her after all."

"Not from what I could see. There was no blood except Sammy's, and only one shot fired. Sammy's gun was on the floor—so he'd drawn—but all the bullets were accounted for."

Nico's drug-induced euphoria dimmed a little. "Sounds like your little girl's a damn good shot."

"Or there was someone else there." Andy frowned. "Seems to me that the first thing she should have done was call me, or failing that, go to the police, and she didn't do either one."

"Shit." Nico spat the word, wondering how the hell everything had gone south so fast. "Who do you think she's working with?"

"No idea. Maybe Connor told someone else. Maybe he told her. Although, based on the conversation I had with her at the diner, I'd have made book against it."

"So maybe she's just scared."

"It's possible." Andy laced his fingers together, a sure sign that he was nervous.

"Look, as far as you know, she trusts you, right?"

"Yeah." Andy nodded, some of the brashness returning to his tone.

"Good." Nico smiled. The drugs were beginning to numb his brain. "Because you're my best link to her. She's had a night to think. You call her; she'll come running. You just have to finesse her a little."

"And then what?"

"You serious?" Nico looked up to meet the man's gaze. "You take her out. Jesus, Andy, you getting soft on me?"

"No," Andy snapped. "But what if I can't find her?"

"You will. You're a fucking detective, for Christ's sake. Besides, I just said she's gonna come to you. She's scared and alone and she needs help. And you, my man, are going to give her just what she needs."

Andy didn't look convinced.

But then, once the man disposed of the girl, he wouldn't be around to debate the matter. His father might have rules about not killing cops, but Nico had no such problem.

Jenny sat on the side of the bed, trying to control her riotous emotions. It was one thing to make promises at dawn, still flushed with the heat of passion. It was quite another to consider them by the harsh light of day—especially alone in a room that looked like it had last been cleaned pre–World War II.

Connor had been gone since noon. Among other things, he was attempting to verify Andy's insinuations about the IAD investigation. If there was truth there, then Connor's information wouldn't be enough to exonerate him. It would be Andy's word against his, and Jenny had already seen how convincing Andy could be.

She'd spent the afternoon trying to sort out the facts, playing the things Connor had told her against Andy's version. She believed Connor, or at least wanted to. But alone, in this room, in light of all that had happened, it wasn't easy. The truth remained that both versions of the story fit the facts.

Except that Connor had saved her from death twice now. But, then, he loved her. There'd never been any doubt about that. The question was about his ability to commit himself to her. To share his life in the fullest possible way.

And the jury was still out on that.

She stared at the phone, trying to resist the urge to call someone. To try to verify the facts herself. Just one little thing might prove Connor was on the level. She chewed her lip, considering the wisdom of such a move. There were two possibilities: calling the police to see if Sandy's murder had in fact been discovered, or calling Sandy's parents. The latter was a minefield. If they knew, then there was every possibility that they were furious with her.

And if they didn't . . . ? Well, Academy Award performances were not her forte.

She sighed, running her hands through her hair, wondering how in the world she'd come to this point. *Be careful what you pray for,* the little voice said, and she almost laughed out loud. For so many years she'd prayed that Connor would let her in. That he would share his world with her, make them a team in the true sense of the word.

So here she was, sitting on a bed in a studio that was probably rented by the hour, waiting for her dead husband to return with news on his allegedly duplicitous partner. Oh, yeah, she'd gotten her wish in spades.

With a sigh, she picked up the phone and dialed. The phone rang once and was picked up by a desk sergeant. Giving her name, she asked for Homicide, and was transferred to a detective. The conversation was brief. The man was curious, but not pushy. There had been no murders in a five-block radius of Connor's apartment.

He asked, of course, if she had reason to believe there had been one, and she lied about something to do with a fight she'd seen on the street. He seemed to accept her answer. Odds were, they had hundreds of calls like hers: people who thought maybe they'd seen something they hadn't.

She hung up the phone with a vague sense of unease, wondering when—or if—Sandy's body would be found. Certainly not at all if she herself didn't find a way to stay alive. Which meant she had to trust someone.

Connor.

She'd made her choice last night. Truth be told, she'd made her choice a million years ago. And it was time to act on that fact.

Her cell phone rang, and she snatched it up, hoping it would be Connor. She stared at the Caller ID, and shivered when Andy's number appeared. He'd been calling all morning—first to assure her that he wanted to help, then to plead with her to let him know where she was.

His voice had held just the right note of concern and comfort. He'd promised his protection, and sworn that the department was doing everything they could to find the people behind all of this. But of course they weren't. She knew that for certain now.

Andy was the enemy.

She gritted her teeth and waited for the disconnect, for the blinking light to signal another message. Typing in the number and then the code, she waited for voice mail to connect, the robotic voice informing her that she had one new message.

She pressed three and waited for Andy's voice, her heart beating as if he were actually on the other end.

"Jenny? It's Andy. I know you're afraid, sweetheart. But everything is going to be okay. I know where you are. We tracked the call to the precinct. Thank God you're okay. I've been worried out of my mind. I'd never be able to forgive myself if anything happened to you. Just hang tight and I'll be there before you know it. Jenny—I swear, I'm going to find a way to make it right."

The robotic voice was back, asking if she wanted to save the message. Jenny hit eight automatically, knowing Connor would want to hear it, then hung up, her head spinning.

Andy knew where she was.

She'd led him right to Connor, her stupid moment of doubt putting his life at risk. Angrily, she shook her head and flipped open the phone. She'd be damned if she'd let Andy get to Connor. She had to stop him.

She dialed and waited as the phone rang,

breathing deeply, trying to force a calm she didn't feel.

"Proctor."

"Andy." Her voice was low, almost a whisper, and she struggled for a more normal tone. "I got your message."

"Jenny? Thank God. I've been so worried."

If she hadn't known better, she'd have believed every word. "I'm fine. But I checked out of the hotel. I just couldn't sit still."

"So where are you?"

"I'm heading for Starbucks. Peace in normalcy. Or something like that." She laughed, the sound more of a croak. "Can you meet me there?"

"Sure." He sounded anxious. Maybe too anxious. But she should be safe in a crowd. And surely Connor would be back soon. "Which one?"

"Corner of Lafayette and Astor."

"All right. You just sit tight. I'll be there in less than ten minutes."

"Thanks, Andy." The words almost choked her, but she got them out, and she was pleased that they sounded almost normal. She disconnected and dialed Connor's cell. He wasn't answering, but she knew he'd check his messages. She told him what had happened, and where she'd be.

Then, just to be safe, she jotted it all down in a message and left it on his pillow.

She knew she was playing with fire, but there was no way in the world she was going to sit tight and let Andy come to her. It was better to be the aggressor. That was what Connor always said. Besides, it was only a matter of waiting, and as long as Andy thought she was turning to him for protection, she ought to be safe.

There was logic in the thought, but unfortunately her heart wasn't buying it. Still, the most important thing was to protect Connor. The rest she'd just have to leave in God's hands. It was, after all, the season of miracles.

Connor waited until a crowd of holiday revelers swarmed past the precinct entrance, and then ducked into the alley. It was a risk, but one he had to take. He needed to know if the IAD stuff was legit. If so, then it meant Andy had strong support within the department. If not, then there just might be a chance Connor could use the information he had and turn things his way.

At least he had the holiday in his favor. Christmas Eve was a traditionally slow day. And the staff would be light. With any luck at all, the personnel office would be empty. He made his way to the back door and, using a passkey, slid inside, back pressed to the wall, hat pulled low over his eyes.

The stairwell was empty, and he quietly made his way up to the third floor. Again his luck held, and he slipped out into the empty hallway, making his way to a closed door on the far side of the corridor.

A man rounded the corner. A stranger. Connor stopped at the water fountain, leaning to drink, waiting for him to pass. His cell phone vibrated against his leg, but he didn't dare answer. He waited to see if it rang again, a signal from Jenny.

It was silent, and he breathed a sigh of relief. He'd check the file, get the hell out of there, and then he'd call her. He counted to three, then lifted his head just as the man disappeared into an office.

So far, so good.

As he'd expected, the personnel office was empty. He closed the door behind him, the frosted glass in the window going a long way toward concealment. The files were in a closet at the far side of the room. Moving quickly, he walked over and opened the door. Luckily, it wasn't locked.

Apparently, officer personnel files weren't worth security measures. Scary.

He closed the door behind him and felt along the wall for the switch, blinking when the light flickered to life. There were six file cabinets lined up against the walls, and it took him three nerve-racking minutes to find the right one. He slid it open and thumbed through the alphabetical listings until he reached the Fs. *Figueroa, Finnegan, Fiske—Fitzgerald.*

He pulled out his file and opened it, skimming the contents. It noted his death, which meant it was up-to-date. It held records of his assignments, merits, promotions, and even a long-ago complaint. Everything was there.

No mention of IAD.

Even if there weren't reports and details, there

would be a flag. Something to note that he was or had been under investigation.

Another of Andy's lies.

If he had the wherewithal to turn Connor over to IAD, he hadn't done it. Which meant two things. First of all, he had no idea that Connor was still alive. Second, he had no intention of letting Jenny live.

Fear shot through him as he remembered the phone call.

Grabbing his cell, he tried to connect, but there was no service in the office.

Stuffing the file back into its cabinet, he shut the drawer, careful to wipe for prints. He wore gloves, but there was no sense in taking chances. Just because IAD wasn't involved didn't mean that Andy was working alone. And Connor didn't want to leave anything behind.

He turned off the light, checked the outer office through a crack in the door, and, once satisfied that it was empty, slipped back into the room. The hallway too was empty, and in moments he was in the stairwell, taking the steps two at a time.

At the bottom, he heard voices and pressed against the wall behind the open door, waiting as two uniforms made their way past him up the stairs. Thank God budget cuts had limited surveillance to the front of the building.

As soon as the men turned onto the landing out of sight, he made his way to the door and stepped out into the alley. It was dark, the harsh lamplight glistening on muddied piles of snow. He fingered his phone, but knew he needed to wait until he reached the anonymity of the crowded street.

The crowds had thinned, people heading home to be with their families. He longed suddenly for the comfort of a fire. For Asa purring on his lap, Jenny curled up next to him sipping champagne.

A taxi honked, and the memory vanished.

He reached for his phone, needing to hear her voice, to make certain that she was okay. He rang her cell, but there was no answer. He left a brief message, then hit the button for voice mail.

What he heard made his blood run cold.

She'd gone to meet Andy.

In an effort to protect him, she'd just made his worst nightmare come true.

CHAPTER EIGHT

Nico Furello was in trouble; there was no denying the fact. His father was close to finding out the truth about his little venture, and if he did, the game was up. The old man had made himself perfectly clear on the matter: If any of his people were caught trafficking drugs, he'd personally see that they were put out of business—permanently.

And Nico wasn't fool enough to believe for an instant that his father's edict excluded him. His father would see him dead just as surely as he was standing here on the corner of Lafayette and Astor, waiting on the only two people left with the potential to bring him down.

Which, of course, upped the ante considerably. He needed them both dead. And he needed it now. But even with cocaine coursing through his blood, he knew he couldn't take them out on a crowded street corner, let alone inside of a Starbucks. So he'd just have to bide his time and wait until the correct moment presented itself.

He tucked his hands into his coat pockets and settled back into the shadows. It was Christmas Eve. A grand night for murder. He shivered against the cold and cursed his situation. This was not how he'd planned for things to work out. Damn Andy Proctor and his nosy partner! He should have known better than to get in bed with a cop. *Shit*.

Maybe his father wasn't so crazy after all. Anthony had always made it a point never to do business with cops, and never to take one down. He always said killing a cop was a quick way to destroy an entire organization. To get the whole fucking NYPD in on the hunt.

But Nico didn't have a choice.

He pulled one last drag on his cigarette and flicked the butt toward an overflowing trash can. Two points. With a little luck, maybe the thing would catch fire. Now, *that* would be a distraction.

He laughed to himself, some of his confidence returning. All he had to do was wait. Patience was more than a virtue, it was a fucking way of life.

Jenny sat with her back to the wall, nursing a nonfat latte. Its warmth filled her, combining with its aroma to create a false sense of security. Normalcy.

Only, nothing was normal.

Andy Proctor popped the top on his coffee and

poured in two sugars. "I was beginning to think something had happened to you." He looked up to meet her gaze, and she struggled to control the tremor in her fingers.

"I was scared." A reasonable explanation, and certainly the truth.

"I can understand that." Andy reached out to pat her hand, and it took every ounce of courage she had not to jerk it away. "But you need someone to help you. To watch out for you. Just because one man is dead doesn't mean there aren't others out looking for you."

"How did Sandy's parents take the news?" She couldn't help the question. She needed him to lie to her. To give her absolute certainty.

Andy stared down at his hands. "It wasn't good. The officers said her mother collapsed." He looked up, his gaze clear, and Jenny resisted the urge to run. All she had to do was stall a bit longer. To set another meeting place, and then let Connor deal with Andy. "They had to sedate her, but I think she'll be all right."

"You're living in a dream world," she snapped, her anger rising. "I don't think anyone ever really recovers from the loss of a child."

His eyes widened, and she immediately realized her mistake.

"I'm sorry, Andy." She reached out to touch his hand. "I didn't mean to sound so harsh. It's just that it's all so fresh in my mind, you know?"

He turned his hand so that his covered hers. "It's me who should be sorry. I shouldn't have been so flip. It's just part of the job, I guess. You have to get tough fast or it'll eat you alive."

In more ways than one, she thought, but swallowed the last of her anger in a grimace. "I don't see how you do it."

"To make the world a better place and all that." Andy shrugged. "I just wish you hadn't gotten caught up in Connor's problems. We ID'd the body in your house. Not a nice guy. Connected all the way to the top, if you know what I mean."

"He was the one following me on the train."

"And you killed him." There was a flash of disbelief in his eyes, and she braced herself. "I had no idea you were such a marksman."

"I'm not." She blew out a breath. "But Connor taught me the basics. And despite the fact that I hate the things, he kept a .38 in the bedside drawer."

"But he wasn't living there anymore."

"I know. I'd forgotten about it. But when I heard someone trying to break in, I remembered it was there. Thank God." She rubbed her arms, her fear the genuine article. "Or he'd have killed me."

"Still, it was a hell of a shot." Andy's eyebrows rose in question.

"Adrenaline and luck." She picked at the edge of her coffee cup. "Look, I know I should have called you. Or the police. But I was so afraid, Andy. And I just needed some distance. I couldn't be in the same room with the body. You understand that, don't you?"

He studied her face and nodded, seemingly accepting her version of events. "I only wish I could have been with you."

"So do you think that now that he's dead, I'll be safe?"

"I don't think so. Connor was mixing with a really bad lot. The kind that don't respect law and order. Until I can run it all to ground, I think you're better off staying out of sight."

She pretended to consider his advice, staring down into her now-cold latte. "Where would I stay?"

"Not at the hotel. If I can find you there, they can, too." He sat back, watching her. "Why don't you come stay with me? My apartment's not that far from here. And since there's no obvious connection, you should be safe there."

"All right." She had no choice but to agree; the trick was to make arrangements to meet him there. "But I need to get my things."

"I can do that for you."

"Don't be silly. You have more important things to do. Why don't I retrieve my stuff and meet you there?"

Andy pursed his lips. "I don't like the idea of your being out there on your own again."

"It'll only be for a few minutes. Besides, with Sammy Lacuzo dead, maybe that'll be the end of it."

His eyes narrowed as he considered her words. "I wouldn't count on it, Jen."

There was something in his tone that scared her, but there was no sense taking more of a chance than she already was. Best to get free while she had the chance. Connor would know what to do next.

"Come on, let's get out of here." She pasted on a smile. "The sooner I get my stuff, the sooner I'll be safe at your place."

He rose, too, falling into step beside her, his body brushing up against hers as they walked through the door. Outside, the cold winter wind whistled around them, swirls of snowflakes glinting in the streetlights.

Andy slid an arm around her, pulling her close, and something hard pressed against her side. She glanced down at the space between them, the hard metal of a gun shining in the half-light. "Your mistake, Jenny," he said, "was mentioning Sammy. I never said his name."

She started to struggle, opening her mouth to scream, but before she could utter a word, he tightened his hold. "I wouldn't do that if I were you. Not unless you want a lot of innocent blood on your hands." He motioned toward a passing mother and toddler.

Jenny shook her head, trying to rein in her fear.

"That's my girl," her captor whispered. "I'm sorry it has to be like this. But if you know Sammy's name, then someone had to tell you. And before we terminate our relationship, I need to find out who."

Connor jumped out of the taxi almost before the man could pull it to a full stop, throwing a wad of bills through the driver's window. He sprinted the remaining distance between the cab and Starbucks, sliding to a stop just inside the door.

Jen wasn't there.

Goddamm it, she wasn't there!

Back on the street he scanned both directions, forcing himself to remain calm. Panic was a worthless emotion. A blur of blue caught his eye, and his heart resumed beating. Jen. It was her scarf. He'd given it to her for Christmas the previous year.

In absentia.

He raced for the corner, rounding it with a sliding sprint. The woman and her companion were only a few yards ahead of him. The man, with his arm around her, was whispering something in her ear. The woman laughed, tipping her head back, her face illuminated by the streetlight.

It wasn't Jen.

Connor cursed himself and stopped. His mistake had cost him valuable time. Backtracking, he made his way again to Starbucks. It was late, and they were closing. A woman with a broom waved him away, but she changed her tune when he flashed his credentials.

"I'm looking for a man and a woman who were in here maybe half an hour ago."

The young woman raised a multipierced eyebrow in question. "The place was packed. There were a lot of couples."

"The guy is white, medium height, cropped brown hair, solid build. Has a military tattoo on his left forearm."

The clerk shook her head. "Except for the tattoo, that describes half of New York."

"I know." Connor nodded in frustration. "Maybe you'll remember the woman. She's also white. Short and really vivacious. The kind that talks with her hands. She has blond hair, probably in a ponytail, and dark blue eyes. She was probably nervous."

Again the woman shook her head. "I'd love to help you. But this is a crazy time of year. There are so many people in and out of here—"

"Wait." Connor held up a hand, reaching for his wallet with the other. He pulled it out and produced a worn photo of Jen. "Here's a picture."

She took it from him, holding it up to the light, then shook her head. "Nope. Doesn't look familiar. But let me ask Javier." She yelled for the guy behind the counter, and he emerged wiping his hands on a dishtowel.

Connor explained himself again, and Javier took a look at the photo, squinting so that he could see it better. "Yeah. I remember her." He nodded. "Decaf, venti, nonfat latte."

"Was she with a man?"

The guy scrunched his face, trying to remember. "Not at first. I remember thinking it was a shame a woman like that was on her own." His smile faded as he met Connor's gaze. "But then another guy came in. I remember him because he just ordered coffee." His disdain was apparent; and had the situation not been so dire, Connor would have laughed.

"Big guy, buzz cut?"

"Yeah, that's one. He was kinda quiet-like. And I remember he went over to sit with the lady."

"How long ago was it?"

"Not too long." Javier frowned, "They talked for a while, and then left together. Maybe twenty minutes ago."

"You saw them leave?"

"Yeah. I was out front, smoking."

Connor's blood pressure ratcheted up a notch. "Did you see which way they went?"

Javier scrunched up his face again, his nose wrinkling with the effort. "I'm not positive, but I think they turned east on Astor, heading toward St. Mark's."

"Thanks." Connor reached out to shake the man's hand, then sprinted out the door and onto the sidewalk. The snow was falling heavily now, coming down in quiet curtains that muffled the usual sounds of the city.

The street was deserted, most people at home with loved ones, enjoying the last of Christmas Eve. Despite the panic that was licking at his brain, he forced himself to stop and think. He needed to consider Andy's options. If the man had plans to kill Jen, he'd want somewhere quiet. But transporting her would be risky.

Which ruled out Andy's apartment, because it was uptown on the West Side. Too far. And too public. Since technically Andy's office was the precinct, that ruled it out as well. It wasn't exactly the kind of place one chose to off a witness.

Connor shivered as his mind summoned a vivid image, but then he pushed the picture aside. He had to keep his cool, or Jen was dead. It was as simple as that.

Nico Furello worked out of a washateria in Hell's Kitchen. Again, it would be too public for Andy's taste. And it would be too easy to document his involvement with Nico if anything went wrong. There was a warehouse near the East River registered in Nico's old man's name that Connor suspected was where Andy and Nico were moving the drugs, but he hadn't been able to get tangible proof. Still, it seemed a likely place for Andy to take Jen. Especially since it wasn't that far away. And if Javier was right, they had headed in the right direction. Connor lifted a hand to hail a cab, then dropped his arm. Better to run. With the weather, he'd be faster on his feet. He'd be able to cut through any traffic and hopefully make better time.

He headed in the direction of the warehouse, tracing the path that Javier had indicated, moving onward through the snow, pushing from a sprint to an all-out run. If the kid had been accurate, Andy had about a half an hour's lead, which could easily mean that it was too late. Hell, truth was, Connor didn't even know for certain that they were at the warehouse.

But Andy was a creature of habit, and it was his best option. Connor simply wouldn't accept the fact that it was too late. He'd walked away from Jen once, and he sure as hell wasn't going to do it again.

CHAPTER NINE

"Tell me who's been helping you," Andy hissed, his frustration evident in the lines of his face.

"You," Jenny answered, trying to keep her voice calm. "You're the one who is supposed to be helping me."

They were in some kind of a warehouse. Open crates and some kind of a workstation were off to her left. A makeshift office was to her right. The rest of the warehouse was filled with pallets of boxes and crates. The lighting was dim, and the room was just barely above freezing. Not the kind of place for holding out. But that was exactly what she intended to do.

"How did you know it was Sammy Lacuzo?" Andy asked, ignoring her barbed comments completely. But then, that seemed to be the routine. He'd ask a question; she'd respond with some kind of noncomment. Then he'd ignore her outburst, instead asking her another question. Tit for tat.

Except that she was sitting in a chair with her hands and feet tied, and Andy had a gun.

"I always make it a point to know who it is I shoot." The minute it was out, she regretted the flip nature of the response. As much as she might wish it so, this wasn't a game.

"Damn it, Jen, I need to know who's helping you." Andy's frustration was edged with something else, and Jenny realized it was fear.

"The big boys too much for you?" she asked, attempting to capitalize on her advantage.

"Hardly," Andy snarled. "Now tell me how you knew Lacuzo."

"There's nothing to tell. I recognized him. His picture is always in the papers." Not that she'd seen, of course, but with papers like the *Daily News* and the *Post*, anything was possible. And she sure as hell wasn't going to tell Andy that Connor was alive.

Andy leaned back against a table that was serving as a desk, tapping his gun against his thigh. "Even if that's true, I still don't buy that you took a pro like him down with one shot."

"I told you, I was lucky."

He shook his head in protest, but she cut him off. "Look, I was on the stairway and he was in the foyer, so the angle played to my advantage." She shrugged, trying to look more at ease than the situation warranted.

"Bullshit." Andy jumped up, his obvious agitation ratcheting up her fear.

"I'm telling you the truth," she snapped, trying to compensate for her quivering insides.

"So where did you learn to shoot?"

She licked her lips. This was going nowhere fast. "I told you, Connor taught me."

"But you said you hated guns."

"I do," she said through gritted teeth, grateful for the anger cutting through her fear. "But you know as well as I do that what Connor wants, he gets." She sucked in a breath, waiting to see if Andy noticed her use of present tense.

"Isn't that the goddamned truth," Andy said, his own anger apparent.

"Andy, there's no one working with me. I swear it," she said, trying to steer the conversation from Connor, afraid her face would give too much away. "I'm not lying to you. And even if I were it'd be par for the course. It's not like you've exactly been honest with me. You're the one working both sides of the street."

"Let's just say I'm making the most of my connections." He shrugged. "When opportunity knocks, sometimes you just have to answer."

"No matter who gets hurt?"

"Yeah." He looked down at the floor, sighed, and then looked up again, his eyes full of regret. "I really do wish it could be different."

"Me too." She swallowed a rush of bile, forcing a smile. "I thought you cared about me."

For a moment his face softened, emotions battling; then he shook his head, as if chasing off offending thoughts. "What I feel for you is moot at

221

this point. You are a danger to me and to those I work with. It's as simple as that."

"It can't be that simple. I'm not a commodity; I'm a person. A person you know really well. I'd even hoped that with Connor gone . . ." She let the words trail off, praying she sounded provocative.

"Too bad." He circled closer, tracing her cheek with the barrel of his gun. "I'd have enjoyed that."

She fought not to pull away, her gaze holding his.

"But it's too late for that." He stepped back, his voice cold. "Besides, you're still in love with Connor. I can see it in your face when you talk about him. Even dead, the bastard has one up on me."

"He was your *friend*." She couldn't help the tone of her voice; Andy's betrayal bit deep.

"He was a self-righteous prick. Thought he always knew what was best. Look at what he did to you."

"No." She opened her mouth to refute the fact and realized the truth would reveal Connor's plan. "Whatever he did, I drove him to it."

"Like hell." Andy's brows rose. "I saw the two of you together, remember? No man ever had it better than Connor. He was just too stupid to realize it."

"And now you're going to do the same thing?" It was a long shot, but if it kept her alive, it was more than worth it.

"What do you mean?" Andy frowned, coming closer.

"I mean that if you kill me, you're throwing me

away, too. Just like Connor. Without ever giving us a chance."

"I'm not exactly an exemplary citizen, Jenny."

"Maybe I don't care." She met his skeptical gaze, careful to keep her own steady.

Andy took a step back, studying her, considering the possibilities.

"Oh, Christ, man, can't you see when you're being played?" A wiry young man with a scraggly beard stepped from the shadows, his eyes colder than any Jenny had ever seen.

"Nico." Andy's voice came out as a squeak, and Jenny realized he was actually afraid of the younger man. Then the name clicked. Nico Furello. Anthony Furello's son.

A killer, with everything to lose.

As if he'd read her mind, Nico pulled a gun, and before she could even open her mouth to scream, he aimed and fired. The report echoed in her ears and she waited to feel something, quietly certain that this time she couldn't possibly escape death.

But there was no pain, only the weight of Andy's body across her lap. Whether Nico had planned to kill him or whether Andy had thrown himself between her and the bullet, she couldn't say. But the facts remained: She was alive. Andy was dead. And Nico Furello had the smile of a feral cat.

Connor moved silently from one crate to the next, his eyes locked on the center of the room and

Jen. He was still too far away to hear what was being said, but he'd seen Nico step from the shadows and kill Andy. And it was clear that Jen was next.

She was sitting on a metal folding chair, her hands and feet secured with rope. From her attempts to kick and swing at Nico, Connor was fairly certain that although she couldn't stand, she also wasn't tied to the chair. An advantage he'd have to use.

The warehouse, too, was a blessing of sorts, for it offered cover. But it also impeded progress, and would make escape difficult, the only open door being about fifty yards behind him.

Crates and boxes were stacked in rows perpendicular to Nico and Jenny, which meant that Connor had to thread his way through the pallets; and to make matters worse, Jen was between him and Nico, which meant that, even when he was close enough, he wouldn't be able to get off a shot.

He pushed through a gap between crates, splinters driving their way into his left arm. Free on the other side, he maneuvered again so that he had Jen in sight. Her back was still to him, but he could see from the set of her shoulders that she was angry. And he bit back a smile. Best not to get on Jen's bad side, even if she was tied up.

Nico was struggling to remove Andy's body, but every time he got close, Jen kicked, connecting with a shin or ankle. Nico's curses carried through the warehouse, and Connor frowned. Noise was an enemy in any situation. But particularly when dead bodies were part of the picture.

He inched closer, assessing Nico, trying to figure out what was wrong. The man was pacing now, waving his hands in the air to underscore his words. The gun pointed alternately at Jenny and the ceiling.

She shook her head, and said something about working alone. Nico seemed to focus momentarily, tracing the line of Jen's jaw with the gun. Connor fought a surge of anger, knowing that if he moved too quickly, Nico would shoot. The prick might not live to tell the tale, but Jen would be dead. And at the moment, keeping her alive was the only thing that mattered.

"I know someone helped you," Nico repeated. "Just tell me who it was and I'll send you on your way."

"Yeah, right. And everyone will live happily ever after." Jen laughed, the sound devoid of humor.

"Bitch." Nico's eyes flashed and he struck her in the jaw with the gun. Connor raised his Beretta, but he held his fire. He was still too far away for an accurate shot, the chance of hitting Jen making the risk too great. "Who killed Sammy?"

Connor held his breath and counted to three, maneuvering among the crates until he was perpendicular to the two of them. He sighted them with his gun, waiting for the right moment, but almost as if he knew he was being watched, Nico shifted positions, again putting Jen between them.

"*I* did." Jen spat out, her voice muffled. "What? You think a girl can't shoot a gun?"

Part of Connor swelled with pride—Jen was definitely holding her own—but it was consumed by horror. What the hell had he gotten her into?

"I ought to shoot you right now," Nico snarled, lowering the muzzle of his pistol.

"But you won't," Jen said. "You can't take that chance. What if there's someone else out there who knows what's going on? Someone who can bring you down, even with Andy and me dead."

Nico's eyes narrowed, but he lowered his gun. Just a little, but enough for Connor to realize that Jen's words had hit home. She was playing the guy like a master. But it wouldn't last forever. Connor finally recognized what it was that had been bothering him.

Nico's face was covered in a fine sheen of sweat, his gun hand shaking ever so slightly. He was nervous, too. His gaze darted around the warehouse periodically, as if he expected an army to jump out and surprise him.

His gait was irregular, jumpy almost. And although Connor might have written it off as nerves, he knew better; he'd seen it too many times before. Nico was higher than a kite, and coming down fast. Which meant his reactions might be slower than normal, his game off. And it was only going to get worse.

Connor reached down beside him, into a crack in the concrete, and pulled a small chunk free. With his left hand, he lobbed the rock across the warehouse, hitting a crate just behind Nico.

The man spun around, gun in hand, and Connor stood up to take the shot, but Jenny was still in the way. Nico moved a step toward the sound, his back still turned, and Connor pushed out of his hiding place, moving toward Jen, his focus entirely on her.

As he reached her, Nico turned, his face contorted with rage. They both fired, the shots going wide, and Connor reached Jen. Her eyes widened with hope, and he smiled, praying he could live up to the faith reflected in her eyes.

Keeping as low as possible, he scooped her into his arms and over his shoulder. Nico's shots luckily missed their mark. Freeing his gun arm, Connor returned fire, but his enemy had retreated to the safety of the crates.

Connor turned to run, but then he heard the sound of another shot, the noise accompanied by hot fire in his shoulder. He stumbled but kept moving, his precious cargo the only thing that mattered. Three more steps and they were safely behind a row of boxes. But Nico was still between them and the door.

Breathing heavily, Connor set Jen on the concrete and worked to untie her hands and feet. When she was free, she threw herself into his arms, kissing his face and stroking his hair.

"You're bleeding," she whispered, her eyes full of tears.

"It's just a scratch." He forced a smile, knowing she wasn't buying any of it, but needing to try to comfort her nevertheless. With a force of will, he pushed her away as another bullet whizzed past them. This one had a velocity that told him Nico was closer.

Jen looked up at him for direction, and Connor placed his fingers against his lips and inched out into the walkway enough to try to place Nico. The warehouse was silent. The only sound was the shrill whistle of the winter wind through the clear story windows thirty feet above them.

No escape that way.

Their best bet was to move toward the door, trying to keep away from Nico at the same time. If the man held his position, they might just be able to circle behind him and get out the door before he realized what happened.

The other option was to leave Jen in place and hunt the man down. Connor had no doubt he'd be able to find him, but the risk was that Nico might find Jenny first, and that was simply more than Connor was willing to dare.

Grabbing her hand, he motioned toward the east wall. Jen nodded, and they began to make their way among the pallets. They were within a few yards of their destination when Connor saw a gap in the crates, and he gestured for Jen to crawl forward into the next aisle.

Following this pattern, they began to make their way toward the door, an occasional noise alerting them to the fact that they were still being hunted. They moved quietly for the most part, and were almost to the door when Jenny hit a rock with her foot, sending it scooting along the concrete.

They froze, crouching behind a six-foot crate, waiting.

Seconds ticked by, turning into minutes, and there was no sound. But that didn't mean anything. Nico might be young, but he wasn't stupid, and even in a drug-induced haze, he'd have heard the noise and capitalized on it.

Jen tilted her head, mouthing the words *I'm sorry.* She was holding it together, but just barely. Connor recognized the signs.

"You're doing fine," he whispered, trying to reassure her. "Just hang on. We're almost out of here."

She nodded and reached for his hand, giving it a squeeze, and his heart swelled with love. He'd taken her for granted for so long. Had put her up on a shelf, just like she'd said. Wanted nothing more than to protect her.

But now he realized he wanted a hell of a lot more than that. He wanted a partner.

He wanted Jenny.

But first they had to get the hell out of here.

Pulling her behind him, he crouched down and moved through another gap in the crates. They were almost even with the door now. He could see the light through the cracks in the boxes, but their cover was ending, the crates petering out with about fifteen feet of open space between the pallets and the door.

If Nico were smart, he'd have moved to cover the distance so that any attempt Connor and

Jenny made to break free would mean certain death. But Connor was betting against Nico. The kid wasn't trained to think tactically. Which might mean he'd been trying to follow them instead.

Connor stopped at the edge of the last row, pulling Jen down beside him. "We've got to make a break for it." He glanced down at her, his gaze locking with hers. "I'm going to try to block you with my body. So whatever happens out there, I want you close to me. Is that clear?"

Her brows furrowed, and he recognized the look. She was going to argue. But he cut her off at the pass, placing a finger over her lips. "There's no time to argue, Jen. This is our best chance. If we're going to make it, we've got to go now. And you have to do as I tell you. It's the only way I'll be able to protect you."

"But who's going to protect you?" she hissed, sparks flying from her eyes.

"Years of experience. Now, come on. We'll debate the merits of equal partnership the minute we're out of here, okay? But right now, we do it my way."

She nodded, the set of her chin indicating that she didn't agree. But at least she was acquiescing. At the moment, that was all that mattered.

"On three," he whispered. "One . . . two . . . *three.*"

They were up, out and running. But Nico was faster, firing from an adjacent corner. Jenny groaned and sank to the ground. Connor turned and fired back, but Nico ran and the bullet went wide. Connor lifted the gun to shoot again, his mind numb with fear, but before he could sight with his Beretta, Nico clutched his chest and fell to the ground. The look of surprise on his face was almost comical.

Connor spun around, and Anthony Furello stepped into the light, followed by three of his bodyguards.

"Don't move," Connor barked, edging toward Jenny.

Anthony held up a hand. "See to your lady."

Confusion mixed with his fear for Jen, and Connor narrowed his eyes, afraid to lower the gun.

"I have no argument with you, Fitzgerald. And you have none with me." The old man took a step closer, both hands raised now, his gun holstered.

Connor nodded once, and dropped to his knees beside Jenny, gently rolling her over, his heart threatening to breakout of his chest as he searched for the bullet wound. Finally he found the tear in her coat, surprised that there was no blood. Ripping the buttons open, he found the envelope with the disk in the inside pocket, the paper torn, the plastic dented. The shot had evidently been glancing, the bullet deflecting off the disk.

Jenny was fine! As if to assure him of the fact, she moaned, her eyes fluttering open. "What happened?" She sat up, leaning against him, her gaze landing squarely on Nico's body. "Did you—"

"No." Connor shook his head, surprised at how sorry he was not to have been able to claim the victory. "It was his father."

Jen frowned, then saw Anthony Furello standing there. Fear flashed across her face, and then surprisingly she smiled. "Quid pro quo?"

The older Furello nodded. "Nico crossed lines that should never have been crossed, and he knew the price for crossing them."

"The drugs," Connor said.

"That and Detective Proctor. I cannot condone the murder of a policeman."

"But you couldn't have known that he'd kill him!"

Anthony smiled. "A good businessman has eyes everywhere. Besides," the old man spat, "Nico was nothing if not predictable." He turned to go, the guards still standing watch.

"But Andy was dirty," Jen called after him. "And Nico was your son."

Anthony shrugged, then stopped and turned, his lined face heavy with grief. "I have no son." He turned again and walked from the building, his men following.

Silence filled the warehouse, the only sound the pounding of Connor's heart.

"What just happened here?" Jen whispered, her hand clinging to Connor's.

"I think the old bastard just gave us a Christmas present."

Jen nodded, and allowed Connor to pull her to her feet. He started for the door, then stopped, realizing she wasn't following. Instead she stood holding the torn envelope. He'd left it on the floor, pocketing only the disk.

"What happened to the divorce papers?" she asked, lifting her head, the expression in her eyes giving the question deeper meaning.

"I burned them the day they arrived." Connor laughed, certain suddenly that everything would be all right. That, as long as they were together, they could conquer anything.

He reached for her hand, pulling her out into the crisp winter air. The snow had stopped and the sky was clear and bright, and somewhere in the distance a bell was pealing. A *Christmas* bell.

And there, under a starry sky, accompanied by the dulcet tones of the bell, Connor and Jenny shared a Christmas kiss.

It was, after all, the season of miracles.

WOUNDED

by Evelyn Rogers

To the readers and booksellers of the world.
You keep the lights shining.

CHAPTER ONE

Halfway through her morning hike, Tessa saw drops of blood against the snow, so close to her path she almost stepped on them.

It took a moment to realize what she was looking at. Mesmerized, she couldn't look away.

Beside the red drops, wandering footprints led from the meadow to her right and up the hill toward the woods. It was the same direction she was headed, both blood and prints slowly being covered by the light fall of snow.

Five minutes later they would have been hidden. But they weren't. It was useless to pretend otherwise.

She held still as the trees, quiet as the crystal mist, and stared at the bright red stains. Someone had passed this way only moments before. Someone in pain. If she hadn't been lost in thought, she might have seen him, or her. It was hard to tell which, though the footprints seemed too large for a woman.

She took the invasion personally, an instinctive reaction, strengthened by her chosen life of isolation. This was her land, her sanctuary. The blood was wrong. It shouted of trouble. The sight of it burned her eyes, yet feeling all this, she could not look away.

Against her will, a forgotten sense of humanity stirred inside her. She tried to ignore it. *Run,* she cried silently, *turn and run, get to the phone, let somebody else handle this.* But she could not move. She could only stand and stare.

Follow the steps; follow the stains, a stronger inner voice ordered. She hadn't realized she still had a conscience. An inconvenience, that's what it was, but it would not go away.

With the snowfall fast obliterating the tracks, forerunner to a predicted storm, she climbed the hill hurriedly, moving with an unexpected sense of urgency, as if she knew the identity of whoever was injured. It wasn't an impossibility, although following her return to her family's Colorado home two years ago, she'd kept herself isolated from everyone except a few neighbors.

But no one would knowingly invade her privacy. She'd made her wishes clear on that count when she first moved in.

Halfway into the hilltop woodland, she spied a dark mound beside a thin, leafless aspen. Heart pounding, she watched the mound for a moment, then glanced around for signs of other intruders. She saw only more skeletal trees, more pristine snow.

The snow was falling faster now. She made her way toward the aspen, her boots crunching against the thin, icy ground covering, her eyes on her destination and not on the trail of blood. Without thinking of her own safety, she knelt beside the body of a man hunched in a fetal position, a smear of blood coloring the ground beneath his right shoulder.

Hesitant to touch him, knowing she had no choice, she pulled off her glove and felt for a pulse beneath the high collar of his jacket. The beat was faint but steady, and when she leaned close to his face, she could feel a brush of warm breath against her cheek.

But he also felt feverish, his skin hot to the touch.

"Wake up," she whispered, shaking the uninjured shoulder gently. She got no reaction.

Quickly she took his measure. He wasn't a big man, which was a good thing. Taking care of a country house all by herself, hauling firewood, hiking, she had built up her physical strength, but with her short stature and slim build, she was hardly Superwoman.

"You're all right," she said in as normal a voice as she could manage. "Help is here. Just hang on and keep breathing."

Slipping off her backpack, with great effort she

maneuvered him around to a sitting position, his back resting against the tree. He flinched once, his only reaction.

She took off the second glove, then fumbled in her backpack for the thermos she always brought with her. Her movements were awkward, maddeningly slow, but she managed to get a cup of steaming coffee held under his nose. He groaned; then as she pressed the cup to his lips, he took a sip, and then another.

She held her breath and studied him, her artist's eye picking out the details. She estimated his age as mid-thirties, a few years older than she. He had handsome features, a strong nose and chin, thick black brows and lashes, medium-length hair startlingly black against the snow. Beneath the thick black bristles and light dusting of snow covering his cheeks, he looked alarmingly pale.

Not only had he lost blood, but without hat, gloves, or scarf, he wasn't dressed for a Colorado winter. The cold was getting to him. His shoes, expensive loafers, were already soaking wet.

What was he doing out in the middle of nowhere? He had no business here. He was a stranger to her. If she'd ever seen him, she would have remembered.

She grimaced when she looked at the bloodstain on the front of his jacket. There was blood on his hands, their unprotected skin a raw shade of red in the frigid air. Long fingers, clean nails, except for the dried blood around the quick of his right fingers, details she took in at a glance.

She also noted the bent little finger of that hand, probably broken in a childhood accident. Somehow it made him appear all the more vulnerable.

She shouldn't care. But still, staring at him, at his helpless appearance, a man who in normal conditions would probably possess great vitality, she felt not exactly pity—she'd had enough of that in her own life—but more a sense of concern, and a rare twisting of her heart.

Without warning, he came to, knocked the cup aside, and jerked forward, sending her tumbling back onto the snow.

"Who the hell are you?" he growled with surprising strength. His eyes darted wildly around the woods. "And where—"

He broke off and slumped against the tree, his strength exhausted as quickly as it came on him. But he managed to keep his eyes open, pinning them on her with suspicion and anger, eyes deep, dark, and filled with accusation, as if she had been the one to injure him.

Tessa's own temper rose.

"Tessa Hampton, if it makes any difference. Mrs. Hampton to you," she snapped. "I'm the one saving your life, unless there's someone you'd like to call. I've got a cell phone in the pack."

For a moment she saw alarm in his eyes, but he grunted and after a slow shake of his head said nothing more.

Shifting her attention to the wounded shoulder,

she didn't bother to be afraid. Fear was for the woman she had once been, in another life.

"I need to take care of that," she said.

But how? She needed something sterile to pack against the wound to stop the bleeding. First-aid class had been an eternity ago in high school, but she remembered the importance of cleanliness.

The cleanest thing she had was her new knit cap. Taking it off, she rubbed one side in the new-fallen snow, then unbuttoned his jacket and flannel shirt and, without looking too closely at the torn flesh, held it against the wound a few minutes, pressing hard, ignoring the whiteness around the stranger's mouth.

Guessing, hoping the flow of blood had stopped, she used her neck scarf to bind the cap in place, winding it around his body and over the injured shoulder. She worked slowly to keep from jarring him. As much as anything, she hated the intimacy required to get the job done. Worse, she couldn't help noticing, and almost appreciating, the fact that he had a broad chest and was obviously in fine physical shape . . . under normal circumstances.

But these circumstances were hardly normal, for either of them. She tried to think of him as a mannequin, the kind used in her high school class, but his flesh was too real, too human.

And too hot. He needed help or he would die in the fast-approaching storm.

At last she rebuttoned his clothes and sat back

on her heels, catching her breath. He had to be hurting. She could see the pain in his pinched lips and in the tightness of his eyes. But he had made no protest, even when she tightened the scarf.

"The snow's coming down harder," she said. "My house isn't far, but I'm going to need your cooperation to get you to it."

"Who's . . ." he began, speaking faintly, then finishing, "there?"

"I've got a wild party going on. We'll get you drunk and you won't know anything's wrong."

She saw no need to tell him the truth: that she lived alone and wanted it no other way. She didn't even accept visitors. But then *visitor* hardly described him.

Without waiting for a response, she packed the thermos and slipped her arms into the straps of the backpack, then, standing and bending over him, put an arm around his shoulders.

He tried to stand, fell back, heaving a sigh of disgust or pain, she couldn't tell which, then made another attempt, this time managing to pull himself to his feet. He was awkward in his movements as he leaned more and more against her until she felt her legs weaken.

"Put your arm around my shoulder," she said, "and put your weight on your feet as much you can."

With only a slight wince, he did as she ordered, his hand hanging limply against the collar of her coat. She took the hand in hers, put her free arm around his waist, and with uneven steps they began the long journey back down the hill.

He could never know what the effort cost her. She hadn't been this close to a man in more than two years. By choice . . . oh, yes, by choice.

Over the smell of blood, and the smell of desperation that clung to him, she breathed in the familiar scent of a man. And she was aware of every muscle he used to help himself down the hill. He was lean, his body firm, nothing flabby or wasted about him.

He was tough, too. Each step had to pull at his wound; the effort to stand upright must be almost unbearable. Yet, except for a sharply indrawn breath every few steps, he held his silence. She was the one who wanted to scream.

She concentrated on their destination. From the hillside, the house, and near it the barn she used as a garage, looked small and vulnerable huddled back from the narrow country road that led to the highway, a band of dark evergreens surrounding the house like a protective wall. Her grandparents had built it long before her mother was born. After their deaths, her mother and father had moved in. She'd been born in the second-floor bedroom, had lived there during her growing-up years.

But they, too, had died, and she'd sold it and moved away. Years later, when she needed sanctuary, it had seemed the right thing to buy it back, along with the surrounding land, and return to the place where she had always felt safe.

She had enough money to live anywhere in the world, but this house, this land, was the closest she could come to having a home. She didn't want to take anyone into its confines.

But on this cold winter's morning she had no choice.

With the snow falling faster, their footprints covered over seconds after they made them, she hurried as quickly as she could, but the going was slow, even downhill. An eternity after they'd begun their trek, she helped him up the back stoop and into the kitchen. The chairs at the table beckoned, but she couldn't stop, afraid that once she put him down, she would never get him up again.

From the kitchen a long hallway led past the dining room to a small living room. She got as far as the sofa. Slipping from her arms, he sat heavily, and it took her several minutes to lift his legs and stretch him out on the overstuffed cushions, propping his head up at one end, using a pillow her mother had needlepointed years ago.

HOME SWEET HOME it said, but he didn't notice.

She wasn't sure he was even conscious, he was so still, so quiet. She felt the pulse at his wrist. It fluttered now, fainter than when they'd been on the hill.

With her own heart pounding, she rubbed his hand between hers, restoring circulation, then did the same to the other, resting them together on his stomach, alarmed that despite her efforts, he remained still and pale, his breathing shallow.

His clothes were wet from his fall in the snow.

She had to get him warm or, despite the fever, hypothermia might set in. First the shoes and socks. Tossing them aside, she wrapped his feet in the afghan lying on the arm of the sofa.

The fire was next. Thank goodness she'd placed the sofa close to the hearth. Moving swiftly, she stoked the banked logs, tossing on a handful of kindling, pleased when the flames shot up. After adding another log, she set her own coat and gloves aside, then turned to find him watching her.

"Oh," she said, startled, not sure why his stare affected her so, except that he was in a place he didn't belong. And he also had the most penetrating eyes she had ever seen.

"Where am I?" he said. He spoke faintly, barely above a whisper.

"Safe. And eventually warm."

But he wasn't listening. He had passed out.

Good, she thought. He was much more manageable unconscious, much easier to take.

Kneeling beside him, she massaged her temples to fend off an impending headache. Maybe she would wake up and find this was all a dream. In reality she was still on her solitary hike, watching the thickening snowfall, wondering idly if the storm would leave her isolated, wondering for how long.

But the stranger lying before her was much too real, his injury far too serious for her to ignore.

Okay, Tessa, time to get to work.

Which meant taking off his wet coat and pants.

The flannel shirt, stiff with blood and torn above the wound, would have to go, too. She had a few oversize men's shirts she wore over her clothes when she was painting. One of them might fit.

First she needed to unwrap his wound and pack it with sterile gauze. Living alone, she kept the necessary supplies on hand. They would come in handy now.

Taking off the jacket took an eternity, since she had to move him slowly in order not to start the bleeding again. But he was shivering. He needed to be warm. It didn't help that the wind had picked up, rattling the windows, almost shaking the old walls. The expected winter storm had struck.

Taking a deep breath, she threw herself into her task. The pants went faster. She was grateful his boxer shorts were dry. But she'd been prepared to take them off, too, if necessary. She'd seen a naked man before.

His legs, long and strong, looked as if they did not belong to the injured parts of him.

After resting the afghan across his body and stoking the fire, she hurried to the bathroom at the back of the house. She returned to find him shivering harder. Her own hands trembled as she opened his shirt, then unwrapped the scarf and tossed the ruined cap aside. The wound, a three-inch slash across his flesh, looked ugly. Blood had coagulated around the edges, and the skin was inflamed and puffy.

The kit she'd bought in town, at the store owner's insistence, contained hydrogen peroxide and sterile gauze, as well as a pair of scissors. Ruthlessly she cut the shirt away from his shoulder, then cut further until the flannel hung in rags and could be eased from his body.

She moved quickly, not thinking about what she was doing, next cleaning out the wound as best she could, ignoring the whispered rambling of her patient. She made out "no," "don't," and she could have sworn "police."

But the last could have been her imagination, strengthened by the howling of the wind.

Aspirin was the strongest medicine she possessed. She dissolved three tablets in water, then lifted his head and forced him to swallow. He got most of it down.

Just as she was settling back, planning to let him get the rest he so desperately needed, he suddenly sat upright, the way he'd done on the hill, but this time he grabbed the front of her sweater and jerked her close, his face twisted in panic.

"Don't call anyone," he demanded, and he shook her. "No one. Promise."

"You need a doctor's care," she cried, the sudden attack leaving her as panicked as he.

"No, no one. You hear? No one. Promise."

He spoke with great anguish, shaking her again, and she could do nothing but nod.

"I won't. I promise. Unless you get worse. Unless I think you'll die."

For a moment he looked at her in wonderment, as if he had never seen her before, then fell back on the sofa, releasing his hold, apparently satisfied.

She stared at him for a moment, wishing she could read his mind. Strangely, she felt a connection to him. She, too, had wanted no contact with the outside world, for what had to be far different reasons, but still the need was the same.

The idea was crazy, her conviction concerning its rightness even crazier, but it wouldn't go away.

After a few minutes, when she saw he was as warm and comfortable as she could make him, she turned to the rest of his clothes, laying them out in front of the fire to dry. The coat was weighted down by something in one of the pockets. Sitting in front of the fire, she investigated and pulled out a gun. Stunned, she dropped it on the rug and stared.

She owned a rifle, carefully locked in a cabinet in the dining room, but she knew nothing about handguns. This one looked as ugly as his wound. She backed away from it, then forced herself to pick it up and hurried to the dining room to lock it beside the rifle. She slipped the key into the back pocket of her jeans.

At that moment the lights flickered, but held. She'd lost electricity before, and she took the usual precautions of assembling lanterns and candles and the battery-operated flashlight she kept in the pantry.

After setting out a package of frozen soup to thaw, she turned toward the phone on the kitchen wall. She'd promised to call no one, but that was before she found the gun. Did that discovery negate the promise? Surely so.

Crushing down a sense of betrayal, she lifted the receiver, but she heard no dial tone. The phone was dead.

A sigh shivered through her. She'd gone against her word—or at least tried to—but even in that she had failed. For a long while she hadn't done much of anything right, except retreat and keep to herself. The stranger had invaded her solitude. Maybe that made them even, a broken promise for a shattered isolation.

The bottom line was that he was the one getting what he wanted. She had told him a cell phone was in her backpack, but she'd lied. She hated the things. And now she couldn't call for the help he so desperately wanted to avoid.

And the gun? He hadn't used it on himself; nor had anyone else. No bullet had caused his injury. He'd been slashed by something sharp, probably a knife.

For the first time since seeing the drops of blood in the snow, she felt flickers of fear. Was her life in danger? She hadn't thought she cared, but she did.

In all her twenty-eight years she had known only one man important enough to die for. But he had been the one to die, leaving her alone.

Except for the stranger.

She forced herself to return to the parlor. Sitting on the floor by the fire, she wrapped her arms around her knees and stared at the man on the sofa, two questions burning into her mind.

What have I done? What am I supposed to do now?

The only answers she heard were the snap of the firewood at her back and the howling of the winter wind.

CHAPTER TWO

Tessa shaded the valleys under his cheekbones, giving him the gaunt look that made him look almost feral, even in sleep. Thicker lashes, thicker brows—he needed both, and she quickly applied them. At last she studied her work and decided it was the best she could do without knowing him further.

Yet she was dissatisfied. She was normally good at drawing, but she had missed the essence of the stranger.

Or maybe it was the uneven light from the fire and the candles scattered around the room that kept her from capturing him as he really was, whatever that could be.

Get real, Tessa. This is a man you don't want to know.

Sometime during the minutes she was casting her attention from model to sketch pad and back again, questioning her sanity, he opened his eyes. Firelight reflected in their dark depths, and despite herself she started. She doubted she would ever get over the effect of his stare.

"What are you doing?" he asked.

"Sketching you," she said. She spoke the truth, but the real truth would have included "keeping you alive."

"In the dark?"

"There's enough light. The electricity's been out almost as long as you have."

He glanced around the room, at the shadows dancing on the walls and furnishings, as if he were truly seeing his surroundings for the first time. He didn't look especially pleased.

"So no radio and no TV."

"I don't own a TV, but I didn't need one to know we had a storm far stronger than predicted. The emergency band on my radio reported power outages over half the state."

"What else did the radio report?"

"Not much. The battery went dead. I forgot to keep it charged."

Was that relief she saw in his eyes? Surely not. It didn't make sense.

But of course it did. He had to be running from someone, something, possibly the law. Despite the warmth of the fire, a chill shivered through her.

"Why?" he asked.

"Why what?"

"Why the sketching?"

Not *Where am I?* or *Why are you helping me?* or even *How long have I been out?*

For someone helpless and needing her cooperation to survive, he had a bad habit of alienating her already fragile goodwill.

She sat up straight. "I sketch because it's what I do. I might ask why you were passed out on my property halfway to bleeding to death or freezing. One of them would certainly have killed you if I hadn't come along."

His answer was a grunt; then he gazed past her into the fire, as if he were remembering things he preferred to forget.

In that, he wasn't alone.

But she wasn't a criminal. Was he? Somehow he didn't seem the type, not that she'd ever knowingly met a felon before.

She set her pad and pencil aside and went into the kitchen for a glass of water. She returned to find him struggling to sit up.

"I wouldn't stand if I were you. You'd only fall and break open your wound."

He dropped his head back on the pillow and stared up at her. "Where am I? And who are you?"

"I thought you'd never ask." She didn't bother to keep the sarcasm from her voice. "I'm Tessa Hampton. This is my home. I found you out in the snow."

"Ah, yes, I remember now. Mrs. Hampton, you said. You made that very clear."

"If you remember my name, surely you remember how we both struggled to get you in here yesterday morning."

"Yesterday morning?"

"You've been in and out of consciousness. Delirious part of the time, too, but the fever broke about noon, more than six hours ago. You'll be happy to know you're going to live. Scarred, of course. The best I could do was pack your wound with sterile gauze, then tape it together as tightly as possible."

"You cleaned it first."

"With hydrogen peroxide. It's all I had. I'm not a doctor. Are you?"

She asked the question rhetorically. To her surprise, he nodded.

"Truthfully?"

"Truthfully." He didn't sound proud. He sounded resigned.

A doctor, was he? That didn't mean he wasn't a wanted man. For all she knew, he could be a homicidal maniac. Maybe she should have bound his arms and legs while he was out, or maybe she was being her usual paranoid self, obsessing over her violated solitude.

In either case, she wished he weren't lying where he was, looking at her with eyes as dark as the night outside the window. Simply lying on her sofa, saying little, he filled the small living room.

She knelt beside the sofa and helped him raise his head. He sipped at the water, staring at her while he did so, and for the second time in the space of a few minutes a chill shivered down her spine. She'd never seen such eyes.

Setting the glass aside, she sat back, putting distance between them.

"When I was out, did I say anything?" he asked.

"A lot of gibberish. A lot of *no*s and *don't*s."

He had also argued with someone, sometimes quite violently. The subject seemed to be money—she got the impression a lot of money—but instinct told her to keep those words to herself. If she felt threatened by him in any way, she had her rifle. And his gun, of course. She couldn't forget he had come to her armed.

He stared silently at the ceiling for a moment. She would have liked to sketch him in profile, awake, meditating, but something told her he wouldn't appreciate her art. A shame. With his strong features and narrow, bristled face, he looked like a cross between a patrician and a Mafia thug, with maybe a bit more of the former than the latter.

He shifted his gaze and caught her staring at him. She did not flinch or look away, though unexplainably her heart caught in her throat.

"I've told you who I am," she said. "Who are you? Or should I just call you Doc?"

He smiled but without humor. "Doc sounds fine."

"You didn't have any identification on you. How do I know you're really a doctor?"

"Take two aspirin and call me in the morning. How does that sound?"

She almost smiled. "Like something I've heard before."

"How about this? I'd like to take a look at the wound."

"Do you have to?"

"Yes, I do." Said with the authoritarian voice she was used to hearing from doctors. It worked better than the "two aspirin" crack.

She forced herself to get close to him again. Patrician, she told herself, not Mafia thug, as she folded back the afghan to reveal his bare chest. He watched her while she worked, but she kept her eyes on her awkward fingers.

Beneath the cover, his skin was warm but definitely not feverish. A scattering of dark hairs across his chest matched the color of his hair, which was tousled from his turning in his sleep.

For a moment she watched the rise and fall of his chest, remembering another time, another man.

"Something wrong?" he asked.

Yes.

"No, I don't want to jar you."

Shifting her gaze, she stared at the tape and the bloodstained gauze. "I'm not good at this. You want me to go slow or fast?"

"Slow. If you're squeamish . . ."

"I'm not."

She took a deep breath. This was harder than he could imagine, but squeamishness had nothing to do with her distress.

He lay back, his mouth pinched, and stared at the ceiling. For all his paleness and lack of vigor, she could feel the life force pulsing in him.

The gauze pulled at the wound, the puckered skin lifting as she eased the bandage away, but the cut, a three-inch diagonal slash across his shoulder, did not open again.

To her, the wound looked ugly, red, and swollen, and the edges weren't holding together as much as she had wanted. He would definitely get through this with a scar. *If* he got through it. She'd told him he would live, but in truth she had no idea whether infection had already set in.

Doc would have to make that diagnosis.

"I can't see. It's too high on my shoulder," he said when she settled back on her heels. "Get a mirror."

More orders. But she went and got a small hand mirror out of the bathroom at the back of the house.

Once again she was on the floor beside him, sitting on her heels as he studied her handiwork, thinking this was as bad as a showing of her paintings when she was forced to watch the critics stroll the gallery. Not that such an occurrence had been frequent. Her husband had humored her in her work, but he'd never taken it seriously.

Quit thinking about him for a moment. As if she could. Gordon Hampton had been the major part of her life and always would be, no matter how many years passed.

A new thought shook her. She hadn't been able to save Gordon from the accident that took his life; maybe fate had sent her this man to make amends.

What a foolish idea. Fate, or God, or whoever ruled the universe, wasn't nearly so kind or so thoughtful. Tessa sighed. The fire was hot against her back, and she ran a hand through her cropped hair.

Holding the mirror high, her patient studied the image of his injured shoulder for longer than she thought necessary, as if he studied it not for the wound itself but for what it represented. Then he dropped his hand, the right one with the curled little finger. Resting the mirror on his stomach, he stared at the ceiling. For an instant there was anguish in his eyes; yet she did not think it was brought on by the sight of his slashed shoulder, not entirely.

"Doc," she said, and he slowly turned his eyes to her. "Whatever it is that's bothering you," she continued, "believe me, I don't care. And I don't care what you've done. All I want is you well enough to leave when the roads open up again. I can fire up my four-wheeler and take you into town. There's a bus station there, a tow service if you've got a car broken down somewhere, telephones, whatever you need."

He didn't say anything, just continued to stare at her as if he were trying to figure her out. Let him try. Others had made the attempt, a couple of psychiatrists, grief counselors, professionals in the field of healing broken souls. They'd done nothing for her, and neither would he.

She stood and picked up the water glass. "I'll get a fresh bandage and rewrap that, unless, of course, you have another suggestion. I've got some chicken soup I can warm by the fire. Try to get down some of the broth. Then, again unless you have a different idea, I suggest you take a couple of aspirins and call me in the morning. I've got a bell that I'll leave by your side. Ring it if you need me during the night. I won't be far away."

Without waiting for a reply, she went to get the gauze and tape. Outside the wind began to howl once again, rattling the windows, reminding her of how completely isolated she was. Isolation had never bothered her before. But this time things were different. This time she wasn't alone.

Sometime during the night, she awoke with a start and sat up in bed. Her second-story bedroom was dark as black velvet. She sat in bed a moment, listening for what had awakened her, but all was quiet. Even the wind had died down.

Out of habit, she tried to snap on the bedside lamp, but the electricity was still not on. Instead, she clicked on the battery-powered emergency lamp she had bought at the insistence of the store clerk in town. Her radio might have died, but the lamp worked just fine.

"Never know what might happen," he had said, "a woman living out here all by herself like you. Colorado winters can be mighty rough."

She had resented his intrusive manner, but now she thanked him.

Easing into her slippers and robe, she took the lamp and went downstairs to the parlor. Doc, or whoever he was, sat hunched close to the fire. She was surprised to see him off the sofa, and alarmed, too. If he was truly mobile, she didn't feel quite so safe alone with him as she had.

She moved closer. He didn't hear her approach, so concentrated was he on his task. She gasped when she saw what that task was. He was feeding her sketch of him into the fire.

"That was mine," she said sharply, an irrational resentment building in her, and she hurried over to retrieve what was left of the drawing.

He pitched the remaining fragments deeper into the fireplace, and she watched helplessly as the edges of the paper curled, turned brown, then burst into flames.

"You didn't have to destroy it," she said. "It wasn't all that bad."

"It wasn't bad at all," he said. Then he looked at her over his shoulder. Flickering firelight cast shadows across his bristled face, and his eyes burned as hot as the flames. "Just don't draw me again. I'll leave here as soon as I can. The smart thing for you to do is forget you ever saw me."

He tried to stand, but he lurched against her and they both stumbled backward to the sofa. She landed against the cushions with him on top of her, his weight heavy, his legs bare against her nightgown. She was smothering, she was dying, she was cast back to another time, another place, another man, the same man whose image never completely left her mind.

But this time the image faded, and she was left seeing only this stranger. Roughly she shoved him off her, not thinking about his shoulder. He winced involuntarily, and she cursed him for being hurt and cursed herself for caring.

She slid off the sofa and started to help him,

but he managed to get himself back to his makeshift bed. She hurried to the kitchen for a fresh glass of water, then set out the bottle of aspirin on the table she had put close beside him.

"You need anything else, please ring that bell. And rest assured, I will not take advantage of you again. You are safe from the maliciousness of my pencil and my obviously inadequate skills." Then she added with emphasis, "Doc."

She was at the doorway to the hall when he spoke.

"Alex. The name is Alex."

She stopped and turned, but he was staring into the fire.

Something in the way he spoke, a lost something, a loneliness she could understand, caused her heart to jolt.

She stared at him for a moment. "Good night, Alex," she said.

Then she hurried down the hall and up the stairs, wondering what had bothered him so much about the drawing she had made of him. It wasn't artistic, she knew that, but it looked exactly like him.

And maybe that was the problem.

But why? He had burned it as if it were the kind of wanted poster she used to see at the post office.

Again she asked herself who he was, and who had slashed him so viciously with a knife. And she wondered if she shouldn't get the rifle, or the pistol, and put it beside her bed.

But no weapon would keep her from remembering the way he had felt lying on top of her. Injured though he was, he was a virile man. Also, there was something vulnerable about him, something in the desperation she saw in his eyes, the grief, the despair, that she could relate to. No amount of rationalizing would make her sympathy for him go away, not completely.

Turning on her side under the comforter, she hugged herself.

"Why did you leave me?" she whispered into the dark, but of course she got no answer. She never did. She tried to conjure up Gordon's face, but for the first time since his death more than two years ago, she failed. An hour ago a momentary relief from his haunting had seemed desirable, but not now.

She began to cry. This was like losing him all over again. She didn't want to. She wanted to cling to his image for the rest of her life, contented with her art and her memories.

But again the only man who came to her mind was the stranger, Alex, as he looked away from the fire and into her eyes. And a moment later, the way he'd stared down at her as they both fell onto the sofa.

For just a moment, afraid as she was, she had wanted to caress his face and to tell him that whatever had caused his pain, he could tell her and she would understand.

She gave thanks for the strength she'd summoned to resist any such foolishness. Tomorrow, if the phone lines still weren't repaired, she would hike down to the road and see if any clearing had begun. Then, whether he—this supposed doctor, this Alex—liked it or not, she would summon help. At the earliest possible moment she would get him out of her house and out of her mind.

CHAPTER THREE

Tessa woke to sunlight and the scraping sound of a snowplow clearing the road. Leaning toward the bedside table, she snapped on the lamp. Its yellow light got lost in the sunlight streaming in through the window next to the bed, but it told her the electricity was back on.

When the scraping sound ceased, she tried the telephone, but the line was still dead. Returning the receiver to its cradle, she lay back, wanting another few minutes of rest. In the stillness she became aware of a tension in the room, an alteration of its usual peaceful atmosphere. It wasn't hard to figure out why. Her stranger, a maybe doctor who was maybe named Alex, stood in the doorway watching her.

The sight of him took her breath—not out of fear, but more just the realization she wasn't alone. To her surprise it wasn't a totally unpleasant feeling.

"How long have you been standing there?"

"Awhile."

His presence must have awakened her, not the noise from the road. He'd been watching her while she slept.

From the moment she'd first brought him into the house, he'd seemed to fill the room he was in. Until now, that had been the living room. This morning, standing where he was, he had brought that power to her bedroom.

Heart beating erratically, she forced herself to study him. He had pulled on his trousers, but the tail of the shirt she'd put out for him hung loose and his feet were bare. The stubble on his face, thicker and blacker than ever, gave him color, made him look almost healthy, until she looked at his eyes. Dark, sunken, bruised. And lost, as if he'd wandered upstairs trying to find out where he was, find out what was happening to him.

If he had questions, she had a few of her own, but she doubted he would tell her the truth.

"The road—" he began, then broke off, swayed, stumbled forward, and grabbed the bedpost for support.

Scrambling from under the covers, her flannel nightgown hanging limp against her nakedness, she helped him to the side of the bed, helped him to sit and take long breaths until each one was steady and he could straighten, holding himself upright on his own.

"You were going to say the road's opening," she said.

"The snowplow woke me."

"Me, too," she said, but she lied. His presence had ended her sleep.

Without thinking, she touched his uninjured shoulder. The warmth, the firmness of his body made the contact feel far too intimate, and she pulled her trembling hand away.

"I won't hurt you," he said, a wry smile on his face. "Right now I couldn't hurt a kitten, and believe me, you're tougher than any kitten I've ever seen."

"You would know because you're a doctor."

"I can see where you might not believe me." He stared at his hands as if he had never seen them before, as if they were not a part of him. "Right now I'm having a hard time believing it myself."

The despair she'd seen in his eyes she now heard in his voice. Something twisted inside her, a tightness, an awareness she hadn't felt in years. Her ears began to ring, as if her blood were pulsing at warp speed. Was it fear? The gun, his wound, the mystery surrounding him should make her afraid, especially as he gained his strength.

But fear was not a part of her emotions. And that was the most unsettling thing of all.

She walked to the window and looked out at the sparkling white world, and at the ribbon of road that meandered in front of the house, providing the rural residents of the county with a lifeline to the town of Benton, the place where she did her shopping for everything except art supplies.

Benton was an old mining town, like many such towns in the state, built on the side of steep hills, slowly losing its residents to the call of the city, every month or so another house shuttered, another For Sale sign posted in the yard.

She was the exception. She had left a long time ago, just like the others, but unlike them, she had returned. To solitude, to a seeking of peace, to a decision about how much, or how little, she wanted to be a part of the outside world. To her, the man sitting at the side of her bed represented that world.

Yet somehow he had become a part of her isolated existence, strangely because he needed her, not the other way around.

Taking a deep breath, she put herself back into her role of nurse.

"There's a bathroom down the hall if you need it."

"I used the one downstairs."

"Then lie down here while I get you some breakfast."

He stared at her a moment. The air in the room crackled. "You want me in your bed, Mrs. Hampton?"

"Not while I'm in it."

"Of course not. It might get crowded when your husband returns."

He couldn't know he was rubbing at her own internal wounds. "You must be getting well. You're getting personal."

Alex was not a man to give up. "He is returning, isn't he?"

"I'm a widow. And I'm not looking for a replacement, temporary or otherwise."

"An unhappy marriage, then."

"On the contrary. No one can take my husband's place in or out of bed."

He nodded. "I'm not intending to try. Curiosity was my only motivation."

"Or you could have wondered whether a man would be getting here as soon as the road is opened."

He glanced around the room, at the four posts of the bed, the folded-back quilt her great-grandmother had sewn by hand for her own wedding, the chest of drawers her parents had used, the old-fashioned wallpaper, the white lace curtains at the window.

"There's no sign of a man in the house, husband or otherwise. And you're not wearing a ring."

"You sound pleased. Why?"

His attention was all on her. "You don't want to know."

"That's the first thing you've said that I believe."

"Smart woman."

He looked at the painting hanging over the chest of drawers. It was a summer view of the hill behind the house, with the aspens in full leaf, their silver-green sparkling in the sunlight. "Did you paint that?"

"Yes, I did."

"It's good."

The compliment pleased her far more than it should have.

"So you're a doctor and an art critic, too?"

His eyes settled on her. "I know what I like."

Neither spoke for a moment. Tessa was the first to look away.

"We've both got cabin fever. Do what you like, rest or come back down. Since you made it up here, I assume you can negotiate the stairs on your own one more time."

Without looking at him again, she got her clothes from the closet and the top drawer of the chest, then hurried to change in the upstairs bathroom. Dressed in jeans and a dark green sweater, she stared at herself in the bathroom mirror. Sporadic sleep over the past few days had brought shadows under her eyes, and she looked pale, far too pale.

What did it matter? She certainly wasn't trying to attract the man. On the contrary, she would be glad when he was gone.

Still, she couldn't resist a momentary satisfaction as she finger-combed her hair. She cut it herself, and it fell into place, blessedly short, softly brushing the edges of her face like a caramel-colored picture frame.

For Gordon's sake, she had worn it long, twisted into a more sophisticated bun for the social events that had been a part of his stature in the state, then set free for the private times that had been the heart of her existence. She had never cared for the parties, the openings, the charity balls, but for him she had been willing to do anything.

When he died in the car accident—he always

drove his Porsche too fast—she hadn't wanted to do anything ever again. This home was as close to that nothing state as she could get.

Until that hike up the hill two days ago.

Downstairs in the kitchen she decided to make waffles and bacon with eggs on the side, enjoying cooking with electricity after two days of balancing cast-iron pots over glowing coals in the living room fireplace.

Again, she felt a momentary pride as she put the can of syrup on the table. During her years back east, she had grown addicted to natural maple syrup, and each Christmas she ordered a case from Vermont.

As she puttered at the sink, she felt more than heard him enter. Behind her a chair scraped and he sat down.

"Don't push yourself too much," she said. "I can bring this to the sofa."

"I'd like it here. It all smells wonderful."

"I'm not much of a cook."

"I've never eaten better."

She almost smiled. He had yet to take a bite.

As she took her place across from him, a silence fell between them. He broke it with a smile and a gentle, "Thank you."

The smile softened his harsh features, and she felt herself smiling in return. Incredibly, she wanted to brush the tousled dark hair from his forehead, to strengthen the connection between them, to let him know she wasn't after his thanks.

Fated or not, somehow he had become her responsibility, and she didn't mind, not in the least.

Before she could say or do anything, she heard a pounding on the front door. He sat upright, the change in him instant, grateful guest morphing into cornered animal.

"Who knows I'm here?"

"No one but me." Resentment rose like bile in her throat. "You think I sent up signal flares?"

He ignored her sarcasm. "Don't answer the door right away."

He didn't wait for her agreement. Instead, he hurried through the door leading to the dining room, his strength restored. His adrenaline must be pumping. So was hers.

A dozen reasons for his panic skittered through her mind, none of them good.

The knocking continued, and she heard a woman's voice call out her name.

Wiping her hands on a towel, she hurried into the hallway and to the front door, surprised to see the draperies were closed on the downstairs windows. Alex must have done it before climbing the stairs.

Then he was there, standing beside the door, where he would be out of sight when she opened it. More startling, at his side he held the gun she'd removed from his jacket the first morning, the one she'd locked into the gun cabinet in the dining room.

Their eyes met.

"It's only a neighbor," she said, speaking softly, her heart in her throat.

Get rid of her, he mouthed.

He didn't lift the gun, didn't make an overt threat, but he didn't have to. The fact that he was carrying it spoke loudly enough.

She opened the door a crack and looked out.

"Mildred Griffin," she said, "what a surprise."

"Had to get out of the house. As soon as the snowplow passed, I headed out on a walk. Thought to check on you, alone here the way you are." She held up a small folding shovel, then nodded back toward the narrow path she'd dug from the road to the porch. "Needed the exercise after sitting around so long."

Tessa attempted a smile. "Thanks for the thought and the effort, but I'm fine, really."

The woman, middle-aged and dressed warmly for the hike, her cheeks ruddy from the cold, peered behind her, clearly wanting an invitation to come in.

Get rid of her.

Why should she do what Alex asked? But she knew she would, and the gun had nothing to do with her decision. Reasons would come later, and very possibly regret.

She'd established her reputation as a loner. It was time to use it now.

"I'll probably be out later." Hugging her sweater tight, she stepped onto the porch and closed the door. "Don't want to let the heat out."

She looked around at the whiteness and at the evergreens and skeletal trees poking through across the rolling landscape, her house and the road the only signs of civilization. Last came the trail Mildred had made. "Quite a storm we had."

The woman sniffed. "We've had worse. But you, being a newcomer, I figured you might have had some problems."

"I've been here awhile. And remember, I grew up in this house."

"Keep forgetting, you keeping yourself a stranger and all."

Tessa had heard the sentiment before. She could see the woman wanted an invitation to come inside. But she wouldn't care for the reception she would get.

Tessa could feel Alex's presence inside the door, gun held tight, senses alert to everything he heard. Now that she was outside, free of the sight of him, her thoughts took a darker turn. She couldn't believe he would shoot, but if not, why had he gotten the gun? And how had he gotten the key to the cabinet?

The biggest favor she could do for her latest visitor was to get her on the road again.

"Look," she said with an apologetic laugh, "I'm right in the middle of something. You know artists."

But of course the woman didn't. The flatness of her eyes and mouth was evidence enough.

"Anyway, I need to get back to it. As soon as the telephones are back up—"

"Phones have been working since midnight," Mildred said with another sniff. "I started to call, but, as I said, I was getting cabin fever and needed the walk."

Too well Tessa remembered the dead line on her upstairs phone. Her heart turned cold, but before she could say anything, her neighbor turned back toward the road.

"If you decide you need anything, give me a call. George and I'll come running, best we can in this mess."

The words were kind, but the cordiality had left Mildred's voice. She was miffed. If she only knew the truth . . .

"Thanks," Tessa said, watching the woman make her way through the deep snow back to the road. All she had to do was call out, to throw herself off the porch and scream for help. Every instinct told her to do just that. He wouldn't shoot her, not the man who had smiled at her in the kitchen, the first human she'd felt connected to in a long, long while.

Fighting against instinct was the knowledge that she would be betraying the man she'd been nursing back to health. She'd seen despair in his eyes, its cause unknown, yet she understood the feeling. She'd felt that dark, deep despair herself.

And so she took a deep breath and went back inside, closing and locking the door before she turned to face him.

"You broke into the gun cabinet," she said.

"It's not damaged. I picked the lock."

"That's hardly the issue, is it? Did you also cut the phone lines?"

"You may find this hard to believe, Mrs. Hampton, but I was trying to keep you safe."

Her name sounded awkward and unfamiliar on his lips, as if he were referring to someone else.

"You're right. I find it hard to believe."

"Okay, I was thinking of my own safety, too."

She stared at him a moment, as if by looking into his eyes, she could tell whether or not he lied.

"Isn't it time you told me how you got cut?" she asked at last. "And where this danger is coming from?"

When he lifted the gun, her heart caught in her throat. Then he turned it and gave it to her, handle first.

"When you locked that cabinet," he said, "you should have taken out the bullets and thrown them away."

Gingerly she set the gun on the table at the end of the sofa, not wanting to hold it any longer than necessary. Then she eyed him critically, her spine stiff.

"Is there anything else I should have done?"

"No. You've been perfect. Now, if you don't mind, I need to sit down. Then we'll talk. Over breakfast."

She stared at him; then, without a word, she found herself following him back to the kitchen to do what he asked.

CHAPTER FOUR

He took a while to speak, eating slowly, deliberately, as if he needed time to gather his thoughts. After an eternity, he pushed his plate aside.

"I killed my brother."

Tessa stared at Alex across the kitchen table. "You what?"

"You heard right. Benjamin Wolfe is dead because of me." He shook his head. "It feels good to speak the truth out loud." He focused on something outside the window over the sink, something distant, something she couldn't see. "Almost," he added, "it almost feels good."

She sat at the edge of her chair and for a moment listened to the two of them breathing. She could smell his despair.

"Were you treating him? Was he your patient?"

"Under the best of circumstances, brother treating brother wouldn't have been wise. Benny's circumstances were far from the best. Neither were mine, but that's another story. The bottom line is that he didn't have to die. Not the way he did. I didn't mean for it to happen. But it did. And I was the cause."

He fell silent and stared at his hands, which were gripped on the table in front of him, his eyes dark with remorse. Her heart went out to him. She felt neither revulsion nor fear, as any normal woman would experience. But she had decided long ago that she wasn't normal.

In the quiet that settled between them, a pause too long, too tense, her mind raced. He had started this confession, or whatever it was. She couldn't let him stop when so much more needed to be said, even if he didn't want to say it and she didn't want to hear it.

As she watched him, a calmness settled over her, as if she were not a participant in the conversation but a rather disinterested bystander. It was the same calmness that had helped her get through her own loss, a pulling back that protected her against the shattering of her emotions. Strengthened by its shield, she thought of the gun she'd taken from his jacket, the gun he had waved at her only minutes ago by the front door.

"You shot him."

He glanced up at her, startled. "Good God, no." Then the remorse returned to his eyes. "But I might as well have pulled the trigger."

She held her silence, sensing he would continue when he could.

"One thing you have to understand about Benny. He's been—that is, he was bipolar. Up one day, on top of the world, then deeply depressed the next, erratic, quick-tempered, even when he was trying to be loving. The signs started when he was a little boy. He was fine when he took his meds, but in the last few years that was none too often. He said they made him feel confused."

"Tranquilizers did that to me. It's why I didn't take them."

Why did she tell him that? She never confided anything personal to anyone. Never.

He looked at her as if he would ask about her own situation, her own history, but she couldn't let him. This was his confession. If he did not tell her right now the truth about himself, about his brother, about his own knife wound, she wondered if he would be moved to do so ever again.

"So if he wasn't shot and didn't die from mistreatment, how did Benny die?" she asked.

"He was shot, all right. In a bank robbery. A robbery in which I was a participant." He nodded at her startled gasp. "If you had a working radio or TV, you would have heard all about it."

"Oh."

She sat back in her chair and studied him. His face looked leaner than ever, shadowed by thick black bristles, his dark eyes sunken and, she saw now, projecting feelings far stronger than remorse. He looked as if he bore the weight of the world on his shoulders.

The strangest thing about this scene was how she did not want to add to that weight.

"Where did it happen?" she asked, trying to keep to the bloodless portion of his story.

"Denver. It was a small bank. The robbery was supposed to be simple.

"But complications arose."

"Yes."

"I can't see you as a bank robber."

"You don't know anything about me."

"I know you've had chances to hurt me. Chances to use your gun. But you haven't."

He attempted a smile. "I'm weak, remember?"

"You've made an amazing recuperation. When I saw you lying in the snow, I thought you were dead. You weren't far from it, either."

"You would have been better off leaving me out there."

She could see no signs he was saying anything but the truth, as he saw it. She hadn't wanted to rescue him, hadn't wanted to find him. She didn't feel the same way now. She didn't want to think about what had changed her mind.

Her own self-analysis would have to come later. Right now she was trying to understand Alex.

He fell into a silence as deep and dark as his eyes.

"I'll make us some fresh coffee."

She jumped from the table and went about the preparations she'd gone through hundreds of times before. Keeping her hands busy seemed very important.

"I don't know if you've noticed," he said behind her, "but I'm having a hard time telling this. At first I thought talking was easy, but it all seems so preposterous, I can't put it into words."

"Start at the beginning."

"I would, but I don't know where that would be. As long as I can remember, Benny was always coming up with schemes. New products he could sell, a dot-com company he wanted me to invest in, a stock someone touted in a bar. He wasn't much of a drinker, but he liked hanging out in bars, said he found his kind there, though he couldn't explain exactly what that was."

"So the robbery was his idea."

"He met these guys—"

"In a bar."

Alex nodded. "I found out what he was planning and tried to stop him. But it wasn't so easy."

He started speaking slowly at first; then the words came tumbling out, one on top of another.

"He told me where they were to meet—rendezvous, he put it—and I went there. A thug by the name of Joseph Agnese was the leader. There were two others, Gabe and one man whose name I never did get. I showed up, trying to tell them—trying to tell Benny, mostly—that they would never get away with the robbery. Agnese wanted to shoot me right away, and Gabe went along. Benny convinced them I could be trusted. It was the third man, the silent one, who bound and gagged me."

He spoke flatly, as if it were the only way to get through his tale.

"The bastard moved fast. He was big and he was strong. Agnese and Gabe were little men, but not this one. Agnese watched, then seemed to understand his purpose without a word being spoken. I would be used as a hostage."

He stood and began to pace the length of the kitchen. Tessa held her silence, letting him work out the tale without interruption.

After a long minute, he began once again to speak.

"Benny convinced them to untie me. He would make sure I did what I was told. The bank was supposed to be a slow one, without many customers on the afternoon we went there. But there was a crowd. I can't say what really happened. I entered in front of Agnese, guns were waved, orders given. Someone threw me a gun, but I stuck it in my pocket. I'm not sure who started firing first. All I know is I saw Benny fall."

The flatness left his voice, and the anguish, the torment returned.

"I ran to him, tried to feel a pulse, but couldn't find one. Then Agnese was jerking me out the door. It was just the two of us. Gabe and the big one were down. On the street, I saw the police cars coming. The getaway car sat in a parking place in front of the bank. I had thought at the time how lucky these guys were to find a place so convenient. But with two of them down, and the police surrounding that car, their luck had run out. The trouble was, mine had, too."

He fell silent so long, Tessa had to speak.

"How were you wounded?"

"Agnese wasn't as stupid as he looked. He'd never intended to take that car. He was carrying a bag of money. He thrust it into my hands and, waving the gun, dragged me to a second car around the corner. All this happened in the space of a few minutes. I didn't have much time to think anything through. I had seen at least one of the bank's customers go down. How do they say it? The police would be shooting to kill."

"My God,"Tessa whispered, her heart quickening.

"I feared Agnese more than the police. I hated him, too. I kept picturing Benny on the bank floor, his life blood staining the carpet. The bastard said the police would never believe I was not in on the robbery. In that moment I believed him. Somehow I grabbed the gun and tossed it out the window. The next thing I knew he had a knife at my throat. I fought and that was when he stabbed me."

"But your coat wasn't cut."

"It was open. He had no trouble cutting deep through my shirt."

Tessa gasped, able to see the struggle in the car. His words coming ever faster, he went on to describe how he fell out of the car, the money bag grasped against his chest, the sirens screaming, Agnese yelling, then taking off. And he spoke about his panic. He knew that part of the city, had been raised nearby, and he knew the side streets and alleys.

"I was losing blood fast. I pressed the money bag inside my coat against the wound and started running, avoiding looking at anyone I passed. The few I saw stepped out of my path, as if they sensed my panic. God knows I wouldn't have hurt them—at least, I don't think I would have—but I didn't trust them enough to stop and ask for help. Then a car came. I stepped in front of it. It screeched to a halt. I pulled the driver out and added car theft to my list of crimes."

"You made it out of the city."

"Damned if I didn't turn into the lucky one. Of sorts. I needed time to think, to decide what to do. Eventually I ran out of gas and abandoned the car somewhere on the highway. I headed cross-country, before the snow started. By then I was feversh, not thinking straight. And all through this I was stupid. I should have gone to the police when Benny first told me about the robbery. But I thought I could talk him out of it. I've talked sense into him with other schemes."

"And the money? You didn't have it on you when I found you passed out on my hill."

"I tossed it the way I had Agnese's gun. It wasn't much of a tourniquet anyway."

"I'm not sure that was smart."

"Probably not. But I wanted no part of it. And I didn't want to be caught with it."

He fell silent, and their eyes met.

"I didn't know about the storm," he said, "and I damned sure didn't know about you."

He stood and came around the table. As she looked up at him, he bent to cradle her face between his hands and brushed his lips across hers.

"Thank you, Tessa Hampton. I don't deserve what you've done for me."

Tessa trembled, waiting for shock, for revulsion, but a different feeling surged within her, a long-dead yearning that suddenly sprang to life.

As if she had known from the beginning this moment would occur, she stood and returned the kiss. No longer was she regarding him dispassionately, as if she were an onlooker to what was happening. She was a participant, not only willing but eager to play her part.

He groaned. She backed away. "I'm hurting you."

"No. You're so alive. So warm. You can't hurt me. Not ever."

Looking at him, wanting him, the warmth of sexual arousal rushing through her, she experienced the sharp bite of guilt, of betrayal. She had thought never again to want a man. One had already filled her life and her heart. But this one wasn't demanding promises, wasn't expecting love. His own promise was more primal, the satisfaction of life's most basic urge.

All this flashed through her mind in an instant. When he pulled her back into his arms, she forgot to think. He kissed her eyes, her cheeks, her lips, each kiss tender. Nothing could have aroused her more. She saw where the kissing must end.

Taking his hand, she led him into the living room, not trusting herself to make it up the stairs. He sat and pulled her to him. Their embrace was gentle and fierce, each trembling from the efforts of restraint and from the kisses they were giving each other.

She began to undress him first, her fingers clumsy with the buttons of his shirt. Parting it, she gave only a brief glance at his bandaged shoulder.

"Stop me if I hurt you," she said, pressing her lips against the hollow of his throat.

"You won't hurt me."

He lifted her chin, and she saw fire in his eyes. She pulled her sweater over her head and tossed it aside. Her bra quickly followed. With the curtains drawn, the only light came from the blazing fireplace. It flickered across her skin. She watched him watching her, and whatever lingering guilt she carried in her heart burned away.

He moved in on her fast, easing her back to the rug in front of the hearth and completing her undressing, his expert hands moving far more quickly and efficiently than hers had done. He turned that same quickness onto his own clothing, moving awkwardly at times because of his wound. When he, too, was naked, he lay beside her to stroke her hair, her throat, her breasts. In the firelight his skin was no longer pale but brown and healthy and eminently touchable.

She closed her eyes and gave herself to what

she was feeling. No image of a man came to mind. Her thoughts were wrapped in black velvet.

As the hunger for him swelled, she found it the most natural thing in the world to part her legs and let him thrust inside her. She had never been given to quick passion. Her personal rhythms were on a slower tempo. But this time with a man almost a stranger, she was a different woman.

She climaxed almost immediately, and he did the same, the gentleness gone, the violence of the moment as overwhelming as it was unexpected, and they clung to one another as the tremors slowed. She held on to him tightly, suddenly afraid of what she might feel now, the expected guilt, the regret, the shame.

She never knew if such ugly feelings would have replaced the sweetness of ecstasy. A hard knock at the door replaced everything with a sharp, irrational fear.

Alex thrust her away, the look on his face absent of anything tender. He was suddenly hard, rough, unyielding.

"Find out who it is and send them away."

She watched in horror as he picked up the gun from where she had placed it. He didn't need to wave it at her. The harshness in his eyes was threat enough. She felt used, hurt, stunned, but not too stunned to act.

Without bothering with undergarments, she pulled on her sweater and jeans, ran a hand through her hair, and went barefoot to the door just as the pounding began once again. Still naked, the white bandage stark against his brown skin, Alex took up his place behind the door as she opened it.

She stifled a gasp. Standing in the shadows of her porch, an officer of the law loomed, tall and broad and strangely menacing, although in a sensible world he would be her friend, and possibly her rescuer.

He gave her a quick once-over, lingering a moment on her bare feet.

"Mrs. Hampton?" he asked. He looked beyond her into the living room. "I'm Sergeant Jenkins with the state patrol. Everything all right here?"

"Of course." Her voice was tight, the voice of someone she didn't know. "Is this part of the after-the-storm service?" She tried, and failed, to make the question sound like a joke.

"No, ma'am, it's not," he answered grimly. "A neighbor of yours thought you were acting strangely when she stopped by earlier. She thought you might be in some kind of trouble."

"Oh, dear," Tessa said with a little laugh, "Mrs. Griffin has quite an imagination."

"I don't know about that, ma'am, but we thought we'd better check out her story. The problem is we've got us a bank robber on the loose. The car he stole was found not far from here. It had been abandoned before the storm hit."

Adopting an expression of dismay, she thought of lying in Alex's arms moments before.

"My goodness," she said, then couldn't keep from venturing, "is he dangerous?"

Jenkins's dark eyes narrowed and his thin lips flattened. "Yes, you could call him dangerous." He looked once again at her feet, then up and beyond, into the interior of her house. "If you don't mind, I'd like to take a look around."

He spoke matter-of-factly, but she sensed a tension in him that made his request far more than polite. Before she could stop him, he was moving past her, his steps determined and practiced. With a sharp intake of breath, she turned, expecting to witness a confrontation.

Or worse. She waited for the blast of a gun.

CHAPTER FIVE

Alex was gone.

She swallowed hard, looked quickly around the room, trying not to call attention to herself or her search. Gone, too, were his clothes, her bra, her panties. Only her shoes and socks remained by the fire as evidence of what had taken place in its heat.

She felt Jenkins watching her.

"I like to warm my feet," she said with a nervous laugh. Quickly she gathered the shoes and socks and sat on the sofa to put them on.

Where was he? The words screamed in her head.

She lifted her head to smile up at the sergeant, but he was already striding into the hall. She followed him into the dining room. He paused in front of the gun cabinet, still locked the way Alex had left it. There was the rifle, her father's actually, and next to it an empty space where Alex's pistol should have been.

But Jenkins couldn't know that.

Still, he was guessing that somewhere in the house the man he sought was waiting, listening. He just didn't know that man was armed.

Heart in her throat, she continued in the sergeant's wake, back to the kitchen and out the rear door, keeping her silence. The snow-covered ground beneath the house's protective trees was marred by only her footsteps. When he had gone out to cut the telephone line, somehow Alex had managed to avoid leaving any trace.

And the lines themselves? Would the damage show? Apparently not, for Jenkins returned to the kitchen with the same grim expression on his face. At any moment she expected Alex to appear, gun in hand, especially when Jenkins jerked open the pantry door.

But Alex had hidden himself well. Physician or not, he was, indeed, a clever man. Where was he? She could not begin to guess.

Jenkins had said he was dangerous. Was he right or wrong? Still feeling Alex's hands on her skin, his lips on hers, she did not know.

One thought occurred: With or without a gun, he was dangerous to her. But he was dangerous in ways the sergeant would not understand, ways she could hardly admit to herself.

When Jenkins was finished exploring the bottom floor—her home was one of the few in the area without a basement—he stood at the bottom of the stairs.

"Please," she said, "go up. There are bedrooms on the second floor, and a bathroom as well. The third has only one room, my studio." At his look of puzzlement, she explained, "I'm a painter." More puzzlement. "I put in windows on all sides to catch the light."

He hesitated, then, just as she'd feared, hurried up the stairs, stopping at her bedroom door, where the bed was still unmade, the sheets tousled as if two people had lain between them and made love. But that particular scene had been played out in front of the living room hearth.

She remembered how Alex had stood in exactly the same place as Jenkins, his presence awakening her like an alarm. She watched the sergeant's tall, broad figure move across the room like a slowly advancing storm, watched his meaty hand open her closet. He peered inside. Again nothing. She felt as if she would explode.

"Sergeant," she said, needing to break the silence, "I promise I'm not being held here under duress."

He turned to face her, his probing eyes dark beneath the brim of his uniform cap.

"That's only one of the possibilities, ma'am."

A totally unwarranted sense of righteous indignation flooded her.

"Do you think I'm harboring a fugitive?"

"Stranger things have happened. Alex Wolfe

had a reputation back in Florida as quite a ladies' man."

Tessa felt as if she'd been hit in the stomach. Somehow she managed a casual, "Florida?"

"Something wrong with that?"

Nothing, except that Alex had led her to believe he was from around here.

Tessa willed her hands not to clench. "Of course not. Denver seems a long way to come to rob a bank."

"There's no telling what the criminal mind will do. Take Ted Bundy, for instance. You remember him from a few years back, right? He had a way with the women and he kept moving from state to state."

"But he was a serial killer."

"A man can break the law in more ways than one. They tend to, actually. Who's to say that's not the way with Wolfe?"

Jenkins spoke the truth. Who was to say?

Still, she knew he was trying to goad her, to frighten her into revealing whatever secrets she might have. But she merely nodded.

"This robbery . . . was anyone hurt?"

"One of the bank's customers was wounded. Three of the robbers went down."

Imagined gunfire echoed in Tessa's mind, and she shuddered. "They must have come in shooting."

"I wouldn't know about that. But the guns came into it soon enough."

She almost asked him about the other man—

Agnese, the robber who had escaped along with Alex, or so he had said. But Jenkins hadn't mentioned two men on the run. Or had he? Her mind was roiling so, she couldn't remember what Alex had told her and what had come from the officer.

No more questions, she vowed, even though she would like to know how much money had been taken. But already she was talking too much. Keep it up and she would give something away.

Neither of them spoke as he finished his search of the second floor. Standing at the foot of the stairs leading up to her studio, he paused.

"Mrs. Hampton, if you have something you want to tell me, you ought to do it."

"You still think I'm hiding him."

His eyes were thoughtful as he looked at her. He was not a stupid man.

"He could have threatened you. You could think he would harm one or both of us if you give any sign of his presence. We already know he's armed."

"You are thorough in your work, Sergeant Jenkins."

"Too much so, some think." He shrugged. "I do what I have to."

She looked up the stairs, certain that Alex had taken refuge there.

"Go on up. You'll find nothing but stacks of second-rate paintings, a couple of easels, and my art supplies."

Silently, she prayed he would not take her up

on the offer, but the prayer went unanswered. He took the steps two at a time, with her hurrying after, but he found only what she had predicted. He made one comment as he took a moment to look through a stack of canvases.

"You're not second-rate."

"Thank you," she said. His grunt made her wonder if he would have dropped her down to third. Throughout her painting career—if she could call it that—she'd received so little encouragement, she couldn't be sure.

At last, he gave up and she showed him back to the first floor and out the front door. One last warning—"Take care, Mrs. Hampton; don't open your door to strangers"—and he was gone. She watched as he made his way down the narrow path Mildred Griffin had dug a couple of hours earlier.

She didn't move from the door until the patrol car was making its way slowly down the narrow road between two high banks of snow. Then she turned back into the house for her own search. She found her quarry in her studio on the third floor, dressed now and going through the stack of paintings much as Jenkins had done.

A ladies' man from Florida, was he? He was tanned, all right. She'd thought his skin was naturally tawny, but now she saw otherwise. As for his reputation with women, she had no trouble believing it. Look how she had fallen into his arms. Her cheeks burned as she remembered just how far she had fallen.

Worse, her heart grew heavy at the thought of his being with other women—lots of them, apparently. The hurt was as disturbing as anything happening to her. It made her feel vulnerable, and stupid, too.

"How did you do it?" she asked.

He looked up slowly. He had known she was there. Where she was concerned, he could intuit far too much.

"I played cat and mouse. I made sure I was where he wasn't. At one point I spent several cold minutes on the front porch."

"He could have seen you."

"He didn't." Then it was back to her paintings. "Do you know what you have here?"

"An amateur's efforts."

"More than that. Way more than that."

Carefully he put the paintings back in place, as if he were handling something of great value, then turned to face her. "Why didn't you tell him I was here?"

Because we'd just made love.

He couldn't know what a shattering thing that was for her. He couldn't know that he'd made a lie out of everything she knew about herself.

She let a shrug serve as her answer.

"You're quite a woman," he said.

"Because I didn't turn you in?"

"That's part of it."

And then he was across the room, pulling her into his arms. As if she had no compunction about what she was doing, no doubts about her-

301

self or about him, she wrapped her arms around his neck and opened her mouth to his invading tongue.

She had known love once, knew how fleeting it could be. She was more than a little in love with this stranger, this dangerous man on the run, and even though it made no sense to subject herself to more pain, more loss, she couldn't help responding to what he wanted from her, what he was doing to her, what they were both about to do.

Danger was proving to be an aphrodisiac as irresistible as love.

He backed her against the wall and thoroughly kissed her. She sucked at his tongue, thrilled by the deep groan her actions elicited. She was playing with fire and she didn't care. With his tongue dancing against hers, he lifted her sweater and caressed her breasts, his hands sure, skillful, enthralling. Her nipples tightened, hard as the erection he pressed between her legs.

Her body wept for him. Impatient, she worked at the fastening at his waist, felt the coarse material give way, and thrust her hand inside his clothes, her fingers itching to hold him, to caress him as he was caressing her.

Success. He was hard, full, slick, moisture already forming on the tip of his sex.

"Tessa," he whispered hoarsely, then backed off, dropping his hands, pulling her hand away from its position of power. For a moment she felt bereft.

"Too fast," he said roughly, then eased her down

to the floor, undressing her, then himself, before he began to explore her body with his tongue. With these simple acts, he made her feel special, regal, a queen being serviced by her slave.

In truth, she was the slave. She would let him do anything. When his tongue reached her breasts, she arched her back to give him better access. He held her by the waist, then eased his hands around to stroke her spine, then lower to her buttocks. Every muscle in her tightened as wine-heavy blood coursed through her veins.

She had always been modest in her lovemaking, willing, eager, but seldom ravenous. She was ravenous now. Spreading her legs, she waited impatiently for his tongue to find its way to her own rigid, pulsing sex.

He teased her, taking his time, kissing her navel, nuzzling her pubic hair. When at last he suckled her where she wanted him most, she went over the edge of sanity. Ecstasy came at her like pounding waves, each stronger than the last, until she was drowning in pure emotion.

By the time she climaxed, she was crying out his name, her fingers raking his shoulders, her eyes closed tight against the sun's rays streaming in through the windows. She wanted the velvet caress of dark, where only feelings mattered, where pleasure was the beginning and end of her existence.

He pleasured her in ways she had never known. When at last her body stilled, he lay on top of her, and she tasted herself on his tongue. It should not have been erotic, but it was.

He eased himself inside her and took his own pleasure, but it was a rapture that they shared, for she found herself climaxing a second time, a special thrill she had never before experienced. Again and again he whispered, "Tessa" against her hair, which was now wet with sweat, her body likewise slick as it moved with his, despite the frigid air only a windowpane away.

At last their passion dwindled into what was almost pain. He held her for a long time, as if he, too, did not want the moment to end, did not want a return to the real world, a world so harsh, so rife with trouble, she could barely contemplate it.

When he spoke, he brought her back to that world fast.

"I'm not using protection."

No shit, she almost said. But she didn't talk that way, didn't even think that way. Not until Alex Wolfe had come into her life.

"Don't worry," she said, keeping her voice light. "I've never been able to conceive."

She lied. Her husband hadn't wanted children, and she had readily gone along with his wishes. If indeed she became pregnant with this stranger's baby, she would not let him know. She had lived alone for two years, taking care of herself without problems, and she knew without any doubt that she could take care of a precious baby on her own as well.

Pushing him away, she slipped from beneath him and gathered her clothes. At the top of the stairs, she glanced backward without quite looking at him. Some things were beyond her strength.

"I didn't hurt you, did I? Your shoulder, I mean."

"No, you didn't hurt me." His voice was flat.

"It's lunchtime. You must have worked up quite an appetite."

"For some things more than others."

She ignored the implication. "I'll take a shower, then see what I can find to cook."

Without waiting for an answer, she hurried down the stairs, questions echoing in her mind, questions to which she had no answers.

What have I done?

What will I do when he's gone?

And the cruelest questions of all: *Who is this man to whom I have given myself? A thief? A killer?*

Impossible. Yet she really did not know.

CHAPTER SIX

After stirring pasta into a pot of boiling water on the back burner, Tessa took out her frustration—her anger, whatever her feelings were—on a package of mixed fresh vegetables. They were wilted and needed all the help they could get, but she didn't do them much good by chopping them so finely they were barely identifiable.

She sprinkled olive oil into a pan, then tossed in the mess and stirred viciously.

Hearing Alex enter the kitchen, she couldn't resist a quick look. Fresh from the shower, his dark hair damp, his skin reddened by the razor she'd given him, he looked as if he wanted to say something, then settled for a solemn nod and, "Smells good."

"Please don't say I'm quite a woman," she said. "Anyone can throw stir-fry over rigatoni."

"I wouldn't know how to stir-fry."

"Then watch and learn."

Her voice was sharper than she'd intended.

"Tessa—"

"Sit down. The food will be ready soon." She closed her eyes and took a deep breath. "Sorry, but I'm out of wine and cheese."

To her own ears she sounded childish, but she was keeping her distance from him the only way she could at the moment. He couldn't know how torn she was, embarrassed, confused, and, worst of all, falling in love.

Falling for a thief, a womanizer, a man she knew nothing about—nothing, that is, except the bad. How crazy was that? About as crazy as she could get.

Unable to look at him straight-on any longer, she kept him in the corner of her vision.

He hesitated a moment, then took his chair, his attention never leaving her.

"Would you care to tell me what's wrong?" he asked.

"Tell me what's right."

He let out a long, slow breath. "The sex."

"True," she admitted, giving him credit. He didn't call what they had done making love. It certainly hadn't been for him, and she was honest enough to admit that anything beyond sexual arousal had been far from her mind when he eased her against her studio wall.

The trouble with women was that after the ultimate act, they began to think about themselves, their partner, about what they had done. It was something men didn't understand.

Dividing the pasta and stir-fry between two bowls, she set them on the table and began to eat as if she had an appetite. After a moment she saw his fork still lay beside his plate.

"Please," she said, gesturing toward his bowl, "I'd hate to think I went to all this trouble for nothing."

She hadn't meant to sound whining. She'd meant to be cool. But how could she when she kept having flashbacks to the sergeant's warnings, then to the way Alex had made her feel?

She pushed the bowl away and looked at him. "Are you really from Florida?"

He looked surprised at the question. "I heard the sergeant. Yes, but I'd hardly call myself a ladies' man."

"Others would, apparently."

"I'm not a monk. Does that bother you?"

"No." She paused. "Okay, a little bit, but only because I don't want to feel used."

"Do you?"

"I don't know."

"You shouldn't. What we've done was no more my idea than yours."

"That's putting things bluntly."

"It came out that way. It's just that I wanted you and you wanted me and we did what comes naturally."

"Now you're making rhymes. Are you making fun of me?"

"I'm trying to understand why you're so upset."

For once she could read his mind. If she didn't like what was happening between them, all she'd had to do was let Sergeant Jenkins know he was in the house. Why she hadn't was something she wasn't prepared to reveal, even if she could put her reason into words.

"You didn't tell me about Florida." Lame, very lame, but not a lie.

"I didn't tell you my father is suffering from Alzheimer's, either, but it's the truth. Or that I decided to move my practice to Denver to be closer to them."

"Them?"

"My mother is his caregiver."

And your brother? The one whose death you caused?

She couldn't bring herself to say the words. But she didn't have to. He brought up the subject himself.

"And I thought I could help Ben."

His story was wild enough to be true. Or was he just layering his problems to capture her heart even more than he already had?

Neither of them spoke for a few minutes. The faucet in the sink began to drip, marking the agonizingly slow seconds. Tessa was the first to break the silence.

"Have you opened your new office?"

"I don't have my Colorado license yet. I'd say getting it looks pretty doubtful right now."

They spoke to each other as if from a distance,

not at all the same two people who had brought each other incredible pleasure a scant hour ago. Without thinking it through, without even meaning to, she was building a wall between them. Walls were safer than warm embraces, or so she told herself.

"Have you ever been married?" she heard herself ask. She hadn't known the question lurked in her mind.

"It never seemed wise. Or maybe I didn't find the right woman."

Have you found her now?

What an absurd thing that would be to ask.

"I found the right man."

His expression didn't change. "You as much as told me that earlier."

"I guess I did."

It was her turn to look out the window and see things he couldn't see.

"My parents died soon after I graduated from college." At his questioning look, she added, "Boulder. I studied art history, you know, something useful in the Colorado woods."

"It's what you had to do."

She nodded. He understood, which didn't mean telling him about herself became any easier.

"I sold this place and moved to New York. Silly me, I thought I would make a big splash. Didn't happen, not even a ripple. I met Gordon at a charity art auction. I'd been hired not because of my expertise in art but because I could pour wine and put out canapés without making a mess."

"A job's a job. At least you were in the right surroundings."

He was being far too reasonable.

"Gordon was older and wiser and richer, and incredibly handsome, but that wasn't why I fell in love with him. He stayed after the auction to help me clean up, then took me out for a late dinner. We were married within the month." She took a deep breath. "Five years later he was killed in a car accident. I found out quickly that the people I considered our friends were really his. And there were always those men who wanted to 'help out' a poor, lonely widow. Especially a rich one."

"A beautiful one, too."

She shifted her gaze to him. "You don't have to say that."

"I was just imagining how it must have been, a lot of men hitting on you while you were still grieving. So you ran. Then I came along."

"Yes, then you came along."

She stared at her hands. *Damn him.* She was trying to put distance between them and here he was making her want to seek comfort in his arms.

"So what do you do now?" she asked.

"The what's not hard. It's the when and how that I can't decide."

He had to turn himself in. They both knew that. He had to tell the truth about everything that had happened. The sooner, the better.

"One thing's stopping me," he added. "I don't want you charged with harboring a fugitive." And then in a deeper, thicker voice, "I can't let anything happen to you."

It wasn't exactly a declaration of love, but it was the warmest thing he'd said to her, and she took it to her heart.

Strange how her standards had changed. She loved a man because he didn't want her sent to jail.

Somehow she gathered strength. "You've got some thinking to do. Go on into the living room. You need some time alone."

He stood but paused in the doorway. "I'm sorry, Tessa."

"For what?"

"For everything."

His apology brought her little comfort. A moment later she could hear him pacing in the hallway before he took refuge in the living room. What was he thinking? About his family? The law? Her?

Despite his apology, she knew she would be at the bottom of his list of concerns.

Somehow they got through the rest of the day with little talk. Night came early. He insisted on sleeping on the sofa, and she went up to her bed. But during the night she could hear him walking about, throwing an occasional log on the fire, fixing himself coffee in the kitchen.

By the time dawn came, all was quiet. Eyes burning from lack of sleep, she pulled on heavy clothes and went down to find him stretched out on the sofa and snoring softly, his long legs tangled in the covers. He slept nude, the corner of one sheet modestly shielding his sex.

All at the same time, he looked innocent and virile and beautiful, his only flaw the puckered wound at his shoulder. It was the kind of flaw that made him appear more masculine. She stared at him a long while before making her way to the kitchen and out the back door.

She'd had a lot of time to think things over during the night. He'd told her he had pitched the stolen money out the window while he was still in town, but Sergeant Jenkins had said the money was still missing. Both men could be telling the truth.

The possibility remained that one of them lied. Only Alex would have a reason.

On the back stoop, she pulled out the small portable radio she'd tucked beneath her coat before coming downstairs. During the night she had recharged the batteries, and she had no trouble finding the twenty-four-hour news station.

At first came weather news, reports of rescues and road clearings. Then the newsman turned to the subject she'd been waiting for.

"The search for convicted felon Joseph Agnese and Alexander Wolfe, the fugitive doctor from Florida, widened to the states bordering Colorado early today when lawmen were unable to find either man despite what they call a careful road-by-road, house-by-house search of the area surrounding Denver.

"Wolfe and Agnese are caught on tape taking part in the robbery of a south Denver bank four days ago. One bank customer was wounded in the heist. Hospital spokesmen have reported his condition as stable. Two of the five gunmen who invaded the bank were killed outright, and a third is critically wounded.

"Money taken from the bank, reported to be in excess of half a million dollars, has yet to be recovered. A ten-thousand-dollar reward is offered to anyone with information that leads to the arrest of either of the men."

He went on to describe the pair, reporting that the doctor had recently closed his Tampa, Florida, practice.

"Reason for the closure is unknown. The public is warned that both men are armed and should be considered dangerous.

"In other news, a five-car pileup on I-25 caused havoc for commuters this morning. . . ."

She snapped off the radio and tucked it out of sight beneath the stoop. The news report made no mention of the car Alex had stolen, or the fact that it had been found not far from her home. Somehow she felt a trap was being laid for her. Silly though it was, she couldn't help feeling she was being watched, even as she sat here at the back of her isolated home.

One thing was certain: No longer could she stay indoors waiting for something to happen, wondering what Alex would do next. Pulling on a pair of waterproof knee-high boots she kept in the storage shed by the back door, she picked up a shovel and looked in the direction of the hilltop where she had found him.

At the time, the snow had been coming faster, and she hadn't looked around for anything else. He had captured her attention, and he'd continued to do so until now.

What if he'd been carrying the money, but in his weakness had dropped it? It could be beside the tree, or down the hill toward the road. He'd said it was in a money bag. A half million dollars must take up a lot of space. But where was it? All she could see around her was snow and more snow.

Refusing to consider the impossibility of her quest, she started up the hill. She would search the area around the tree, then start down in the direction from which he must have come. The sky was cloudless, so brilliantly blue it looked painted, and the early-morning temperature seemed cold enough to freeze spittle, but she was carefully bundled, and her exertions added to her warmth.

In the deep, soft snow, progress proved slow. She welcomed the concentration it took to move only a few inches up the hill. Working this hard, she couldn't think. Her plan, if she had one at all, was to dig around the tree and down the side of the hill Alex must have taken. Success was highly doubtful, but she had to do something besides sit around and worry.

Remembering was difficult, too. Remembering every minute of every hour since he'd come into her life.

A half dozen yards up the hill, Alex's sharp voice stopped her.

"What the hell do you think you're doing?"

She turned to face him. Standing behind her in the poor path she'd managed to clear, he had on the jacket he'd been wearing when she'd found him. Like then, he wore no cap or gloves.

"You'll freeze to death," she said.

"Then answer my question fast. Unless you've decided my death is preferable to my presence."

"That's ridiculous," she said, and meant it.

"Is it? You're looking for the money, aren't you? You don't believe I threw it out the way I said."

Tessa didn't know what to believe, or what to tell him. If she confessed her feelings for him, he would laugh. And she would cry. Salt would keep the tears from freezing; they would run freely down her cheeks.

She threw the shovel at him. He caught it easily.

"If it's up there, you find it yourself. But please don't touch me again. When you touch me, I believe everything you say. My husband used to tell me I was a rotten judge of character. He was right about most things. He was probably right about that."

She made a wide berth around him, not looking back, not wanting to see him watching her with those dark eyes that so easily hid what he was feeling.

Except in moments of passion. When he'd held her, heat had flared in their depths.

The memory of that heat made her run. She ar-

317

rived at the back door panting. Pulling off her boots, she tossed them beside the stoop and hurried inside, closed the door, and leaned back to take a few settling breaths.

Her breathing turned shallow. Something was wrong. Or at least changed. She couldn't say how she knew or what the something might be, but her senses were definitely on the alert.

Had Jenkins returned? She couldn't remember whether or not she had locked the front door last night, and she had no idea whether Alex had done so.

Heart pounding, she stepped into the hallway. An arm circled her neck, and she was pulled sharply back against a hard body.

"Well, well," a man's voice whispered nastily into her ear, "Doc has found himself a way to keep warm in all this cold."

CHAPTER SEVEN

Tessa clawed at the arm, unable to breathe. Awkwardly, futilely, she kicked out, but she was truly trapped.

"Be nice and I'll ease up."

The voice was like rancid oil. It took all her willpower to hold still. Her assailant took a long time before moving his arm.

But he didn't release her completely. Trembling, she gasped for air.

"I'll bet you've been real nice to the doctor, haven't you? Maybe you could be nice to me, too."

His laugh was as chilling as his hold on her. She tasted bitter bile.

"Wouldn't that be something, him coming in and finding your legs spread? He owes me. He owes me a lot."

She could hear the fury in his voice. She fell limp, then suddenly threw herself forward, taking him by surprise. Freed, she stumbled, then righted herself and turned to face him. He was short and dark and grizzled, his features sharp as a ferret's, his thin lips twisted into an ugly grin. But his unblinking raisin eyes told her he was not amused by what she had done.

This had to be Joseph Agnese, the robber who had escaped along with Alex. The look of him—the evil in him—was far worse than anything she could have imagined.

She refused to give way to panic. Where had Alex put his gun? Could she get to the rifle before Agnese caught her again?

Impossible.

He knew she was helpless as much as she did.

"Alex will kill you."

She threw out the words as if they could protect her, but in her heart she was praying for his safety as much as for her own.

"He can try. But I don't think he will once he finds out I've got you."

"I mean nothing to him."

"That won't work. I watched you two on the hill. I saw the way he looked at you when you were walking back toward the house." Again the grin. "I'm not stupid, bitch. But I'm mean. Real mean."

Agnese pulled a knife from his coat pocket and clicked it open. A wicked six-inch blade sprang from the ivory handle. "I cut him, but you must know that. I missed his throat. Give me any trouble, I won't miss yours."

Tessa's skin crawled. She knew he spoke the truth. Yet the more he spoke, the calmer she got. And she managed a smile. That shook him. She could see the uncertainty in his evil little eyes.

Without warning, he came at her. But she was as quick as he. She ran for the front door. His shadow loomed in front of her, his arm raised, the outline of the knife as clear as in a photograph. Despite herself, she let out a scream. From behind her came his primal cry.

And for the first time in her life she was paralyzed with fear. In her awkwardness, she tripped. The slashing knife caught the sleeve of her jacket. She heard the fabric tear as she fell to the floor. Twisting away, she narrowly avoided a second swipe of the knife.

Growling, Agnese stared down at her, legs akimbo. He rubbed the blunt edge of the knife against his obvious erection.

"I like it when women fight."

Tessa couldn't imagine any woman *not* fighting him. She scooted back as far as she could, her back against the wall, hating herself for lying so passively on the floor in front of him, having to listen to him, look at him. But she could do little else; raw fear robbed her of thought. Nothing she had done to escape had worked. Even her heart was barely managing to beat.

Agnese knelt beside her and thrust the point of the knife against her throat.

"Call to him," he growled, "yell out. He might not have heard that pitiful scream of yours. We want him hurrying to your rescue."

His eyes narrowed until they were no more than small black specks in his narrow, grizzled face. When he leaned close, his sour breath filled her nostrils.

"I want the money. Get it for me."

She swallowed. The point of the knife pricked her skin. In her mind she could see the bright red blood trickling out against her white skin, staining the collar of her coat.

Stall, that was all she could think of. Calling out to Alex, bringing him running into the house, could get him hurt worse than anything her feeble nursing skills would be able to handle.

Besides, judging from the greed and cruelty warring in Agnese's eyes, she would be dead before Alex came crashing through the back door.

"He doesn't have the money."

She spoke scarcely above a whisper, unable to do anything else with the knife at her throat.

He eased the pressure and sat back on his heels. "What are you talking about? I saw him run with it."

"He threw it out of the car he stole. He was still in town. Someone must have picked it up."

"How do you know that?"

"He told me."

Agnese rubbed the back of his hand against his mouth, giving her a good look at the knife and at the drop of her blood on the tip. Slowly his grin returned.

"The bastard's a liar. And so is his bastard brother. The bank job was supposed to be simple."

"And it wasn't?"

Keep him talking. And think. Think.

"Benny paid. And so will his little brother."

She studied him without seeming to. He was a small man, as Alex had said, small and wiry, but obviously too strong for her to overcome. And Alex? His wound had left him weak. He could make love, but he wouldn't last long in a fight.

The one thing he had that Agnese could not match was intelligence.

For a moment she looked past Agnese, her eyes flaring; then she returned her gaze to him.

"Trying to make me think he's behind me?"

"Of course not. You're too smart to be fooled by anything like that."

"You need a real man. When this is over—"

He didn't finish. Alex hit him in the head with the shovel, and with a groan he slumped forward, landing on top of her.

She squeezed her eyes closed. "Is he dead?"

"No such luck," Alex said.

He took him by the scruff of the neck and rolled him away from her. Agenese's head lolled as he lay with his back on the hallway carpet. A trickle of blood ran down his temple. She stared at the knife he held in his hand, unable to move.

But only for a minute. With a cry she scrambled to her feet and pressed her back against the wall.

Both she and Alex stared at the unconscious Agnese. He didn't seem nearly so evil now.

She was about to throw herself into Alex's arms when a bullhorn sounded outside.

"Okay, Wolfe, Agnese, we know you're in there. We've got you surrounded. Come out with your hands raised."

She recognized the voice of Sergeant Jenkins.

This was like a scene out of a movie, except that movies never tore her to pieces the way reality had managed to.

"Are you all right?" Alex asked.

"Fine. And you?"

"Other than being scared shitless, I'm doing all right."

"Is that your professional diagnosis?"

He stared at her for a long minute. "I've never heard you joke before."

"There's a lot you don't know about me."

"You're right. I'm wondering if I'll get the chance to change that."

Tossing the shovel aside, he walked toward the front door. "Stay back until it's safe."

Then he was outside and she heard orders barked and people running, and before she could draw a deep breath, her house was filled with big-booted strangers in uniform, their guns held tight.

She was whisked into the arms of a female officer and dragged outside, with orders to keep her head low.

In all the confusion, she got close to Alex only

one more time, when he was being dragged toward a police car, its lights flashing.

Looking at her solemnly, he managed to get out one last message: "I won't bother you again. I've already harmed you enough."

Stunned, she watched as the car took off down the road, its siren blasting.

"We need to get you to a hospital."

She looked at the policewoman, who had remained close by her side.

"No, I'm all right."

"Procedure, Mrs. Hampton. We need to know what those men did to you."

It was not delicately put.

"I said I'm all right. I'll sign whatever release you need."

"But you're bleeding."

She touched her throat. She'd forgotten all about the knife.

"Joseph Agnese threatened me with a knife. Dr. Wolfe saved me."

The policewoman, a small, attractive brunette, nodded. "Stockholm syndrome. It happens in cases like this."

"You mean where the victim sympathizes with her captors? Let me get a gun to Agnese and you'll see how much sympathy I have for him."

She stared after the fast-disappearing car. "Nobody hurt me. Frightened me, true, but fear goes away."

And in time so did a broken heart.

CHAPTER EIGHT

"Lovely, my dear, perfectly lovely," Simon Hughes gushed.

Tessa smiled at the compliment. Hughes was curator of Denver's most successful private art gallery. He was studying one of her landscapes as he spoke.

"With a few bold strokes you've managed to capture the essence of winter," he added. "I feel its chill."

To prove it, he shivered.

"You're too good to me."

He patted her arm. "After all you've been through, my dear, you deserve all the goodness you can get." He wrinkled his finely sculpted nose. "But in this case I speak the truth."

He looked around the main room of the gallery. "Just look at the crowd."

"Curiosity seekers," she said, giving way to the heaviness that never quite left her heart.

"They might have come to see the woman who survived days as a hostage, but they're staying to admire her work."

He signaled to the young woman passing a tray of champagne. Taking a glass, Tessa thanked her. Too well she remembered the time she'd spent doing exactly the same thing back in New York.

And now here she was at her own show, with one of the New York critics in attendance. Maybe he, too, had come out of curiosity, to see the freak who painted, the widow of one of the Big Apple's charity leaders, the woman who had gotten through what the press called a "harrowing experience" without harm.

Except, of course, for her broken heart. That was something she kept to herself.

Alex.

She dared let herself think his name. She hadn't seen him alone since he was taken into custody two months ago. She'd spoken to his lawyer often enough, and to the one she'd hired to act as her spokesman.

But Alex himself had been unavailable.

I won't bother you again. I've already harmed you enough.

With those words the real harm had begun. But she couldn't tell him the way things were with her, not then, not now.

She wasn't sure he cared.

The good news for him had been that Benjamin Wolfe had not died from his gunshot wound. But he'd been comatose, drifting close to death, before at last waking to confess his part in the robbery and his brother's innocence.

Within a week Alex was no longer a suspect, even though the bag of money had yet to be found, despite the offer of a substantial reward.

Not so Agnese, who remained in jail awaiting trial.

And Tessa had come out of her own self-imposed prison to pursue the showing that was taking place on this cold spring afternoon.

Sipping the champagne, she was accosted by several art patrons as effusive as Hughes. From across the room, he gave her the sign that another of her works had been sold. Each time she nodded, pleased but not quite satisfied. The money didn't matter, only the fact that another someone wanted a work of hers hanging in his or her home.

For that, she was alive enough to be glad.

Pasting a smile on her face, she mingled. And then suddenly she became aware of a change in the room, an unexpected silence, all heads turned toward her, more than a few looking behind her.

She turned, and her heart stopped.

"Alex." She tried in vain to smile. "You've come to my show."

Somehow she managed to keep her voice light, a miracle, since he was looking handsomer than he did even in her midnight imaginings. He was dressed in a dark gray suit, pale gray shirt, and red tie, his hair trimmed, his face shaved with a better razor than she had been able to provide him.

With tanned skin and an alert look in his eyes, he looked healthy. But he also looked hungry, and not for any canapés. As he leaned close to brush his lips against her cheek, she could have sworn he growled.

He backed away. "You're a success. I'm not surprised."

"You never know how one of these things is going to turn out."

And you never know who is going to show up.

"How's the family?" she asked, as if there were nothing unusual about his presence, nothing wrong with his having ignored her for two months.

"Benny's coming along. He's forced to take his meds in jail. Right now he swears he won't ignore them ever again."

"That's good."

"He's said it before."

"And your parents?"

"The same."

"And your practice?" she asked, doggedly cheerful. "Have you gotten your license yet?"

His mouth tightened. "I'm working on it. Look, Tessa, if I'm making you uncomfortable, just say so and I'll leave. When I read about this, I couldn't stay away, but it may not be the brightest idea I've ever come up with."

"No, it's fine. And very considerate of you."

What was she doing? Considerate? She'd like to tell him what he could do with his consideration.

But not here. They were already making spectacles of themselves simply with small talk.

She might as well give the crowd something to really talk about.

The girl passed with the champagne tray, and she deftly set her glass on it, then in one smooth motion took Alex's hand and practically pulled him across the room, the crowd parting to let them pass. She didn't stop until they passed through a door marked STAFF ONLY. As the door closed, she turned to face him.

"I've got a few things to say to you, Dr. Wolfe—"

He stopped her with a kiss. Wrapping his arms around her, he held her tight and deepened the kiss until she thought she might drown.

When he let her go, she blinked and stared up at him, pressing her fingers against her mouth. "Don't think you can come in here and get away with just anything you want to do."

His face darkened, and suddenly she laughed, surprising herself as much as she surprised him.

"But of course you can," she said. "I've already proven that, haven't I?"

"Marry me."

That stopped her for a moment. "We barely know each other."

"Yeah," he said with a grin, melting her heart, "but I kinda thought that's how you do things."

"I have to be in love first."

"There's that."

"And I have to be loved."

"No problem there. I'm crazy in love with you."

"So where have you been the past two months?"

"Trying to save your reputation. And get my life together again."

"I don't care about my reputation. Actually I'm a heroine, or don't you read the papers? Although there was some speculation in the columns about how we passed those days snowed in."

"That's no surprise. Mainly I had to get my life together so I could ask you to share it. Feel free to say no."

"Do you mean that?"

"Hell, no. You do and I'll hold you captive again."

"That wasn't exactly the way it was."

"No, but it's a nice fantasy."

"Do you really fantasize? You seemed so practical."

"I was under duress."

"That makes two of us."

He stroked her hair, then dropped his hand. "We're talking too much. I'll ask again. Will you marry me?"

"I hadn't planned to get married ever again."

"Change your mind."

She stepped closer to him and lifted his hand, brushing her lips against the crooked little finger. "How did that happen?"

"Benny. We were little boys."

"Say no more."

"Tessa . . ." He sounded threatening.

"Yes, I'll marry you."

He kissed her again, gently at first, then with enough passion to curl her toes.

"We've got lots of details to work out, where we'll live, whether to have children, little things like that."

"We live together wherever you set up your practice, I'm not pregnant but I want babies, I plan to keep painting, and I'll teach you to cook. That should take care of everything."

She unfastened his tie and messed up his hair. "I've got to mess you up a little bit so you can't go back out there and run away from me again. You've already got lipstick smeared across your face."

"Is there a back door to this place?"

"No, but there's a back bedroom that I've been using while I was getting the show ready."

She led the way to the small room. When they were in its confines, beginning to undress each other, she put a hand on his to stop him.

"I never told you how terrified I was."

She didn't have to tell him when or why.

"When I heard you scream, I went out of my mind."

"You saved both of us."

"Of course I did. I told you I hadn't married because I hadn't found the right woman. When I did, I couldn't lose her."

She could see he spoke from the heart. And for the first time in a long while, her own wounded heart felt healed. When she took him in her arms, she was flying, soaring, delirious with the joy of being alive.

EPILOGUE

A Small Town in Idaho
Two Months Later

Dorothy Montgomery stood at the foot of the bed and watched her husband sleeping. The sound of his snoring soothed her. It was proof he still lived.

He needed surgery, and would get it, thanks to a benevolent society that took care of the state's emergency cases. But what about the months of recovery before he could return to his construction job?

Clitus had always been a strong man, a proud man, who took care of his wife and son. But a bad heart had robbed him of that strength and, almost as bad, of that pride.

Their savings would soon be gone, and Dorothy's job as a cafeteria worker in the local high school could hardly make up for the loss of his salary. Going to the side of the bed, she was brushing her lips against his forehead when the front door of their two-bedroom house slammed shut.

"Mom!" ten-year-old Tommy Montgomery cried out.

Dorothy hurried out to shush her son, closing the bedroom door behind her.

"Your father's sleeping," she said softly. "You know not to disturb him."

A look of excitement danced across her son's upturned face. He wasn't in the least subdued.

Tommy was a loving son, bright and handsome with his shock of wheat-colored hair and sprinkling of freckles across his nose. He was also sensitive to their problems. She hadn't seen such a smile on his face in a long time.

He struggled a moment to catch his breath.

"You shouldn't run like that," she admonished. She knew she was overprotective, but she couldn't have both men in her life suffering ill health.

"You know that dump down by the Chevron station?"

"The illegal one? The one the city keeps trying to close down?"

"Yeah, that one. It's a good thing it's still open."

"And why is that?"

"You better sit down, Mom. I've got something for you, and I'm not sure you won't pass out when I tell you what it is. Splat, you'll be stretched out on the floor."

The boy had an active imagination, and he made her grin. If sitting down would humor him, she could easily comply.

Settling her thin frame in the well-worn rocker that was her husband's favorite chair, she rested her hands on her jeans and gave her son the solemn regard she knew he wanted.

"Okay, I'm ready. So what have you got? I assume it's something you found at the dump." She couldn't keep from adding, "Even though I've told you there are rodents and all kinds of vermin in that stinky mess."

"I look in the dry parts, that's all, and I found this bag."

He paused for dramatic effect.

"What was in the bag?" she asked, playing her part, thinking maybe some shoes or clothes or replacements for the missing pedals on his bike.

"Money. Lots of money."

"Play money."

"No, the real stuff," he said, stiffening, showing the pride he'd inherited from his father. "I know what the real stuff looks like."

Despite her instinctive skepticism, Dorothy could feel her heart beat faster.

"So show me."

"I'll have to bring the wagon inside. I had it down there in case I found something. Boy, did I ever!"

He ran out, not waiting for permission. In a minute he was back, wheeling inside the big red wagon he'd gotten as a birthday present when he was six. Yellowed newspapers lay stacked on the top, covering his treasure from curious eyes.

He got to work removing the papers, setting them carefully aside, as if he wanted to postpone the unveiling as long as possible. He gave up the neatness when he was half-done.

"There!" he said, stepping back and pointing to a dirty gray canvas bag in the bottom of the wagon.

Dorothy knelt beside the wagon and opened the bag. Stacks of money lay inside, jumbled stacks of hundred-dollar bills. She picked up one of the bills, rubbed her fingers against it, then sat back on her heels and stared at her son.

"Where did you say you found this?"

"In the dump," he said impatiently. "Mr. Sloan at the station said I could keep anything I found there, anything at all. He said trucks come in the night and just dump stuff off, and as far as he was concerned, the trash was there for the taking."

"But this isn't trash," Dorothy said, too dumb-struck to say more.

"Not to us, but it was to some truck driver. I figure he was driving along, somebody threw the bag in his truck without him knowing, maybe a robber or somebody—"

"That's absurd."

"You tell me how it got there."

"I don't know. But your idea sounds too preposterous. Things like that don't work out for people like us."

"We're as good as anybody," he said in protest, the pride kicking in again.

"Of course we are, but . . ."

She looked at the bag of money, took out another bill, and held it to the light.

"Looks okay, doesn't it?" Tommy asked. "There must be a million dollars in there, maybe a billion."

"Not that much, but there's a lot."

The bill didn't look counterfeit, but she would have to take it in to the bank to find out for sure.

And what if it was real? What would she do with it and all the rest of the money?

Dorothy Montgomery had her own brand of pride, the kind that came with being an honest woman. She needed to show her son what that honesty entailed.

"What we need to do is take this money to the bank, and call the sheriff—now don't look like that; you know we have to. If we're meant to have any part of it, we'll get us a nice reward."

"And if we don't get anything?"

She hurried around the wagon and gave her son a giant-sized hug.

"We will, Tommy. I've got a feeling that everything is going to turn out just fine."

Her euphoria held as they hid the money beneath the load of paper. After checking on her husband, she started toward town, holding on to her son's hand on one side and on the other gripping the handle of the rattling old wagon.

As they walked, she thought over Tommy's explanation of how the money got in the dump. A robber throwing his loot—wasn't that the word?—in the back of an unsuspecting driver's truck. That had been the story. What an imagination the boy had, and she loved him all the more for it.

At the filling station, Mr. Sloan stared at them in puzzlement. Grinning, Dorothy nodded in greeting, then as he waved cheerily, she continued on her way, humming an old song her mother had taught her when she was Tommy's age.

Under the circumstances, "When You're Smiling" seemed the right accompaniment for her parade.

A KISS TO DIE FOR
CLAUDIA DAIN

Women are dying. Pretty women, lonely women, women who give their hearts to a man who promises happily ever after, but delivers death.

He steams into Abilene on the locomotive, a loner with a legend attached to his name. Jack Skull claims he is tracking a murderer, but Anne feels as if he is pursuing *her*. It seems every time she turns around, she comes face to face with his piercing blue eyes.

Though she's sworn matrimony is not for her, somehow she finds herself saying "I do." When Jack takes her in his arms and lowers his lips to hers, reason flies out the window, and she can well believe his will be a kiss to die for.

EVELYN ROGERS
More Than You Know

Toni Cavender was the toast of Hollywood. But when a sleazy producer is found brutally murdered, the paparazzi who once worshipped Toni are calling her the prime suspect. As a high-profile trial gets under way, Toni herself finds it hard to separate fact from fiction.

When an unmarked car tries to force Toni off a cliffside road on a black, wet night, the desperate movie star hires detective Damon Bradley to find the truth. Someone is out to destroy her. Someone who knows the lies she's told . . . even the startling reality that lying in Damon's arms, she feels like the woman she was destined to be. Yet Toni can trust no one. For she has learned that hidden in the heart of every man and woman is . . . *More Than You Know*.
